P9-DHI-361

Praise for the national bestselling League of Literary Ladies Mysteries

"This highly addictive series continues with a clever story-line, quirky characters and an ideal island location. As the mystery evolves and the main character realizes the parallels to Agatha Christie's famous novel, the suspense intensifies, and the twists and turns keep on coming."

—*RT Book Reviews*

"Kylie Logan has created a cast of characters with whom readers will feel invested, as their histories are played out throughout the series . . . The plot, a surprisingly complex one in this third of the series, never suffers from the focus on character development. Literature, the struggle of authors, and friendship among women make this an absorbing read—a spookily good book with an even greater mystery."

—Kings River Life Magazine

"Logan has fun with this unusual story, intimate setting, and feisty characters, and readers will, too."

—*Richmond Times-Dispatch*

"This is one of my favorite series. What could be more fun than a mystery series that is about a reluctant book club? I love how the mysteries run parallel to the book the League of Literary Ladies are reading." —MyShelf.com

"One of my favorite cozy mystery writers . . . What great characters Kylie Logan has created." —Fresh Fiction

Berkley Prime Crime titles by Kylie Logan

Button Box Mysteries

BUTTON HOLED
HOT BUTTON
PANIC BUTTON
BUTTONED UP

League of Literary Ladies Mysteries

MAYHEM AT THE ORIENT EXPRESS
A TALE OF TWO BIDDIES
THE LEGEND OF SLEEPY HARLOW
AND THEN THERE WERE NUNS
GONE WITH THE TWINS

Chili Cook-off Mysteries

CHILI CON CARNAGE
DEATH BY DEVIL'S BREATH
REVENGE OF THE CHILI QUEENS

Ethnic Eats Mysteries

IRISH STEWED

Gone with the Twins

Kylie Logan

BERKLEY PRIME CRIME
New York

BERKLEY PRIME CRIME
Published by Berkley
An imprint of Penguin Random House LLC
375 Hudson Street, New York, New York 10014

Copyright © 2017 by Connie Laux
Penguin Random House supports copyright. Copyright fuels creativity, encourages
diverse voices, promotes free speech, and creates a vibrant culture. Thank you for buying
an authorized edition of this book and for complying with copyright laws by not
reproducing, scanning, or distributing any part of it in any form without permission.
You are supporting writers and allowing Penguin Random House to continue to
publish books for every reader.

BERKLEY is a registered trademark and BERKLEY PRIME CRIME and the B colophon
are trademarks of Penguin Random House LLC.

ISBN: 9780425282960

First Edition: March 2017

Printed in the United States of America
1 3 5 7 9 10 8 6 4 2

Cover art by Dan Craig
Cover design by George Long

This is a work of fiction. Names, characters, places, and incidents either are the product
of the author's imagination or are used fictitiously, and any resemblance to actual persons,
living or dead, business establishments, events, or locales is entirely coincidental.

If you purchased this book without a cover, you should be aware that this book is stolen
property. It was reported as "unsold and destroyed" to the publisher, and neither the author
nor the publisher has received any payment for this "stripped book."

For Hooligan Apollo,
who really is gone with the wind

ACKNOWLEDGMENTS

Every book is its own adventure, and *Gone with the Twins* is no exception. Brainstorming, research, plotting, planning. If it were a linear process, it would certainly be easier, but of course, the creative mind doesn't work that way. In reality, it's more like brainstorming, researching, oh no that's not going to work, brainstorming again, etc.

The good news (and it's really amazing when you think about it) is that the book does get written, and as always when a book is finished, I have plenty of people to thank:

My agent, my editor, the writers in my brainstorming group who so generously share their time and talents. Thank you Shelley Costa, Serena Miller, and Emilie Richards! To my email buddy, Maureen Child, thank you for listening to me not only plot and plan, but moan and complain, too.

And of course while all this creativity is going on, there's real life to deal with, too. Thank you to my family, who help get me through the everyday joys and chores and problems. David always reads my first chapters to make sure I'm telling just enough to get readers reacquainted with my characters and not too much to overwhelm them. Thank you for the first look!

Gone with the Twins gave me a chance to revisit South Bass Island, and as always, I have to thank everyone there for being so welcoming. If you're ever near Lake Erie, pay them a visit!

◈ 1 ◈

"Fiddle-dee-dee!"

The real question—at least for me—wasn't where Chandra Morrisey had found the elegant white lace fan she swept back and forth in front of her face when the exclamation oozed out of her, but where on earth her exaggerated Southern drawl had come from. South Bass Island, three miles from the Ohio shore in Lake Erie, is not exactly dripping with Spanish moss or known for its grits.

"The woman has more nerve than Carter's got liver pills." As if to reinforce exactly what I was thinking, this added pronouncement from Chandra had more Southern belle aplomb than had ever been heard north of the Mason-Dixon Line, and to emphasize it, she tossed her head in a way that made her blunt-cut blond hair bob in the summer sunshine that streamed through the windows of the Island Yacht Club. Her eyes narrowed, she shot a look across the room to where Vivien Frisk held court, two men on either side of her. "She thinks the sun comes up just to hear her crow."

"Whatever!" It was early, but when a waiter walked by with a tray full of drinks, Kate Wilder grabbed a mimosa and downed half the glass in one gulp. "Bea, who can we blame for creating this monster?" she asked me. "And is it ever going to end?"

Believe me, I felt Kate's pain.

"It's my fault," I admitted. "I'm the one who said she could choose the book for this discussion."

"*Gone with the Wind*." Kate rolled eyes the same color as the club's neatly manicured lawn. "I guess it's a good thing we're not reading *Dracula* or she'd be running around biting necks."

"I know who her first victim would be." I slid a look across the room just in time to see Vivien toss back her head and laugh. Like everyone else on South Bass, I knew Vivien's reputation was anything but spotless.

Cutthroat.

Vindictive.

Selfish.

I'd heard all those words and more uttered in the same sentence as Vivien's name. Still, Chandra's reaction was over the top. Even for Chandra.

Interested, I stepped back and watched the drama that played out in front of me. Chandra, resplendent that morning in a long yellow skirt, an orange top, and sparkling sandals, shooting daggers of death across the room at Vivien, who looked pretty (as always) in a white summer dress dusted with a tiny print of green flowers. The dress had a nipped waist, a wide skirt, and a neckline that was just high enough to be appropriate for the occasion, and just low enough to show off the smooth sweep of Vivien's milky shoulders to best advantage.

Vivien batted her dark lashes and pouted at the middle-aged man stationed on her left.

Chandra ground her teeth.

"You knew she would be here," I said. "You knew she was hosting the event. Maybe you shouldn't have come."

"Y'all can't be serious." In one slick move, Chandra spun away from watching Vivien, tapped the fan closed, and whacked me on the arm with it. In a ladylike way, of course. "How could I not come and pay my respects to Mizz Estelle? Why, everyone just adored Mizz Estelle."

"And no one ever called her Mizz Estelle." Clearly the charm (oh, how I use the word loosely!) of Chandra's Southern persona had not penetrated the aura of pragmatism that Kate carried like a shield. When she glanced Chandra's way, her lips were set in a thin line. "It was always just Estelle. Or Ms. Gregario, to those who didn't know her well. You know that, Chandra. You knew the woman all your life."

"Ex-act-ly." It says something about just how far gone Chandra was when she dared to *tap-tap-tap* the sleeve of Kate's gray linen jacket with said fan to the beat of the syllables. "Which is precisely why I knew I had to be here." She sighed and pressed a hand to her heaving bosom. "There is a certain honor we owe the dead, and Mizz Estelle's passing, it surely affected me clear through to my bones. Even with being so upset and all"—she lifted her chin and clenched her jaw—"I knew I had to be here to honor her memory. Just like we should all express our admiration and appreciation for those brave young men who gave their all for the noble Confederate cause."

"Really?" Let's face it, there's only so much even I can take. When that waiter zipped by again, it was my turn to grab a drink. I held the stemmed glass in a death grip and pinned Chandra with a look. "Could you drop the Scarlett act? We get it. We really do. You love the book we're reading."

"I more than love it!" Chandra's sigh tickled the morning air. "I want to live it. It's so wonderfully romantic. So completely absorbing. So absolutely—"

"Phony." It may have been just a coincidence that this opinion popped out of my mouth exactly at the moment Levi Kozlov walked into the gathering to honor island real estate agent Estelle Gregario's life.

Then again, maybe it wasn't.

Once upon a time, long ago, in a galaxy far, far away and in a universe even more unrealistic than Chandra's notion of the antebellum South, I couldn't think of romance without thinking about Levi. But that was before I fell into bed with him—and found out afterward that though I'd always known him as the owner of one of the island's most successful bars, he was actually a private investigator who'd been hired by my (former, once I learned what was going on and fired him) attorney to live on the island so he could keep an eye on me.

The truth had come out a couple of months before, and still, just thinking about it made my blood pressure rise and my blood boil in response. Even a sip of mimosa didn't cool it off.

Which didn't mean I couldn't be an adult about the whole thing. I mean, more of an adult than I'd been when I found out what a conniving, weaselly rat Levi was and whacked him over the head with a wet mop.

I set the thought aside and, ever the adult, refused to back down. She might not be Scarlett O'Hara, but for the moment at least, Chandra was my role model. When Levi headed in our direction, I lifted my head, set my chin, and steadied my shoulders, just as Chandra had done a few minutes before when she sang the praises of the dead Rebs. It wasn't easy to keep my cool, considering how delicious he looked. Khakis, a crisp blue dress shirt unbuttoned at the neck, a navy blazer. Levi is tall, broad, and golden-haired. He's got a chipped-from-granite chin, a voice so husky it sounds like he's just slugged down a shot of really good brandy, and a sculpted-by-the-gods chest. The rest of him is mighty fine, too. I know this from firsthand experience.

When he stepped over to say hello, I managed a tight smile.

His own smile was far more relaxed. Or at least it looked that way, and I silently cursed him for being able to carry it off. He blessed Chandra, Kate, and finally me with that megawatt smile, and I did my best to ignore the tiny flame of heat that licked my insides. "No Luella this morning?"

"Working her little fingers to the bone over on the boat of hers!" Yes, Chandra really did press the back of one hand to her forehead and close her eyes in forbearance as if she were the one who was toting that barge and lifting that bail. "She'll be along. Don't you worry," she added for Levi's benefit.

He glanced my way, his honey-colored eyebrows raised.

With a wave of one hand, I told him to ignore our ingenue.

"So . . ." As the owner of Wilder Winery, Kate has the instincts of an astute businesswoman and the experience of walking a fine line when it's called for. She glanced from me to Levi and I swear I could see the wheels working inside her head—she wondered which of us would crack first.

I guess she knew it was sure to be a draw because she filled the uncomfortable moment with small talk.

"Estelle sold you the bar, didn't she?" Kate asked Levi, even though she already knew the answer. "She sold Bea her house, too."

This was no secret. Not to Levi or to anyone else.

A waitress drifted by, and he grabbed a glass of sparkling water from her tray. "She was a classy lady, and as smart as they come. A lot of us have good memories of Estelle."

"And not such good ones of that niece of hers." Chandra was so busy swiveling a look in Vivien's direction, she actually forgot the Southern drawl. "She's as sneaky as Estelle was honest. As nasty as Estelle was nice. Rumor has it her real estate agency isn't doing well at all. That's no surprise! She should have known better than to go up against Estelle when it came to island real estate. Who would want to deal with a woman like Vivien? She's lower than a snake's belly in a wagon rut."

From the Southern belle she so wanted to be, this particular comment might have packed a little more oomph. Without the accent and coming out of regular ol' Chandra, who'd been an island resident since she was born and made her living reading tarot cards and crystals for tourists, it made me bite my lip to contain a giggle.

Kate didn't bother to hide her laughter and Chandra didn't appreciate her reaction one bit. She sniffed. "You've heard all the same stories I have, Kate," she snapped. "Even with as desirable as island real estate is, Vivien practically has to get on her knees and beg people to be her clients. Why, even when she was sick, Estelle closed more deals. Vi-vien"—she bit the name in two—"Vivien hasn't made one sale since last fall. Not since she sold Tara to—"

Chandra snapped her mouth shut and a color that matched her flamingo-pink nail polish raced into her cheeks. She squeezed her eyes shut. "Sorry, Bea," she mumbled.

Irritation bristled up my spine and my stomach clenched. I covered my reaction with a careful sip of my drink and stepped just the tiniest bit to my left, farther from Levi. Better that than having him pick up on the fact that every muscle in my body tensed.

"You don't have anything to be sorry about, Chandra," I said. "It's no secret that Tara is open for business or that it's a B and B that competes with mine."

Chandra may be our island flake, but she has a heart of gold. Of the four Ladies in our Literary League—me, Kate, Luella, and Chandra—she's the one who always lets it all hang out, emotion-wise, the one who's the softest touch, the one who might be a little wacky, but is never mean. Her gray eyes misted. "I know, I know. But they're stealing all your business. Tara is filled to overflowing and has been since summer started, and your place . . ." She brushed a hand against her cheek. "Well, I know you've had empty rooms, Bea, and you've never had empty rooms before, and you know it's just because Tara is new and people are dying to see it, I mean because of the fabulous decorating and the charm and how they're playing up the whole Southern plantation thing. And with the Civil War costume party gala they're hosting next weekend to raise money for the island's historical society . . ."

Chandra's cheeks paled and she swayed inside her sparkly sandals. "Oh my goodness, I shouldn't have chosen *Gone with the Wind* as our book this month! I never thought of it. I swear, I never did. I just wanted to pick a book that was wonderful and romantic. If I'd made the connection between that Tara and our Tara—"

I might be irritated but I wasn't heartless. I managed a smile and put a calming hand on Chandra's trembling arm. "I told you, none of it is your fault. You're right—tourists are always interested in what's new. That's why they're flocking to Tara and the gala."

"And because of the Twins, of course." Kate's words were as acid as the expression on her face, and she didn't apologize for either. "Oh come on, we all know it's true. It's like watching a car accident. Even if the wrecked cars are on the other side of the highway, everyone rubbernecks. They can't help themselves. Most peoples' lives are pretty dull, so they live vicariously through the people they call celebrities. They don't care who those people are or what they're famous for, all they want is a taste of the drama. Those Champion twins are—"

"Business people. Like all of us are business people." I congratulated myself—I had actually made this sound as logical and unemotional as I'd hoped I would. Tell that to the sick feeling in the pit of my stomach. This was the second summer that Bea & Bees—my charming Victorian inn—had been open for business, and for the first time, I'd had a rash of cancellations, days with no phone calls inquiring about rates and open dates, weeks with no hits on my website, and no comments on those travel review sites, except for a one-star bashing from some guy named Juan who claimed his room wasn't clean, the neighbors were loud, and breakfast would have been better had he picked it up at a fast-food joint.

Yes, Chandra is my neighbor.

And yes, she can sometimes be a little loud, especially when she's celebrating a full moon with one of her legendary bonfires.

But just for the record, my rooms are spotless, I'd never had a guest named Juan, and the breakfasts I serve at my B and B are the best on the island. Hands down.

None of which changed my current predicament. Thanks to the tourists who flocked to Tara and eschewed Bea & Bees, for the first time I was having to advertise discount specials.

I had deep pockets; it didn't hurt my wallet as much as it did my pride.

"You know, Bea, you could fight fire with fire." The little singsong voice Chandra used when she said this warned me that whatever she was going to suggest, I wasn't going to like it. "If you let people know that you're really . . ." She had the good sense to look around and lower her voice. "That you're really FX O'Grady, the famous horror writer, they'd come running to your place. Heck, I could probably rent out rooms at my house just so people could sit next door and get a look at you."

She was right.

And I wasn't any more willing to budge on the topic than I had been when I shared the secret with my friends just a couple of months before.

"I'm not looking to cause a sensation," I said. For like the one hundredth time.

"You know, I hate to admit it when Chandra's right." Kate had already finished her drink, so when the waiter came by, she gave him the empty glass along with one of her dazzling smiles. "You could attract attention," she said.

"Except that I don't want to attract attention." I firmly ignored Levi when I said this, since his whole purpose for being on South Bass—well, before I fired the attorney who was signing his paychecks—was to make sure little ol' celebrity me stayed safe from the fans who would no doubt besiege me if they knew I was trying to live a normal life out of the limelight. "I want people to stay at my place because it's beautiful and the food is fabulous and the view is terrific. I don't want them to stay there to look at me."

"Unlike some people, who like to be the center of attention."

Yes, this sounds so nearly catty, I expected it to come out of Kate's mouth. Which was why I was surprised—and paid attention—when Levi spoke up and glanced toward the entrance to the bar.

I was just in time to see the double doors fly open and a stream of sunshine—like a spotlight—fill the entryway. There was a figure outlined against the blinding light: a man with dark hair, long legs, and a million-dollar . . . Well, I was going to say smile, but honestly the expression that outshone even the summer sun was more of a smirk.

Who shows up at a memorial service with a smirk on his face?

I wasn't the least bit surprised when the man stepped inside and the doors closed behind Zane Donahue. Dark-eyed, square-jawed, and ruggedly handsome, Zane was a summer cottager who was as well-known for the lavish parties he threw as he was for the size of the boat he kept docked there at the club, the skill of his water skiing, and the fact that he liked nothing better than parasailing, fast cars, and faster women.

"Oh, this ought to be good," Kate mumbled. "You know what happened between Vivien and Zane, don't you?"

Of course I did.

Everyone on South Bass did.

A year earlier, Zane Donahue had purchased a summer

home on the island and Vivien Frisk had handled the sale. South Bass is only four miles long and a mile and a half wide; land is scarce, prices have skyrocketed over the years, and, according to the island grapevine, Zane had paid upward of two million for the four-bedroom house with its view of the lake. He needed only one thing to make it perfect, and that was no problem for a man like Zane. Though his lot wasn't big, there was just enough room for the in-ground pool he'd planned.

Room, yes. But that pool was never going to happen.

"An Indian burial mound." Levi must have been thinking what I was thinking, because when I snapped to I found him shaking his head. "How could Vivien not have disclosed that when she showed him the property? How could she not have mentioned that there's an Indian burial mound right outside his back door?"

"He'll never build that pool," I added.

"And he'll never forgive her for not disclosing all the facts." Like I said, Kate was as down-to-earth as anyone I'd ever met. Ever practical, she said what we were all thinking. "He's going to have her tied up in lawsuits from now until forever."

"And she's not the least bit happy about it," Chandra purred and grinned. "Bless her heart!"

Zane pulled a plastic box of orange Tic Tacs out of his pocket, shook out a few and popped them in his mouth, then nodded hello when he passed the tight groups of people who stood around waiting for the official memorial service to begin, but it was easy to see that he wasn't paying attention to anything or anyone—anyone but Vivien Frisk.

Jaw tense, arms pressed to his sides, he strode across the room to offer his condolences on Vivien's aunt's passing.

Or maybe to make sure Vivien would show up for their next court date with the poor mediator who was in charge of acting as a referee between these two high-charging Type A egotists.

"I'm not here because of you." Sharp as rifle shot, Zane's voice could be heard clearly across the room. He stood directly in front of Vivien with his back ramrod straight and his feet slightly apart, and the four men who'd been hovering around her like bees around a particularly gorgeous flower slowly drifted away.

"Your aunt was a wonderful woman," Zane said.

Vivien stood and fluffed her skirt. "It runs in the family," she said.

"Then maybe you and Estelle weren't really related."

I was pretty sure Zane wasn't going for funny, but Vivien laughed. The sound was light and sweet. She smoothed a hand over her shoulder-length brown hair. "Oh, Estelle and I were related, all right. She taught me everything there is to know about the real estate business."

"Like how to cheat your customers?"

Even Vivien wasn't prepared for him to be that blunt in public. A muscle jumped at the base of her jaw and her hands folded into fists.

We all held our breaths.

And let them out again with a collective *whoosh* when the doors swung open again and Quentin and Riva Champion walked in.

Vivien shot them a look, and from where I was standing, I couldn't tell if she was relieved by the interruption or sorry they'd spoiled her fun.

Zane backed away and a moment later, I saw him on the other side of the room at the bar.

As for the rest of the crowd . . . well, the Vivien/Zane smackdown might have provided a few weeks of juicy island gossip, but once Riva and Quentin arrived, Vivien and Zane might just as well have rocketed to Pluto.

The Twins were in the house.

"Good morning! So nice to see you! How are you today?"

They worked the crowd like seasoned politicians, hands extended, smiles on their faces . But then, they'd had plenty of experience. Riva and Quentin, see, were the twin son and daughter of Hollywood megastar Desiree Champion. All the best boarding schools, all the most sensational relationships, all the most fabulous parties for their sweet sixteens and their twenty-firsts. They wouldn't even be closing in on thirty for a couple more years and already they were mini-celebrities in their own right; glowing moons that traveled in Desiree's orbit, spent Desiree's money, and, in the case of Riva, even married (ever so briefly) one of Desiree's exes.

And then, two years before, the news broke over the country like the cold slap of a tsunami—Riva and Quentin had been kidnaped from their mother's Malibu mansion by Desiree's long-time business manager, Orrin Henderson. Along with a priceless trove of Civil War–era coins, the twins were gone with the . . . well, as much as I hate to say it, they really were gone with the wind. No trace of them. No ransom note. No nothing. Nothing but a media circus that was as predictable as it was all-encompassing. Newspapers, magazines, cable and network news. Every media outlet on the planet was focused on—as they were called throughout the frenzy—the Twins.

Just as quickly and mysteriously as they had disappeared, the Twins resurfaced a year later when they arrived at a police station in the middle of New Mexico with a harrowing story of imprisonment, torture, and abuse. One day, Henderson had left the home where he had held them captive and he'd never come back, and Henderson—and those coins worth millions that he'd made off with—was never seen again. Riva and Quentin made a miraculous and heroic escape.

It doesn't take much imagination to picture the all-new frenzy that started up once the Twins arrived back on the scene. They were young, they were beautiful, they had a tale to tell, and they told it on every talk show in the world, in a bestselling book, and, according to an interview I'd recently seen with them on a network morning show, in a soon-to-be major motion picture.

So what were they doing on South Bass? According to another interview I'd just recently read in our local newspaper, they were on the island in search of peace and tranquility.

Call me stonyhearted, but to me that might be better accomplished if they'd stop giving interviews, making personal appearances, and letting themselves be photographed for the cover of everything from *People* to *Vogue*.

In their quest for the quiet life, they'd bought what was then a defunct inn through Vivien Frisk's real estate agency and converted it into Tara, their homage to the Southern plantation life Chandra so loved. With twenty rooms, Tara was far larger than Bea & Bees. Add to that the over-the-top Victorian decorating scheme and the notoriety of its owners and, well . . . honestly, I could almost understand why the place was booked solid (according to the island grapevine) for the next year. Winter months included.

Which didn't mean I had to like it.

"They're hosting Tuesday's meeting of the Chamber of Commerce at Tara to go over last-minute details for the gala," Levi remarked, watching the Twins sashay their way to where Vivien waited to greet them. "You going?"

I wasn't sure if he was referring to the meeting or the gala so I kept my answer neutral, but I refused to look Levi's way. He always knew when I was lying and I didn't need to see that in his eyes. "I'm a big supporter of the Chamber of Commerce."

I watched the Twins chat with Vivien and wondered if there had ever been that much vivacity—that much beauty— in any one place at any one time. The Twins were tall and both of them were golden-haired and blue-eyed. Riva was shaped like a strand of angel hair pasta. Not everyone's idea of the perfect female body, but photographers loved her. Quentin had the build of a natural-born athlete, sleek and lean. I'd seen any number of women swoon in his presence, but frankly, my dear, he wasn't my type, and at that particular moment and standing next to Levi, I didn't want to think about who was.

Luckily, Vivien provided a distraction when she clapped her hands to get everyone's attention.

She glanced around the room and when I did, too, I noticed that Zane Donahue had disappeared. "We'll have lunch and share stories about Estelle in a little while. For now, we're going to lay a paving stone in her honor outside on the club's fabled Walkway of Captains. If you'd all like to join me . . ." She motioned toward the door and lead the procession.

We followed Vivien out into the summer sunshine. The walkway she talked about featured paving stones that honored many island residents and visitors, and I carefully trod over names I recognized, as well as many who'd been members of the club long before I arrived on South Bass. The walk began out at the street and continued past the front doors of the club and around to the back, and that's where Vivien headed and where we gathered around her when she motioned toward the ground at a spot where a strip of lawn met the walkway. Beyond that was a sweeping view of the lake, where boats bobbed in the blue water. It was a fitting spot to honor Estelle, who had always loved spending time out on the lake.

In her honor, we stood quietly and watched while Vivien got to her knees with the help of two brawny club employees. The stone with Estelle's name on it had already been set in place, and most of it was already bonded to the stones around it by what looked to be fresh cement. Vivien would be adding the last of the cement with the trowel one of those club employees handed her.

She paused for a moment so the manager of the club could flash a picture to commemorate the event, then dipped her trowel into the container of cement another employee held out to her.

The quiet that settled around us was interrupted only by the calls of the lake gulls that wheeled overhead and, somewhere off in the distance, the strains of a jaunty Jimmy Buffett song, which came from a nearby bar and was punctuated by the slamming of a car door.

We bowed our heads. I'm sure that's why we never saw Zane Donahue run up behind Vivien.

Not until it was too late, anyway.

"You think you can treat me like this?" His voice rumbled over the lawn and startled the couple of gulls who were snoozing nearby and they took off screaming. "You're a thief, Vivien. A liar and a thief."

And with that, he poured a bucket of water over Vivien's head.

❮❮◆ 2 ◆❯❯

Since I was standing close to Vivien and right in the splash zone, I had to change clothes when I got home, and wash my hair, too, to get rid of the smell of chlorine. Which, I suppose, wasn't nearly as bad as what Vivien—madder than the wet hen she so resembled and swearing a blue streak—must have gone through after the crowd scattered and the memorial service fizzled. The cops were called, or so I heard the next day when the watery assault was the only thing anyone on the island could talk about. According to those in the know, official statements were taken and complaints were duly filed.

Something told me I'd hear all the gory details that evening. Vivien was selling off her aunt's possessions and I was scheduled to meet her at Estelle's house at seven thirty that Friday. It wound up being a glorious summer evening, complete with cotton ball clouds I knew would reflect the light of the setting sun and produce a fabulous array of pinks, oranges, and reds, and I hoped my business would be concluded in time for me to enjoy it. The lake itself was the color of sapphires, and a pleasant breeze took the edge off of what had been a warm afternoon. I grabbed my checkbook and a light jacket and, rather than brave weekend traffic, decided to walk. Estelle lived close to downtown Put-in-Bay, the heart of the island's hopping social scene, and the last thing I wanted to do was negotiate my way through streets crowded with summer tourists.

Just a few minutes after I left home I was standing in front of our fabled island merry-go-round, a tourist hot spot, listening to the music of the carousel organ and watching the young and the old whirl around and around on chickens and pigs and the island favorite, Pete the Perch. Farther down the street, I sidestepped groups of partiers and passed the historic hotel and any number of bars and restaurants, already busy, that I knew would be packed until the wee hours of the morning.

Estelle's house was close to Mother of Sorrows Church, where just a couple of months before, I'd accompanied a group of nuns who'd come to the island for a retreat and were instantly embroiled in a mystery, and I glanced toward the gray stone building just in time to see a man duck behind it. Tall, dark-haired, athletic. If I didn't know better I would have thought it was Zane Donahue, but after what I'd heard from Chandra, who was once married to island police chief Hank Florentine and who got the inside scoop on these things, Zane and Vivien had been ordered to stay far, far away from each other. Tossing water on Vivien during what should have been a solemn ceremony was one thing, but even Zane wasn't high-handed enough to ignore a police order and show up near Estelle's when Vivien was handling her late aunt's estate.

The house Estelle had lived in all her life was an unassuming bungalow with a gigantic old rhododendron bush up front and another between it and the house next door, which had a Frisk Realty "For Sale" sign in the front yard. There were flower boxes on the windows that some friends of Estelle had kindly planted and kept watered throughout her illness, and even from a few houses away, I could see that the boxes still brimmed with red impatiens and purple pansies but they were drooping now that Estelle was gone and Vivien wasn't tending them.

I could also see that I wasn't going to be alone.

"Hey, I didn't know you were coming by."

When I stopped on the sidewalk directly across the street from Estelle's to consider my options and wonder if there was any chance I could slink away and pretend I didn't hear him, Levi turned from where he was just about to walk up her front steps.

So much for options. And slinking away.

"Vivien must have decided to get a couple sales out of the way at the same time," he said. "That's why you're here, too, right?"

Act like an adult, I reminded myself, and ever the adult, I knew when I was well and truly trapped. I looked both ways before I crossed the street. There were times on the island—winter and weekdays during spring and autumn— when I wouldn't have had to bother. But this was June, and with so many tourists on the loose in the golf carts that were the island's preferred mode of transportation, I wasn't taking any chances.

"You're buying something from Vivien?" I asked Levi

when I joined him on the slate sidewalk that led up to the house.

"An old rolltop desk. I saw it back when I bought the bar and Estelle handled the deal. We came over here to sign the papers and I told her if she ever wanted to get rid of it, I'd be first in line to take it off her hands. She remembered." He was dressed more casually that evening than he had been the day before when we were at the yacht club, and he poked his hands into the pockets of his (nicely butt-hugging, but it's not like I noticed or anything) jeans. "She gave me a call just a couple of days before she died and said the desk was mine if I wanted it. For a price, of course."

"Estelle was nothing if not a smart businesswoman." I smiled at the memory. "She called me, too, about a Queen Anne curly maple highboy I admired when she invited some of us over for cocktails one night. Mid–eighteenth century," I said, "and it's going to cost me a small fortune, but it's worth it."

"And you can afford it."

He hadn't meant the comment as anything more than a casual reply, but let's face it—I was a little touchy when it came to my background and Levi's treachery.

I clutched my hands at my waist.

He pretended to study the single fat cloud that drifted high above our heads.

There didn't seem to be any point in standing there and being uncomfortable. "We should go in," I finally said. "I'm sure Vivien is waiting for us."

"Right." He turned to the house. "You in a hurry?"

It was the first time I stopped to think that a Friday evening in the summer was probably the worst time for Levi to be away from his bar. "Go on, go right ahead." I stepped back to let him up the stairs first. "I've got nothing going on tonight and no one staying at my place." Did I somehow manage to make this sound like it was no big deal? "You go." I made a little shooing motion with my hands. "Get your business over with so you can get back to the bar, then I'll take care of what I need to do."

"Not what I meant." He put a hand on my arm, and don't ask me why, but I let him. I let him leave it there, too, at least for as long as it took for the heat of his skin to seep into mine. That's when I couldn't control a shiver, and that's when he let go. "Everything is under control at the bar. We're busy, but not slammed. I don't need to get back for a while. I thought if you weren't busy we could—"

Could what, I could only imagine, but I didn't find out, and maybe that's a good thing. A sleek and very shiny black BMW Z4 roadster convertible purred up to the curb, and first Riva, then Quentin Champion, got out.

"Oh, is this a party? I love parties." Riva giggled and, like it was the most natural thing in the world, wound an arm through Levi's. "Especially when there are handsome men around."

"More of a buying expedition than a party," he told her.

Riva managed another giggle. "That's exactly what we're here for, too. How cool is that! Vivien told us she's getting rid of some of her aunt's stuff and, well, you know how it is." Though she hadn't bothered to even look my way before she closed in on Levi, now Riva slid a grin in my direction. "When you have a busy inn, you need all sorts of furniture. Actually, I'm surprised we had the chance to get away at all this evening. Aren't you surprised we had the chance to get away this evening, Quentin?" She turned to her brother, who might have been listening if he weren't so busy watching two young, leggy ladies walk by.

With a flick of her corn-colored ponytail, Riva turned back to me. "Well, it is amazing that we had a chance to get away. I mean what with all the people staying at our place this weekend. Is it always this busy in the summer? Are you filled to the rafters this weekend, too?"

"Bea's place has the best reputation on the island." Like he had all the practice in the world (and for all I knew, he did), Levi managed to untangle himself smoothly from Riva's grip. He put a hand on my shoulder. "Her place is always busy."

"Which means we really should get down to business here," I announced and retreated from Levi, from the emotions that erupted inside me at his touch, and from the sly smile on Riva's face by racing up the front steps. I'd already raised my hand to knock on the front door when something caught my attention from the direction of that big rhododendron. The plant twitched, I swear it did, and I guess Levi noticed, too, because he walked over to that side of the house.

"You need some help, Cody?" I heard him ask.

The answer was muffled. But then, the man who Levi was talking to was behind the rhododendron bush.

"How about you come on out of there and say hello?" It might have sounded like a friendly suggestion, at least to anyone who knew Levi well. But Cody obviously wasn't one of them. Or maybe he just wasn't about to argue with a guy nearly twice as tall as he was.

When he stepped out from behind the bush, I recognized Cody Rayburn even though we'd never formally met. He worked at the island's only gas station and I'd seen him there a time or two, tinkering with cars. He was in his thirties, short, and scrawny. His long, dark hair stuck out the back of his red baseball cap, and that evening, he was wearing a dark T-shirt and jeans dotted with oil stains. He scrubbed a finger under his nose.

"How ya doin'?" Cody asked no one in particular.

"You can't be here to buy something from Vivien." How Riva decided this so quickly was anybody's guess. Or maybe just one look at Cody and she knew he wasn't an antiques-loving kind of guy.

"You looking for something?" Levi asked him.

Cody backstepped his way closer to the porch and farther from Levi. "Just heading home," he said. "Taking a shortcut, heading home. Thought I'd stop in and talk to Vivien for a while. She's here, ain't she? She said she would be here tonight." He cocked his head and looked at the house. "I'll just hang out here with you and talk to her for a while, maybe have a beer or two. We do that all the time, you know," he added as if someone might challenge his statement. "I stop in and we have a couple beers and a couple laughs."

Knowing Vivien, I wasn't convinced, but hey, who am I to judge? Again, I turned to knock on the door. Again I was interrupted, this time when a green motor scooter zipped into the drive.

"Vivien here?" A man with hair the color of walnuts whipped off his helmet and joined us on the porch. "I'm supposed to meet her here this evening. Alex Canfield." He shook hands all around. Well, except when it came to the Twins. One look at them and his eyes got as wide as hubcaps. He blushed and stammered something about what an honor it was to meet them.

"I've got to get to work over at the Yardarm," Alex said once he'd recovered. "You know, that new restaurant over near the marina. I just wanted to stop in really quick because Vivien said she was getting rid of some of the old tools in Estelle's garage. When I was a kid I used to come over here to cut the lawn and I remember that Estelle had this incredible tool that belonged to her grandfather. Cast iron, three-strand rope maker from 1901 with some old rope still attached!" He spoke these last words on the end of a reverent sigh. "That rope maker made me fall in love with antique tools. I can't wait to get my hands on it, and maybe some of Estelle's other old stuff, too."

"Join the crowd." This time, I didn't wait for anything to interrupt me. I rapped on the front door.

There wasn't any answer.

"Well, that's weird." Levi took the steps two at a time and stood on the porch next to me. "I know she said seven thirty, and—"

I checked my phone. "It's after."

I knocked again.

Still no answer.

"She keeps an extra key over there, in that phony rock." When Cody Rayburn spoke up, we all looked to where he was shuffling a nervous little dance on the front lawn. He shrugged. "Hey, like I said, me and Vivien, we're friends. She told me about the extra key. You know, in case that old aunt of hers ever needed anything and Vivien couldn't be here to help her. She told me where the key was so that I could stop by and lend a hand."

Levi and I exchanged looks, and we didn't have to utter a word. Vivien and Cody were about as much of a friendly couple as the Gulf of Mexico and an oil spill. Even when he produced a key from inside the faux rock, I wasn't convinced.

Rather than use a purloined key to get in the house, I tried the doorknob. The front door swung open.

"Vivien!" I called out to her. "It's me, Bea. I'm here. I mean, uh, we're here! A bunch of us are here." I stepped into the living room. Levi was right behind me, Riva was behind him (and standing a little too close if you asked me), then Quentin and Alex, with Cody bringing up the rear. "I came to pay you for the highboy."

Considering what she was charging me for the dresser, I thought Vivien would have come running, but there was no sign of her.

Come to think of it, there was no sign of the highboy, either. The last time I'd been to Estelle's it was in the living room directly opposite the front window. Now that spot was empty.

Automatically, I stepped farther into the small, neat room, with its smoky gray walls and white woodwork, and looked around. There had been other, smaller things I'd told Vivien I'd be willing to purchase along with the highboy: a pair of silver candlesticks and an old lamp that had long ago been converted from oil to electric. It had a glass shade decorated with blue and green flowers and wasn't my style, but it would look good in one of my guest rooms and would be a nice memory of Estelle. The lamp was gone, too.

"She probably just ran out for something," Riva declared and plunked herself down on a dark gray couch with rolled arms and elegant wooden feet. The couch was as understated and sedate as vivacious Estelle never was, but one look at the rug on which it stood—squares inside squares in shades of red and green and yellow—and I couldn't help but remember Estelle's exquisite taste. As a matter of fact, when

I'd visited to share a drink with Estelle, I'd sat right where Riva was sitting. It was the perfect spot from which to admire the curly maple highboy.

"What's the sour face for?" Levi had the sense to keep his voice down when he leaned close and asked.

"My highboy." I waved at the empty spot along the wall. "Where's my highboy?"

"Maybe Vivien's out back helping someone load it into a van or something," Levi suggested. He swallowed his words when I gave him a look. Vivien helping someone do manual labor? Not in this universe, and we both knew it.

"Maybe she's got a sort of staging area for the stuff she's selling," I said, and I made my way through the living room and into the dining room in search of the highboy. Quentin Champion followed along, and once he fell into step behind me, Levi trailed him. So did Cody and Alex.

As it turned out, there was nothing in the dining room but a table piled with archive boxes, and nothing in the kitchen except appliances, an oak table, and a collection of cookbooks with a sign taped to them that said *Library Donation* in Estelle's loopy handwriting.

No curly maple highboy.

I paused to consider this while I dragged out my phone and called Vivien. The only number I had for her was for her office, but for all I knew, she'd been delayed by an impending real estate deal.

No answer.

I tapped the phone against my chin.

"Let's try her cell number," Levi said, and he pulled out his own phone, checked his list of contacts, and called.

From somewhere in the house, we heard the strains of "Sexy and I Know It."

"That's it," Cody chimed in. "That's Vivien's cell phone."

I shushed him with the wave of one hand. "We need to listen to know where the ring is coming from."

But by then, the snippet of song had ended.

Levi dialed again and we all held our breaths and bent our heads to listen.

We actually might have been able to locate the direction of the sound if Riva didn't saunter in and chirp, "What are you guys doing?"

We groaned in unison and Levi tried one more time.

This time when Vivien's phone rang, we were ready for it.

"Basement," Cody said, and pointed to a door at the far end of the kitchen.

"I don't think so," Alex said. He pointed in the other direction, past the dining room and back toward the living room. "It sounded to me like it came from upstairs."

I wasn't comfortable proposing that we go off in different directions and search. It wasn't my house, and other than Levi, who I knew a little too well, I didn't know any of these people. "We'll check upstairs first," I suggested, and when we trooped back into the living room and up the stairs and stopped at the top of the landing where there was a hallway and the open doors of three rooms, Levi dialed the number again.

Nothing.

As if we'd choreographed the move, we all turned on our heels and headed the other way. Riva, the last one to have joined our little procession, was in the lead when we walked back into the kitchen and toward that closed basement door.

"I . . . I don't want to go down there." She eyed the door and wrapped herself in a hug, and as much as I'd been trying to pay as little attention as possible to the story of the Twins and their lives in captivity, I couldn't help but remember something about how she and Quentin had been tied in a dark basement by their kidnapper for days on end.

Call me a sucker, but I moved to the front of the crowd and opened the basement door so Riva didn't have to, and this time when Levi dialed Vivien's number, the music was loud and clear.

"I'm sexy and I know it." A gravelly voice ground out the words to a driving techno beat. "I'm sexy and I know it."

"Down here," I said, though I guess I didn't have to. I felt along the wall for a light switch, flicked it on, and started down the basement steps.

"I'm sexy and I know it."

Apparently Levi thought we should make sure about the ringtone.

There was nothing special about Estelle's basement. At the bottom of the steps, all of us but Riva—and Quentin, too, I noticed—stepped into a rectangular room where there were some boxes stacked, a ping-pong table, and an old sewing machine.

"I'm sexy and I know it" came from somewhere on my right.

There was a door there, and beyond it, Estelle's laundry room. When I swung open the door, I could just make out the shapes of a washer and a dryer. There was no light switch on the wall and step by careful step, I inched into the room, swinging my hand over my head. My fingers smacked a long pull chain that turned on a single lightbulb hanging from the ceiling in the center of the room.

"I'm sexy and I know it," the man with the gravelly voice sang again.

Only when I saw Vivien, she was looking as far from sexy as it was possible to get.

She lay on her back on the tile floor, one arm thrown over her head, her hair spread out behind her like a dark halo. Her right leg was bent in an impossible position, and her dress, a summery little number with bright flowers all over it, was bunched up around her thighs. Her eyes were open. So was her mouth. There was a raw red mark around her neck and an odd-looking contraption lying next to her head.

If I had to guess, I'd say it was a cast iron, three-strand rope maker from 1901. The rope that was still attached to it was wound around Vivien's neck.

"Nobody move." Levi had the good sense to stop the rest of the group at the door of the laundry room, and by the time I turned to him, my heart in my throat and my stomach doing flip-flops, he had already called the police.

❖ 3 ❖

"So . . ." Police Chief Hank Florentine was a bulky guy with a bullet-shaped head and a buzz haircut. He had big hands and a stubborn chin, and he didn't smile nearly enough. Then again, in his business, I guess he didn't often have the opportunity. Once Levi had called him, we'd stepped out of the laundry room and back into the main basement, and just a few minutes later, Hank arrived. He glanced from me, to Levi, to Alex, to Cody. The Twins were still upstairs. Lucky them—they hadn't had to look into the face of their dead real estate agent.

Hank already had a scowl on his pug-ugly face, so when it folded in on itself, I knew he was even more unhappy than usual. "What are you doing here, Cody?" he asked, and maybe Cody Rayburn was smarter than he looked because he had the sense to step back and try to blend in with the wall. "You know better."

"I do. I really do." Cody's head bobbed. "But I was just passing by, see, and all these people were coming in here to Estelle's and they invited me to come inside, too, and—"

Cody knew he'd said too much and that we were bound to dispute his version of the story; he clamped his lips shut.

Hank scratched a hand along the back of his neck. "I'll need to take each of your statements," he said, and I guess he knew we wouldn't take issue because he never even looked at me or Levi when he added, "Bea and Levi, here. I'll start with you. Then you can help out with the rest of them."

I knew I should take this as a compliment. In the little over a year I'd lived on South Bass, I'd assisted Hank in solving a few murders. He would never come right out and say it—and I would never expect him to—but I knew he appreciated my insights and my help. As for Levi . . . an all-too-familiar uncomfortable thumping started up behind my ribs . . . Levi was, after all, a professional private investigator. He was the ideal ally.

"Let's leave these guys to do what they have to do," Hank said, glancing toward the laundry room door and the paramedics who were at work in there. "We'll go upstairs." He gave Cody a laser look. "And we'll talk."

Hank let Alex and Cody go first, and we followed. When we got to the living room, he told a uniformed officer to keep an eye on Quentin, Alex, and Cody and looked around for Riva, who, her brother informed us with a wave at the closed door of the powder room, was currently indisposed.

"Estelle had an office upstairs," Levi suggested. "You could take everyone up there and interview them privately."

Hank nodded, and we followed him up the stairs.

The moment I stepped inside the office and caught sight of the golden oak desk that dominated the far wall, I could see why Levi wanted to buy it. It was a beauty, at least five feet wide, complete with a row of cubbyholes across the top back and a dozen little drawers under those. Estelle had obviously cherished the desk—the polished brass hardware twinkled at us in the evening light.

"So . . ." Hank sat down in the chair in front of the desk. There were two chairs across from the desk, both upholstered wing chairs I had a feeling were designed to put Estelle's customers at ease. I sank into the one to the right of the window that looked out over the street. Levi took the chair on the other side of the window. "Who wants to start?"

"We were here to buy furniture from Vivien," I said.

"Both of you? Together?" The note of skepticism in Hank's voice was anything but professional, but I guess I couldn't blame him. Levi and I were as discreet about our breakup as we'd ever been about what we had of a relationship. But Chandra is my next-door neighbor, after all, and she doesn't miss a thing. She doesn't much care who she talks to about the things she sees and hears, either, and I was sure that by now, she'd told Hank all about how Levi and I were on the outs.

"Not both of us together," Levi clarified. "I was supposed to be here at seven thirty to see Vivien."

"And that's the time she told me to stop by, too," I added.

"And the rest of them?" Hank asked.

"The Twins said they were here to look at furniture," I said, filling Hank in. "Alex Canfield told us he stopped by to look at some old tools. Cody Rayburn—"

"Ah, Cody Rayburn!" Hank leaned back and his chair squeaked. "What do you know about him?" he asked both of us.

Levi shrugged. "He works at the gas station. Once in a while he shows up at my place and drinks too much."

"And he was hiding in the rhododendron bush when we got here," I added.

Thinking this through, Hank tipped back his head and pursed his lips.

"You don't look surprised," I said.

"We'll talk about it later," Hank replied. "How well did you know the victim?" he asked me.

"Hardly at all," I admitted. "We'd met a time or two, and I was at the memorial service yesterday, of course. Before that, I talked to Vivien on the phone the other day. You know, to arrange to meet here tonight. She knew what I was coming for. She knew that Estelle wanted me to have the highboy. We talked value and we agreed on a price. And the highboy, by the way," I pointed out, because it never hurts to let a professional know these kinds of things, "isn't here."

"Not here?" Hank didn't sound as interested in the missing highboy as he did in wondering why this was important.

I filled him in. "I came here specifically to buy the highboy. The highboy isn't here."

"You think someone stole it. Was there any sign of forcible entry?"

I thought back to when we'd all arrived. "The door was open," I told Hank. "But the doorframe wasn't scratched and I haven't seen any broken windows."

"And nothing inside the house looks as if it's been disturbed?"

"You mean except for the highboy that wasn't where it was supposed to be? No," I told him.

"Probably not a robbery, then. Ms. Frisk must have known her killer if she let the person in," Hank mumbled. While we were talking, he'd taken a small notebook and a pen out of his pocket and, pen poised over the page, he looked Levi's way. "How about you?" he asked. "Did you know Ms. Frisk?"

"A bit."

Not a surprising comment from Levi. After all, it's a small island and something like two hundred people actually stay put throughout the winter. We were all bound to bump into each other now and then.

Levi shifted in his chair. "We dated for a while," he added.

I'd already sat up like a shot and uttered an amazed, "What?" when I realized it was not only an overreaction, but pretty tacky, too, and way too revealing. I could have kicked myself. I sank back into the wing chair and wished I could disappear, but even that didn't keep me from noticing Levi turn my way.

"It was just a couple of times," he said, and he was talking to me, not to Hank, because Hank hadn't asked anything about how often Levi and Vivien might have seen each other. "Last spring. After you and I—"

Hank cleared his throat just in time. "So, Levi, obviously you can tell me more about Ms. Frisk than Bea can."

Levi's shrug wasn't exactly convincing. "She was . . ." He pressed his lips together. "Well, I guess anybody who ever met her knew that Vivien was bright and attractive and—"

"She was sexy and she knew it," I sang.

"I suppose some people might say that." Like we were the only two people in the room, Levi kept his eyes on me. "I thought so, too. At first," he added, almost a little too quickly. "But the more time I spent with Vivien—"

"How much time was that?" The question didn't come from Hank.

A muscle bunched at the base of Levi's jaw. "Not very much. Then again, it didn't take me very much time to realize that she was full of herself and demanding."

I knew my smile was tight and so sweet, it could have rotted teeth. Ask me if I cared. "I suppose that all depends on what she was demanding and who she was demanding it from."

"Well, not what you're thinking," Levi answered quickly.

"As if you'd know what I'm thinking."

"I thought I did. Back before . . ." He twitched his broad shoulders. "You can't expect that I'd just sit around every night all night by myself and—"

"Like I did," I snapped. "Every night. All by myself."

"Which is fine if you're into the whole tortured, lonely artiste thing."

"Tortured, lonely artiste!" I sat up and slapped the arms of the chair. "Is that how you think of me? Because let me tell you something, buster—"

"All right, you two." I guess Hank knew the only way he was going to get our attention was to hop out of his chair, come stand in front of us, and give us a glare of monumental proportions. "I don't know what's going on between you two. I don't want to know," he added, with one hand out like a traffic cop to stop us just in case we were about to tell him anything personal. "All I know is that I'm investigating a murder. And having you two sitting here squabbling like angry cats isn't helping me. So you"—he swung around in my direction—"you wait until I ask for your opinion. And you"—this time he turned to Levi—"you are going to tell me anything you can about Vivien Frisk."

Hank knew it was all he needed to say. He stalked back to his chair, sat back down, and picked up his notebook and his pen. "You dated her," he said to Levi, recapping what we already knew and forcing me to reconsider what it meant. "And you said it was when?"

"Back in the spring. We went out"—Levi had to think about it—"twice. We went out twice. Once for coffee, and Vivien was so picky and so demanding of the barista, I was amazed anyone could be that particular about coffee."

He knew I was particular about my coffee; I was perfectly justified in giving him a sour smile.

"I cut her some slack. I figured she was having a bad day," Levi continued. "Then, about a week later—"

"That's why you have her cell number!" Yeah, sure, Hank had told me to keep my mouth shut but the pieces fell into place and I couldn't help myself. I dug my fingers into the fabric arms of the chair. Better that than letting Levi see that I was shaking. "I had her office number, and that's the number I called when we came into the house. But you, you had her personal number. You have her in your contacts."

"Yes, I have her in my contacts."

"And even though you thought she was . . . what was that you said, picky and demanding? Even though you thought she was picky and demanding, you never deleted her from your contacts?"

Levi slapped one arm of his chair. "So I never deleted her from my contacts. Big deal! I've never deleted my grandfather's name from my contacts, either, and he died three years ago!"

"That's different," I announced, folding my arms over my chest and plunking back in my chair. "Dying isn't the same as dating."

"Sometimes it's just as painful," Levi growled. Something told me he wasn't talking about Vivien Frisk.

"Don't even start!" Hank snapped when I opened my mouth. "I told you, Bea, you keep quiet. If you two want to duke it out after I'm done here, you have my blessing. Right now, you're slowing me down. And I don't appreciate it."

With thumb and forefinger, I pinched my lips shut. While I was at it, I bit the inside of my cheek, too.

"So, about a week after you and Ms. Frisk went out for coffee . . ." Hank hauled in a deep, calming breath and let it out slowly, but that didn't fool me. His voice still simmered with aggravation. "Then what?" he asked Levi.

"She called one evening. Vivien called. She asked if I'd like to meet her for dinner. I wasn't doing anything." He cast the briefest of glances in my direction. "I told her sure. After we got to the restaurant, it took me about a minute and a half to realize we really didn't have anything to talk about, and besides, that night, she was even nastier than she was when we went out for coffee. She criticized every little thing our waitress did, she complained about the food, she talked about herself nonstop. Yes, Vivien was vibrant and sexy." Another look in my direction. "But she wasn't my kind of woman. She called again a few days later and asked about lunch and I told her I was busy. She must have gotten the message because I never heard from her again."

"But you came here tonight anyway," Hank remarked.

"Believe me, it wasn't Vivien's charms." Levi pointed toward the rolltop. "It was to buy that desk."

"And where were you, say, two or three hours ago?" Hank asked.

"That's when you figure she was killed?" Levi didn't

even need to think about it. "At the bar, checking in an order from our beer supplier. There were plenty of people around. They can tell you I never left there all afternoon."

"And you?" Hank turned my way.

"Me? Why would I kill Vivien? I told you, Hank, I hardly knew the woman."

"Looks like you don't have to know someone well to have really strong feelings about her," he said.

"Look . . ." I twined my fingers together and leaned forward, my elbows on my knees. "I had nothing against Vivien. And I certainly couldn't have been jealous or mad at her for dating . . ." Call me a coward, but I couldn't make myself say the name. "I couldn't be mad at her because of who she dated, because until just a couple of minutes ago, I had no idea who she dated. As to where I was this afternoon . . ." I thought back. "I went down to the ferry just after noon to pick up a food order from a specialty shop on the mainland. After that I stopped at the grocery store for things like bread and milk, and then at the newspaper office to place an ad. I went home, did some paperwork, read a couple chapters of *Gone with the Wind*, took a nap."

"Anybody see you around the house?" Hank asked.

I swallowed down the realization that it was actually harder to admit I had no guests than it was to convince Hank I had no alibi. "No. But I did see some people over at Chandra's briefly, and I talked to them, too, so they could vouch for me. I went out to the front porch to chase Jerry the cat away from my flowers and I saw there were some people at Chandra's front door. I called over to them, asked if they needed help. They said they had appointments for tarot readings and Chandra wasn't home."

I can't imagine why this interested Hank in the least, but he made a note of it in his book.

"And then?" he asked.

"They got in their golf cart and left."

"Time?"

"Four. Maybe five. Does it matter?"

"It might," Hank conceded. For him, that was sharing generously. He tapped his notebook with the tip of his pen. "Did Chandra talk to Ms. Frisk at that memorial service yesterday?"

"Not that I saw," I told him. "But speaking of that . . ." I weighed the wisdom of mentioning Zane Donahue to Hank and decided I'd let him be the judge of whether I was imagining things or not. "When I got here this evening, Zane Donahue was across the street. Well, it might have been Zane Donahue," I added in the interest of full disclosure. "I didn't get a really good look, so I can't really be sure. But it could have been him. He was heading around to the back of the church. You know what happened at the yacht club yesterday. You know he and Vivien—"

Hank groaned. "Don't even remind me. Those two were always going at each other. Sickening. And you say he was here?"

"I said he was across the street. If it was him. I didn't see him near the house."

"I didn't, either," Levi added, "and I got here just a little while before Bea did."

"I'll keep that in mind," Hank remarked. "Now, as for Chandra . . ."

"Chandra thinks Vivien was a lousy, dishonest, nasty person," I told him, and okay, yes, so I emphasized the *nasty* just a little too much and made sure I was looking Levi's way when I did. "That's not news, Hank. There aren't many people on South Bass who have much good to say about Vivien."

"Chandra more than most," he replied, and glanced from me to Levi. "You two don't know, do you? Well, maybe you wouldn't, being newcomers to the island. Chandra, see, was once married to a man named Bill Barone."

I knew Chandra had three exes and that Hank was number three. "Bill, was he number one? Or was he her second husband?" I asked him.

"He was the first," Hank said. "Chandra was in her twenties and Bill was older by ten years or so. He was a pilot over at the airport, and from what I've heard, he was a nice guy."

"You didn't know him." It seemed like a no-brainer, but Hank would understand that I had to have all my ducks in a row.

"It all happened before I came here," he admitted. "I wasn't born on the island like Chandra was and like Bill was, too."

"And you never met him after you came here?" I asked.

Hank shook his head. "He was already dead by then. Sad story. Got sick. Leukemia. There was nothing they could do, and he died young. But not before . . ." He let out a long breath through his nose. "Vivien didn't grow up here on South Bass. The way I heard it, she came here from the mainland when she was in her twenties. She was at loose ends, looking for work, and Estelle, well, you know what a nice woman Estelle was. She offered to teach Vivien the ropes of the real estate business."

"And then Vivien turned around and opened her own real estate company and stabbed Estelle in the back," Levi said.

"Something like that." Hank nodded. "But that's not all

she did. You see, once Vivien arrived here . . . well, you knew her, both of you. It only took two minutes in the room with the woman and you knew she was the type who, when she set her sights on a man . . . well, unlike you, Levi, most of them weren't smart enough to know when to call it quits. You cut and run. A lot of others didn't have the good sense. Bill Barone was one of them."

I couldn't have been more surprised if Hank had told me he could sprout wings and fly. "You mean . . ." I stammered.

"Vivien stole Bill Barone away from Chandra. Yeah, he was years older than Vivien, but he had some money and a good reputation, and I hear he was a good-looking guy. Vivien set her sights on him and never let up. She was Bill's widow. And Chandra never forgave her for what she did." Hank shook his head slowly back and forth. "It's no surprise to anyone who knows her that Chandra doesn't keep her feelings to herself. More than once, I've heard her say that she hated Vivien Frisk and wanted nothing more than to see her dead."

❰❰ 4 ❱❱

Chandra had been done wrong by Vivien Frisk.
    Serious wrong.

But that didn't mean . . .

While Hank was downstairs corralling the next person he wanted to interview, I chewed over the situation—and everything Hank seemed to be implying when he brought up Chandra's name.

It didn't take long to make up my mind.

"No way," I mumbled.

"You're thinking about Chandra."

I'd been so deep in thought, I'd forgotten Levi was there. Or at least I would have forgotten if that little thrill of excitement that shot electricity through the air every time he was around weren't tickling over my arms and prickling along the back of my neck.

With a *harrumph* under my breath, I told the prickles and the tickles to get lost.

It helped that I had other things to think about—Hank had pretty much come right out and said one of my best friends might also be a killer.

"No way," I said again.

"She does tend to get carried away." I didn't need Levi to point this out. He didn't know Chandra nearly as well as I did.

Unless he'd dated her, too, somewhere along the line.

The thought was unworthy of me, not to mention preposterous, and before I could let it upend me or sour my mood even more, I told myself to stick to the matter at hand.

"You know her, Levi. Yeah, sure, Chandra can be something of a drama queen. She proved that yesterday by acting the way she was acting just because we're reading *Gone with the Wind*. But you also know that she doesn't have a mean bone in her body. Besides, if she was going to kill Vivien, you'd think she would have done it years ago. Why wait until now? She's been married twice since Bill Barone. She's had plenty to keep her occupied."

"But seeing Vivien yesterday might have—"

"Awakened long-suppressed hatred? Please!" I'd already rolled my eyes when I realized it was childish and that Levi probably couldn't see me well, anyway. The light was quickly fading in Estelle's office.

Gathering twilight.

Summer breezes.

A guy who also happened to be a terrific lover not two feet away.

I wasn't taking any chances; I flicked on the light on the table between my chair and Levi's, and just to be sure I could well and truly banish the romantic ambiance that was gathering, I got up and turned on the desk lamp, too.

"Chandra doesn't suppress anything," I reminded him. "Not for long, anyway, and certainly not for years."

"Maybe not, but you of all people should know that there are depths to peoples' minds that most of us will never understand."

He was talking about the books I wrote, not about me personally, but talking about the books I wrote only served as a reminder of his treachery. No, not his treachery when he actually went out on two dates with Vivien, though come to think of it, that didn't make me feel any more charitable toward Levi. I mean how he'd led a double life: bar owner and Bea watcher. I was talking about what a rotten, lowlife stinker he was.

All I had to do was keep reminding myself how true that was.

I plopped back down in my chair and crossed my arms over my chest.

"It's not going to ever get better if we don't talk about it." His voice was as gentle as the summer night, as soothing as the breeze that flowed through the window and caressed my cheek. I hated the way he always seemed to know what I was thinking about. Especially when I was thinking about him.

"Maybe I don't want it to get better," I told him.

"I don't believe that."

"Why?" I'd already turned in my chair to look his way before I realized it wasn't a good idea. It was the blue eyes. I'd always been a sucker for guys with blue eyes.

I stayed strong. "There's really nothing for us to talk about," I pointed out. It wasn't the first time, and something told me it wouldn't be the last. "You lied."

"And you didn't?"

I might have been able to handle this comment in my usual levelheaded way if he hadn't added a tiny little click of his tongue to the end of it. Like he had every right to be offended.

Equally offended, I popped out of my chair and marched toward the door. "You can tell Hank—"

"What?" Our police chief just happened to show up with Cody Rayburn right behind him. "That you're eager to help me out? Thanks, Bea." The way Hank plowed into the room, I had no choice but to step back. Or get run over. Cody toed the carpeting just inside the office door, and with no place else to go, I dropped back into my chair.

There was another chair in the corner, a mahogany Chippendale with a crisply carved back and a seat upholstered in damask the color of autumn leaves, and Hank pulled it over in front of the desk and motioned to Cody to take a seat. Honest, I'm usually not obsessive about dirt but the thought of Cody's oily jeans against that lovely fabric and I couldn't help myself. There was a small throw pillow embroidered with violets on my chair, and I whipped it out from behind my back and plunked it on the chair just as Cody sat down.

"What are you doing here, Cody?" Hank asked.

Cody rocked back and forth, flattening the pillow to make it comfortable. "You're the one who brought me up here, Chief. You said you wanted to talk. About—"

"That's not what I mean and you know it," Hank snapped. "What are you doing here, Cody?"

There is only so long anybody can stand up to Hank's withering glare, and though I didn't know him, my guess was Cody had less backbone than most. He flicked his tongue across his lips. "It's like I said . . ." In the soft glow of the lights I'd turned on around the room, Cody looked even more anemic than he'd looked out in the daylight. He had what my grandmother would call "poor skin," pockmarked and sallow. He had what my grandmother would call "bad hair," too. It stuck out from the back of his baseball cap in greasy clumps. I'm not sure she would have recognized sketchy when she saw it, but I sure did. From the moment I set eyes on him, I had decided Cody Rayburn was sketchy.

"I was just passing by," he told Hank, as bold as brass. "On my way home from work. It's like I told everybody. I mean, them . . ." He made a gesture toward me and Levi. "And those other ones, those people downstairs. I was just passing by, and sometimes Vivien, she—"

Hank leaned forward in his chair. "She what?"

It seemed a simple enough question but maybe Cody knew Hank better than I did. And maybe for all different reasons. Maybe he knew he'd never be able to hold his own beneath the flash of aggravation that sparked in Hank's dark eyes.

Paler than ever, Cody sank back in his chair. "You know Vivien and me, you know we were friends, Hank."

"I know you thought you were Vivien's friend."

Cody scrubbed a finger under his nose. "Ain't that the same thing?"

I'd never thought of Hank as an especially patient person, but I saw now that I was wrong. A cop is part law enforcer, part social worker, and part mediator, and though he didn't like his softer side to show, this particular cop was good at all three.

Or maybe he just knew that if he let his frustration out, he'd never be able to stop himself from blowing his cork.

Hank clutched the wooden arms of the antique desk chair, but his voice was soft and even. "She had an order of protection against you, Cody."

This was news. To me, and to Levi, if the flash of surprise on his face meant anything.

My spirits lifted. We had a viable suspect. A viable suspect who wasn't Chandra.

"You weren't supposed to be within five hundred feet of Vivien," Hank reminded Cody.

The smile that touched Cody's lips was surprisingly sly. "I wasn't near her. I was out in front. In front of Estelle's house. No way I knew Vivien was here."

"That's not what you told us." So okay, Cody didn't appreciate it when I piped up; eyes narrowed, he shot me a look. Ask me if I cared! "You told us you used to stop by and have a couple of beers with Vivien. You said that's why you were here tonight. And you knew where Estelle kept her hide-a-key."

That fire flared in Hank's eyes. "Is that so?" He made note of it in his little book. "You want to explain that, Cody?"

"I didn't . . . I mean, how could I know where that key was? I was just . . . I just guessed, that's all. When these people here, when they said they were supposed to meet Vivien and there was no answer when they knocked, I figured there had to be a key around somewhere. And I guessed. Heck, Hank, you know it, half the people on the island keep a spare key in one of them fake rocks."

"Half the people who own cottages on the island haven't been stalked by you."

"Do I look like the kind of guy who needs to stalk a woman?" Cody braced one scrawny arm along the back of his chair, leaned back, and lifted his chin. Something told me the preening was for my benefit, and I wasn't sure if I should laugh or cry. "Vivien was nuts," he said, his voice sharp. "She told you I was bothering her, following her around, showing up at all the places she used to go."

Hank nodded. "That's exactly what she told me. And she convinced a judge, too."

"Well, doesn't it figure you'd all believe her and not me?" His mouth twisted with disgust. "'Cause I tried to tell you the whole story then, Hank. I tried to tell you the truth when Vivien got that order of . . . of whatever it's called. Me and Vivien, we used to get it on together once in a while." He gave me a broad wink. "If you get my drift."

I did, and it made my skin crawl.

"Then I told her I couldn't see her no more," Cody added. "My old lady was pregnant, and—"

"And you were having a relationship with Vivien and with another woman? At the same time?" Okay, so my question shouldn't have come out sounding more like *no way, no how* than it did a simple request for clarification. But then, it was hard to believe one woman would be attracted to Cody. Two? At the same time?

"Hey, you don't know what you're missing until you give it a try," Cody said, his smile sly.

I got the message, but then, I guess Levi did, too. A throaty growl came from that side of the room.

I guess Cody heard it, too, because he dropped the come-and-get-me act. "Vivien, she started following me," he told us. "You know, after I dumped her. I'd stop for a beer at a place like Levi's, and there she was."

"True?" Hank asked Levi.

His shrug was barely noticeable. "They may have been in the bar at the same time. I can't say."

"I always got there first," Cody said. "And then Vivien, she'd come in after. If you was paying attention, you would have seen that. She was following me."

"She wasn't following you tonight." I felt duty bound to point this out. "You were hiding in the rhododendron when Levi and I got here."

"I was looking for something," Cody insisted.

So I had every right to ask, "What?"

He tugged his earlobe. "I was here helping Estelle once. Helping, you know, clean up the yard in the spring. And I lost a ring."

I didn't give him time to think about it and cook up some cockamamy story. "What did it look like?"

"Hank!" Cody looked toward the chief. "What's the deal here? Why is this chick asking questions?"

"Her name is Ms. Cartwright." The tone of Hank's voice said all Cody needed to know. "And Ms. Cartwright is here because I asked her to be here. So is Levi. If they want to ask questions, they can ask questions."

"And I want to know what your ring looked like," I said.

Cody's top lip curled. "Gold. With a silver skull in the center of it. Ask my old lady. She gave it to me last Christmas."

"And you liked it so much, you lost it last spring and didn't decide to look for it until today?" Levi gave Cody a level look.

"I didn't want to bother her." Color touched Cody's ashy cheeks. "Estelle, I mean. I knew she was sick. Everyone on the island knew she was sick. She was a nice lady, and I didn't want her to see me poking around in her bushes because, you know, I didn't want her to worry. I didn't want to bother her."

What had Levi said about how I understood that there were depths to people's minds that could be unfathomable?

Maybe so, but even I couldn't tell if Cody was lying.

I suppose Hank couldn't, either, which is why he kept pushing.

"So you were here looking for a ring. And what time was that, Cody?"

He shrugged, sniffed. "I left work around five, stopped for a shot and a beer. Not at Levi's place," he added just in case Levi happened to mention that he hadn't seen Cody there. "I had one shot and one beer. And then I started for home. I'm not crazy enough to try and drive around here on a Friday night. I walked. And since I was walking right past Estelle's and I knew there was no way I could bother her anymore"—another shrug said all he needed to say about that part of the equation—"I figured I'd look. You know, for my ring."

"And what were you doing before that?" Hank asked.

"I told you, I had a shot and a beer."

"Where?"

"Gordon's. You know, over by the ice-cream shop."

I knew Hank would be sure to check. "And before that?" he asked.

"I was at work."

"Can someone verify that?"

I knew exactly what Hank was digging for—an alibi—but it took a moment for Cody to catch on.

"You think I killed Vivien?" His voice was tight with outrage. "Heck, why would I do a thing like that?"

Hank lowered his chin and looked Cody in the eye. "You want a list? How about because she was afraid of you? How about because you were stalking her? How about because you were obsessed with her?"

"Obsessed." Cody waved away the thought with one hand. "There are plenty of fish in the lake, Hank."

"So who can tell us where you were this afternoon?"

Obviously, deep thought wasn't Cody's strong suit and he spent a minute getting his memories together. "Phil was off today. My boss," he added for my and Levi's benefit, though he didn't have to. Since there was only one gas station on the island, I'd dealt with Phil more than a few times, and I was sure Levi had, too. "I changed the oil for some guy with a cottage over on Columbus Avenue. Big guy named . . ." Thinking hard, Cody snapped his fingers together. "Jason, maybe. Or something like that. Jason or Jackson. Yeah, that's what it was. Jackson. Jackson Moody."

I knew Jack. He was active in the local neighborhood association. I bet Hank knew him, too, but he made a note of the name, anyway.

"And what time was that?" he asked Cody.

"What . . . what time did Vivien die?"

Hank actually smiled. But not like it was funny. "I'm the one asking the questions. What time did you change the oil in Jack Moody's car?"

Cody's face screwed up with the effort of concentration. "Three. Four, maybe. Yeah, closer to four, I think."

I had a feeling I knew what Hank would ask next so I didn't feel guilty butting in. "And Jack waited there at the gas station while you worked on his car?" I asked Cody.

He shook his head. "He said he was going to walk downtown and see what was going on. There's supposed to be some kind of party in the park tomorrow night. He said he was going to see, you know, what bands were playing."

When Levi commented, he made it sound like the most natural thing in the world. "So Jack Moody can't say if you were there at the gas station the whole time."

"The oil in his car wasn't changed when he left, and it was when he came back." I had to give Cody credit—it was a remarkably on-point observation. "That proves it, don't it, Hank? That proves I was there the whole time."

"Maybe," Hank conceded. "You know we'll ask around."

"Go right ahead." Cody stuck out his bottom lip. "You'll see. You'll find out I was there. Why would I kill Vivien, Hank? I loved her."

"Then why did you break up with her?" I asked him.

"I didn't . . ."

That's the problem with being a liar. Sometimes it's hard to remember where the truth ends and the lies begin.

The three of us sat patiently and waited to see what other trouble Cody could get himself into.

"I didn't officially break up with her," he said.

"You told us you did," I reminded him. "You said that's why she started following you, why she started telling lies about how you were stalking her."

"We talked about it." To Cody's ears, this sounded plausible; he nodded. "I told her I was thinking about breaking up with her. You know, on account of my old lady and the kid. But Vivien, she was pretty upset about it. And I told her . . . I told her, you know, that maybe we could talk about it. And that's when she started following me around. You know, so she could try to convince me to change my mind. Vivien, she was nuts about me."

Hank stood up. "I'll be in touch, Cody."

"Sure. Sure, Hank." Cody stood, too, and walked out the door.

"There's your killer," I said, motioning toward the door as soon as Cody closed it behind himself. "You can't possibly think it was anyone else. That guy's a stalker and a liar. He can't keep his own story straight."

"And he might have an alibi," Hank pointed out.

I knew I wasn't going to convince Hank, but I had to try. I had to remind him, "Chandra might, too."

❦ 5 ❧

Alex Canfield was next up, and I have to admit, as soon as he walked into the room, it was hard for me to keep an air of objectivity. Oh, I don't mean he was some kind of handsome hunk and I couldn't keep my mind on my work. I'm way too levelheaded for that sort of nonsense. But Alex was friendly, neatly dressed, personable. He had a good smile, an easy manner, and a sort of openness that, before I'd met my share of murderers, I would have instantly seen as a badge of honesty.

These days, I didn't need to remind myself not to be fooled by any of it.

I knew better, right? Charming can hide cunning, and there's often something shady going on behind a dazzling smile.

If I needed any more proof, I only had to look Levi's way.

"I hope I can help." Alex tossed aside the pillow I'd pitched on the chair and slipped into the seat Cody had just vacated. He looked from one of us to the other. "What do you want to know?"

"For starters, what you were doing here tonight," Hank said.

Hands flattened on his knees, Alex sat up straight. "It's like I told these folks . . ." He glanced at me and Levi. "When I got here, I told everyone I was here to pick up some of the old tools that once belonged to Estelle's grandfather, and her great-grandfather, too. I'm really into antique tools."

I wasn't sure if anyone else caught what I'd just heard. I leaned forward. "That's exactly why we were all here," I told Alex. "Only everyone else who came said they were here to buy things from Vivien."

It took a few seconds for him to catch on, and when he did, Alex's cheeks flushed. He might not be classically handsome—his chin was a little narrow and his ears were a tad big—but Alex was nice-looking enough. A broad smile added an air of little-boy sweetness to his face. "I see what you mean! I said—"

"You said you were here to pick up the tools," I reminded him. "So you must have paid Vivien for them sometime before today."

Alex shook his head, and a curl of nut brown hair fell onto his forehead. "I was going to buy the stuff. I mean, I offered to."

"And Vivien didn't take you up on it?" I was glad Levi asked the question so I didn't come across as too pushy.

"That's right," Alex told him. "After Estelle died and I called and told Vivien how I'd always admired the old tools, I said right away that I was willing to pay whatever she thought was a good market price. I even had a list I made from auctions I saw online. I didn't want her to think I was trying to shortchange her. And Vivien, well, she told me not to even think about paying. She said I should stop by this evening and pick up whatever I wanted."

"Definitely not what she said about the curly maple high-boy." I folded my arms over my chest. "Any idea why she was feeling so generous?" I asked Alex.

"Well, that's exactly what I asked her."

Hank sat with pen on paper, ready to take note of what-ever Alex had to say. "And what was her answer?"

"She said she didn't need the money." Alex's brows dropped over his eyes and he wrinkled his nose. "It was awfully nice of her."

"And completely out of character," Hank commented. "I mean, let's face it, we all might not have known Ms. Frisk well . . ." His gaze went ever so briefly to Levi, and I barely controlled myself; I wanted to jump up and give Hank a high-five for the moral support. "But I think we all know that she didn't have a reputation as a woman who was espe-cially charitable."

"Well, no." With a little cough, Alex cleared his throat. "I don't think she thought I was a charity case or anything. I think she was just being nice. You know, for old times' sake."

I could take a chance and guess what he was getting at, but let's face it, there's not much room for guessing in a murder investigation. I was perfectly within my rights when I blurted out, "You mean you dated Vivien, too?"

Alex didn't hold the question against me. I mean, not like I figured Levi did when he scowled in my direction. "I'm sorry, I should have explained myself better. I just figured on an island this size, everyone knows everyone else's business," Alex said. "Vivien and I, we started seeing each other last fall. Sure, I dated her."

"You and everyone else." Yes, I mumbled the words. Yes, Levi still heard them. That would explain the sour face.

"So she liked you." This came from Hank, and believe me, I wasn't fooled into thinking he was getting all touchy-feely. This was important information in terms of any motivation or alibi Alex might have, and Alex's motives and alibi . . . well, they were important to the investigation. Besides, sticking to the facts allowed Hank to sidestep what I think he was worried might turn into another Bea versus Levi smackdown. "She wanted you to have the tools because you were her boyfriend."

"Ex-boyfriend," Alex admitted.

"Let me guess—you went out with her twice."

Alex looked at me as if I'd lost my mind. "Twice? Why would you—"

"What Ms. Cartwright means . . ." Elbows on knees, Levi leaned forward, but not before he aimed what he thought was a withering look in my direction. He should have known better—I'm a New Yorker. I don't wither easily. "Vivien . . . er, Ms. Frisk, was known to have had a number of relationships, and some of them didn't last very long."

Alex laughed. "I'll say! And I'm not talking out of school here. I'm not gossiping. Everyone knows that Vivien had that way about her. You know, men just couldn't resist her."

"Some men."

My stage whisper wasn't lost on Levi. But then, it wasn't meant to be.

Alex went right on as if I'd never spoken. "I honestly don't get it. I don't understand why any man—well, most men, anyway—who dated her even once wouldn't want to keep dating her. Vivien is . . . well, I guess now I have to say *was*." His lips pursed and his eyes lowered, he took a moment to adjust to this new reality, then twitched his shoulders. "Vivien was beautiful. She was funny. She had that certain something, you know? If she was in a room, you wanted to be right there next to her talking to her. If she was dancing, you couldn't wait to get out on the floor and shake a leg. She was just that kind of woman. So yes, we did go out more than twice. Way more than twice. I liked her."

Like.

This was a word I had never heard associated with Vivien Frisk.

Not from Levi, even when he admitted he'd been seeing Vivien.

Never from Chandra, that was for sure.

In fact, now that I thought about it, I realized that even Estelle Gregario, though she'd never spoken ill of her niece, had never said a nice thing about her, either.

"It isn't often that someone speaks so highly of someone they've broken up with," I commented. "If Vivien was so wonderful—"

"Oh, don't get me wrong!" Alex laughed. "Vivien could be a handful. The woman had an ego the size of Texas! But you're wrong about me breaking up with her. Vivien, she dumped me."

"And still, you're so pleasant about the whole thing."

It would have been a benign sort of comment if Levi or I had made it. Coming from Hank, Alex paid a little more attention. He cleared his throat.

"You're asking me if I was angry."

It wasn't a question, but Hank gave him plenty of time to answer.

When Alex finally did, he added a shrug. "I guess I was," he admitted. "At first. I thought everything was going pretty well between us. And then one day, Vivien told me she didn't want to see me anymore."

"Did she say why?" I asked him.

Another shrug didn't fool me. There was more to the story than Alex was willing to talk about.

Hank didn't miss it, either. "This is a murder investigation, Mr. Canfield," he reminded Alex. "If there's anything you know . . ."

He sighed. "She told me she'd met someone else. She said he was the love of her life."

Once a fiction writer, always a fiction writer, and in addition to maybe helping with a murder investigation, these were the sorts of details that always whetted my appetite when it came to devising stories and understanding motivations.

Everybody's motivations.

"I don't suppose this was last spring?" I asked. "I don't suppose she threw you over for some bar owner who—"

"Oh, come on!" Levi groaned. "You don't go out twice with some guy you know from around town and decide he's the love of your life. At least most women don't. So just forget about it, okay? It's not important. It was never important. It was coffee."

"And dinner," I reminded him.

The noise he made from deep in his throat reminded me of the thunder that rumbles out over the lake when a storm rolls in from Canada. "And dinner. Okay. Coffee once. And dinner once. But I guarantee you, Vivien sure didn't break off a long-term relationship with Alex just to have coffee with me."

He had a point.

Rather than admit it, I turned back to Alex, "Did she say who that other man was?"

Alex frowned. "She never mentioned a name. And honestly, I never asked. I didn't want to know. You know, once you do, you start comparing yourself to that other person. That's never healthy."

He couldn't have known how spot-on the comment was. I started a mental list:

Vivien Frisk:

A little older than me, and Levi, too, for that matter, but that didn't make much of a difference. Vivien was lively, flirty, and more worried about her makeup and her wardrobe than she'd ever been about her business practices. People noticed her—even people who didn't agree with her questionable ethics—and being the center of attention was what Vivien was all about.

Bea Cartwright:

Way more accomplished, and I'm not just saying that because I need the ego boost. I was a bestselling author. I'd had movies made from my books, and a TV series, and heck, even a Broadway musical that had won more than a few awards. I'd chucked over the limelight in the name of finding some peace and quiet, and I'd hidden my true identity from even my closest friends until I'd been outed thanks to Levi, hiding behind glasses I didn't need and afraid to let the real me shine through, because if I did, I'd be besieged by fans and hangers-on, as I had been back in New York.

Of course men were attracted to Vivien Frisk.

She might be sneaky and dishonest.

But at least she wasn't a phony.

Not like me.

"Vivien, she talked a lot about how she'd never known real love before."

Alex's statement snapped me out of my dark thoughts and back to the matter at hand. "So the guy she dumped you for . . ."

"All I know is that he has plenty of money," Alex said. "Vivien told me that. Maybe that's why she didn't want me to pay for the tools. Maybe he was taking care of her and she didn't have to worry about money anymore."

"Maybe," I admitted. "But you did say this happened in the spring, right? Which means that's probably when she met this new guy, this love of her life. But that's the same time—"

"She was seeing me. Yeah, I get it." Levi crossed his arms over his chest. "I guess she was hedging her bets. Rightfully so, since I wasn't interested. And it explains why she didn't much care when I didn't want to see her again."

"What it doesn't explain . . ." Hank had clearly had enough of this let-it-all-hang-out analysis of Levi's dating habits. He swiveled in his seat, the better to pin Alex with a look. "It doesn't explain how you felt when Ms. Frisk broke off your relationship."

"Like I said"—Alex squirmed in the Chippendale chair— "I was mad. At first. Hey, who wouldn't be? Things were going well. At least I thought they were. And when she told me it was over, well, it knocked me for a loop. She kicked me to the curb."

"But then . . ." I met Alex's glance.

"Then I found out I had never known what real love was,

either. See, once I stopped seeing Vivien, I met someone else, and I've never been happier. That's what made me realize that getting dumped by Vivien . . . well, it was the best thing that's ever happened to me."

"So you're not still angry at her?" I asked.

"You mean, did I kill her?" As if the very idea struck a nerve, Alex winced, and when he spoke, his voice was clogged with emotion. "Like I told you, I liked Vivien, and you know, I was sitting down there, downstairs"—he glanced toward the closed office door—"and I was thinking about how the whole thing doesn't feel real. Vivien dead? It's like someone told me the sun has stopped shining. But once I let the horrible reality seep in . . ." He shifted in his seat.

"I've been thinking about it," Alex said. "And I don't think any of you will be surprised when I tell you that Zane Donahue killed Vivien."

"You have proof?" Hank asked.

Alex instantly shook his head. "Do I need any? Come on, we all know that the two of them . . ." He puffed out a breath. "It was one of the things Vivien talked about. A lot. No matter how often we were together or what we were doing, the subject of Zane always seemed to come up."

Hank made note of it. "Because . . ."

"Because he's a lunatic," Alex told us. "Because she was afraid of him. Poor Vivien! All she ever did was sell the guy a house."

"She didn't disclose the burial mound," I reminded Alex.

"Except she did." He looked from one of us to the other. "What kind of person do you think Vivien was?" Fortunately, Alex didn't give us time to answer. He went right on. "She told me the whole story. How Donahue saw the property and fell in love with it. He told her right then and there that he was planning a swimming pool, and she told him there was no way it was ever going to happen."

"That's not what Zane Donahue says," Hank reminded him.

Alex frowned. "Of course it isn't. Of course he'd lie about it. Zane Donahue thinks he's God's gift to the island. Like all his good looks and all his money and all his swagger can get him whatever he wants. But the truth of it is, he changed his mind about the house after all the papers were signed. Some other property came up for sale. Some bigger house with a better view. He wanted to get out of the deal and buy the other house. He was looking for a way out, and he glommed on to the story about the Indian mound. I'll tell you what, hearing his lies spread all around town, it broke Vivien's heart. And then when he took her to court, well, that's when things really started to get ugly."

I could have asked, but I knew this was Hank's territory, so I let him go right ahead. "Ugly how?"

"Threats," Alex said. "Angry phone calls. Public scenes. You all heard what happened at the memorial service yesterday, right?" Of course he knew we had, so he didn't bother to give us time to respond. "Who does that to a woman in mourning? Who creates that sort of scene? I only wish I didn't have to work and I had been there. I would have popped Zane Donahue right in the nose. The man doesn't have a decent bone in his body. I'm telling you, if you need a suspect, Zane Donahue is your man. He killed her. I'm sure he killed her."

"Did you ever hear any of these threats yourself?" Hank asked him.

Alex thought about it for a moment. "Well, there was one time this past winter when Vivien and I were out for dinner. We were just leaving the restaurant as Donahue was coming in. Really, if I'd seen him there at the door, I would have waited to leave until he was seated. Or taken Vivien around the back and out another door. I wasn't paying attention. I wasn't quick enough. And before I knew what was happening, there he was, right up in Vivien's face."

"What did he say?" I asked.

Alex wrinkled his nose. "He was grumbling. Talking low. You know, like somebody does when they're making a threat. So everything he said . . . I don't know. But I did hear one thing clearly. I heard him say that whatever happened to Vivien, she deserved it."

As if he remembered hearing about the incident from Vivien, Hank nodded. "She filed a report."

"And couldn't sleep for days, poor dear." A muscle jumped at the base of Alex's jaw. "She was just that upset."

Believe me, I wasn't making light of the incident. Back in New York, I'd once had a stalker; I knew these kinds of things were serious, and that they could escalate. Still, I had to point out the obvious fact. "That was an awfully long time ago."

"There have been other threats since then," Alex said. "Vivien told me. It was always the same sort of thing from Donahue. He'd see her down at the marina or in the park or somewhere around town and he'd say things like 'You'd better watch out.' Or 'You don't know who you're messing with.' Or 'You'll be sorry.' I don't have one little bit of doubt. Zane Donahue killed Vivien."

"Maybe," Hank conceded. "Maybe not. You can be sure we'll check on Mr. Donahue's whereabouts this evening." His gaze flickered briefly to mine. "In the meantime, I still have to ask . . ." Hank got ready to write down the answer. "Where were you this afternoon, Mr. Canfield?"

"You mean before I got over here? Well, of course that's

what you mean. You're looking for an alibi, aren't you? It's just like on those cop shows on TV—only this, this is real. And it feels weird." A shiver snaked over Alex's shoulders.

"I was home. All day," he said. "I'm a bartender over at the Yardarm and I've got the late shift tonight. I had lunch and took a nap and I didn't get out of bed until about an hour before I came over here."

"Can anyone verify that?" Hank wanted to know.

"Absolutely. That new love of my life I mentioned earlier? We weren't out of each other's sight, not since we both got in from work last night. We were together all day."

"I'll need a name," Hank said. "And a phone number. I'll need to talk to her."

"Him." Alex's grin said it all. "Told you I had something of a revelation once Vivien was out of the picture. And I have her to thank for it. If she'd never dumped me, I wouldn't have met John and realized I'd been hiding my true self all these years. I wouldn't be as happy as I am now. So you see . . ." He stood and took a piece of paper off the desk so he could scrawl a phone number. "John's cell," he explained, handing the paper to Hank. "He'll tell you we were together and that will prove I didn't kill Vivien, right? Really, I had no reason to kill her. Thanks to her, I'm a very happy man. Can I . . . can I go to work now?"

Hank told him he could, and once Alex was out of the room, he grumbled, "We're getting nowhere fast."

"We've got Cody," I reminded him. And then, before he could say something crazy about Chandra, I added, "And it sure sounds like Zane Donahue has motive."

"Motive isn't proof." Hank scraped a hand through his buzz cut hair. "And heck, if none of that stuff about the burial mound is true to begin with . . ." he said a single word under his breath and though I didn't catch it, I could well imagine what it was. "I've got people to talk to, and plenty of sorting out to do."

"And don't forget the Twins," I reminded him.

Hank waved a hand. "They just moved here. What do they know?"

"Vivien sold them Tara," I reminded him. "And you know Vivien—maybe she was lying to Alex about how she told Zane all about the burial mound." Neither Hank nor Levi disputed that this was a possibility. But then, they'd both known Vivien. One of them better than the other. "If Zane Donahue is telling the truth and Vivien really did swindle him, maybe the Twins have some complaint against her, too. Maybe—"

My phone rang and I didn't get the chance to finish.

I answered, and it took just about three seconds of listening before my heart jumped into my throat and I jumped out of my chair.

"I've got to go," I told Hank and Levi, though I think they probably could've guessed that, since I was already on my way out of the room. "That was my security company. There's been a break-in at the B and B!"

❖ 6 ❖

It's amazing how fast lights and sirens cut through a crowd, even on a Friday evening on an island that's known for partying.

Not that it was my idea to head out in Hank's squad car. I was all set to hoof it back to the B and B but he insisted, pointing out that the department would have to respond to the call anyway, and since we were already together, it just made sense. He left a uniformed officer in charge at Estelle's and before I had a chance to voice an opinion (I had a feeling Hank didn't want to hear it), Levi hopped into the car, too.

"I'll take the front," Hank told Levi the moment we'd skidded to a stop in the driveway. "You go around the back."

"And me?" I asked, but it was already too late. Moving faster than any guy his age should have been able to, Hank was already on the front porch and Levi had sprinted around to the back of the house.

I can move pretty fast, too, but really, there didn't seem to be much point. Instead of trying to compete with either of them, I did my best to control the queasy feeling in the pit of my stomach that had erupted the moment I'd gotten the call.

A break-in.

My mouth went dry and my heart battered my ribs.

Standing out on the walk, I looked over the Victorian monstrosity of a house, with its teal paint accented with purple and terra-cotta and the distinctive brick chimney that hugged its outside all the way from the ground level to where it towered over the roof. I'd lived there for just about eighteen months, and when I'd bought it, all I was looking for was a place to hang my hat and hide out from the world. At the time I started searching for a home far, far away from New York, the location didn't matter as much as it being isolated did. The house itself didn't matter, either, except that I knew I wanted a place that was big enough to be an inn and provide this way-too-famous-for-comfort author a little cover and a whole lot of peace and quiet.

I hadn't found either.

I mean, not if I counted the number of murders I'd been involved with since I'd come to the island.

What I had found, though, was a home.

The realization hit like a physical thing, somewhere right between my heart and my stomach, and I pressed my hands to the spot and whispered a prayer that everything was all right inside the house.

While I was at it and anxious to quiet the sickness inside me, I had a look around.

No suspicious cars in the area.

No activity in the tiny park overlooking the lake across the street.

No footprints on the slate walk that led up to the front porch, but then, that would have been too easy. It had been a dry late spring, so I really didn't expect to see any.

In fact, the only sign of life there in my little corner of South Bass was the flick of the beaded curtain on one of the windows of Chandra's house next door.

I wasn't the least bit surprised. I knew better than to think she'd miss something as exciting as a police car with lights flashing in my driveway.

I joined Hank at the front door.

"They didn't attempt to get in this way," he said.

"Then it had to be the back door." By the time I had decided this, Levi was already on his way around to the front of the house.

"They tried back there," he called out and poked his thumb over his shoulder toward the backyard. "The door-frame is scratched and someone smashed one of the glass panels in the door. That's when the alarm went off, and it must have scared them away. I don't think they got in."

There was only one way to find out.

While Hank went around back and called the station to have a cop come over and dust for prints, I punched in my security code and opened the front door.

"I'll go in first." Don't ask me how he got up the front steps so quickly, but Levi put out a stiff arm to stop me.

"Really?" I stepped back, my weight against one foot. "You said it yourself—he didn't get inside."

"I said it didn't look like anyone got inside." Because I had no choice, I had to wait until he stepped into the entry-way before I could follow him.

Back when I purchased the property, it was what Estelle Gregario had described as "one holy heck of a mess." She was absolutely right. Four thousand square feet on the first two floors alone, and over the years, the size of the home and the cost of maintenance had overwhelmed each of its previous owners. One by one, they had finally just stopped trying, and by the time it was up for sale again and Estelle showed me the house, the neglect more than showed. Peeling paint, pitted floors, holes in the walls. The electricity had needed a complete overhaul. The plumbing had to be totally replaced. Decorating—one aspect of moving that I'd always enjoyed—was the least of my worries, not when I had to think about weight-bearing walls, a new slate roof, and the army of island critters who had decided that even a crumbling house beat living out in the wild.

Fortunately, thanks to all those bestsellers and movies and, yes, the TV show (residuals are a wonderful thing), I didn't just have deep pockets—I had endless resources, and the good taste to pull off a miracle. These days, Bea & Bees shone, baseboards to ceilings, front door to back.

The stairway that led up to the six suites of rooms I rented to island visitors was directly opposite the front door. Every step was spotless. The banister gleamed. The parlor was on my right and I peered inside—with its leather furniture and the Oriental carpet in shades of tobacco and red and green, it was perfect. The hardwood floor of the hallway in front of us that led to the kitchen reflected the soft glow of the overhead lights.

The antique tall case clock behind me ticked to a steady beat.

Not so my still-racing heart.

"It's pretty quiet." Yeah, Levi already knew that, but I'd learned early on in investigating murders that it never hurts to point out the obvious when my stomach's in knots and I'm finding it hard to pull in my next breath. "Nobody's here."

"We don't know that. Not for sure." He moved down the hallway. "I'm going to take a look around, and I don't suppose there's any point in telling you to go back outside." He knew better than to wait for my answer. "Just stick close, okay?"

I bit my tongue. Sticking way too close to Levi was what had caused all my problems in the first place.

Rather than remind him—and myself—I dutifully followed him when he carefully walked through the entire first floor, including my private suite off the kitchen. I had a small sitting room there, a bathroom, my bedroom. The last time we'd been in there together . . .

Rather than think about it, I forced myself to concentrate on Levi opening closet doors and looking under the bed.

There was no sign that anyone had been there, and none of the mess I was sure there would have been if someone had ransacked the house.

"Anything missing?" he asked.

I glanced around my bedroom. A few months earlier, I would have been tempted to give him a sultry smile, motion toward the bed, and say, "Yeah. You, me. Over there." I kept my mouth shut. The opportunity for that kind of easy banter had passed us by, and after all this time, I was surprised the realization was still so painful.

I cleared the thought away with a cough and opened dresser drawers and my jewelry box. I'd never been flashy when it came to jewelry, but my great-grandmother's pearls were one of my prized possessions. They were right where they were supposed to be.

"Nothing," I told him. "Everything's fine."

"We're still not taking any chances." He walked out of my suite and instructed me to lock the door behind me, and we did the same thing in the rooms upstairs. Levi checked out everything, even the attic, though the door to Suite 6 that led to the attic was locked.

By the time we dragged back downstairs, I felt like a wet rag that had been wrung out and tossed aside. I leaned against the black granite breakfast bar in the kitchen.

"Thank goodness no one got in," I said.

To which Levi responded, "We still haven't checked out the basement."

I let him handle that on his own and made coffee while he did, watching with more than a little interest as Hank and a cop I knew as Officer Jenkins worked their forensic magic on my back door.

"Nothing." Levi tramped back upstairs and into the kitchen, and when I waved toward the coffee mugs on the counter, he grabbed two, filled them both, and handed one to me.

Over the rim of his cup, he watched me cradle my mug in two hands. "You okay?"

"I'm . . ." I would have liked nothing better than to slough off the whole thing, but then I'd have to deny the *rat-a-tat* going on inside my rib cage. "Why would anyone want to break in?" I asked him and myself.

His shrug said it all. "Nobody home, quick in and out. Grab anything you can to sell or pawn. That's pretty much how these folks think. Except . . ." He'd been about to take a sip of coffee, and he paused, the mug halfway to his mouth. "A B and B isn't the best target, is it? There are usu-ally people coming and going, especially on a summer evening. And you never know who might be hanging around, upstairs in a room or out in the garden. Seems pretty nervy."

"Unless everyone on earth knows I don't have any customers." I didn't mean to sigh. It was a sign of weakness, and it was unworthy of me, too, but I just couldn't help myself.

"Hey!" He put down the mug and lifted a hand, and I had a feeling he would have pulled me into a hug if I hadn't warned him off with a look. "Every business is cyclical. You know that. Right now, all the tourists are enamored with the Twins. But folks will come around. You'll see. Tara isn't nearly as nice as this place. Your house is more off the beaten path, and it's way quieter."

"Apparently a little *too* quiet or someone wouldn't have taken the chance of breaking in." Since my words were so sour, I added sweetener to my coffee and stirred. "Do you suppose they'll try again?"

"Hey, none of that talk." Levi refilled his coffee mug and, watching him, I realized I hadn't even tasted mine yet. I sipped.

Halfway back to the breakfast bar, he stopped. "If you're worried, I could stay here tonight," he said, and added instantly, "That's not what I meant."

"I know what you meant." I slid onto one of the high stools in front of the bar. "I can take care of myself."

"You've made that eminently clear."

I took a drink of coffee. "Is that a compliment?" I asked him. "Or a criticism?"

He had the nerve to offer me one of those grins that sizzled along my skin like heat lightning. "A little of both, I guess." He set down his coffee cup. "You know, the thing with Vivien . . ."

I waved away whatever he was going say. "I know. It was just coffee. And dinner. Really, it doesn't matter. I get it."

"Back at Estelle's, you didn't act like you got it."

"I was surprised, that's all." Rather than take the chance that he'd figure out I was lying, I went to the fridge and grabbed a jar of salsa, and on my way back, I took a bag of tortilla chips out of the cupboard. "I don't know about you"—I dumped the salsa into a bowl—"but I haven't eaten and it's late and I'm hungry—and really?" There is only so much aplomb a girl can fake. I plunked the empty jar on the counter top at the same time I sent a laser look in Levi's direction. "How could you be fooled by a woman like Vivien?"

"I wasn't fooled. It's not like I was head over heels in love with her or anything. I was just looking for something to do. You know, some way to pass an evening in a pleasant way. Somebody to talk to."

"You own a bar. You've got hundreds of people to talk to."

"You know what I mean. And I bet I'm not the only one. I bet you've had a couple of dates since . . ."

Since what, he didn't have to say, but in case he had any ideas about whether he should, I instantly lifted my chin. "I have not," I told him. "Not one. And even if I had, it wouldn't have been with someone whose reputation around the island stinks."

"That's for sure." He had the audacity to grin. "You picked me, didn't you?"

I plunged a chip in salsa, popped it into my mouth, and crunched. "So, did you have a good time?" I asked Levi.

"You mean when I went out with Vivien? I told you. Not especially. She was kind of annoying, yeah, but that wasn't the worst part. The worst part was . . . oh heck, Bea!" He slammed his coffee mug on the counter, and ceramic meeting granite caused a short, sharp ring that reverberated through my sternum. "The worst part was that no matter what she said or what she did or how charming and funny she tried to be, I couldn't stop thinking about you."

I am not often at a loss for words, and even when I am, I can usually cover pretty quickly. Still, I froze, a chip almost to my mouth, and salsa dripping on the kitchen counter was pretty much a giveaway.

I guess it was a good thing that I was saved when my front door burst open and Chandra zipped down the hallway. "Hank's in the driveway," she called out as if I didn't know. "What's going on, Bea? What's wrong?"

At that particular moment, what was going on and what was wrong had less to do with Hank, the break-in, or even the dead body back at Estelle's than it did with me and Levi, eyes locked over that bowl of salsa on the counter, at a loss for words and grappling with wayward emotions.

Levi recovered first, and, looking more than a little relieved at the interruption, he turned to Chandra when she came into the kitchen. "Somebody tried to break in."

Chandra was dressed in a white gauzy top and white capris, and she blanched to the same pale shade as her ensemble. "Break in?" She caught sight of Hank and Officer Jenkins at the back door and her top lip curled like she'd bitten into a lemon. "You mean here? A break-in here?"

"They didn't get in," I told her and poured her a cup of coffee. "I guess they tried, but Levi looked all around. There's no sign that anyone got inside."

Chandra pressed a hand to her heart. "Thank goodness!

We don't need that kind of bad news on the island, do we? Not at the start of summer when the tourists are flocking in and things are going so well."

Only things weren't going all that well.

I told Chandra about Vivien Frisk and waited to see her reaction.

One second. Two seconds. Three.

I knew she'd heard me because Chandra's plucked eyebrows sank over her eyes. But she didn't say a thing. In fact, all she did was stare straight ahead into space.

"Chandra?" After I figured I'd waited long enough, I closed in on her, inserting myself into her line of vision just in case she'd forgotten I was there. "Are you all right? You heard me, right? You heard me say that Vivien is—"

"Dead." The single word oozed out of Chandra like the whispered *Amen* at the end of a prayer, and I couldn't help myself; I wondered whether she was giving the dead the reverence that is their due—or thanking her lucky stars that a long-held wish had come true.

Since I didn't like the second possibility, I concentrated on the first, and on the gravity of the situation. "Hank says he's going to want to talk to you," I told her, and just as I'd hoped, the words snapped her back to reality.

"I don't see why." She grabbed a chip and dipped it in the salsa, and her gaze flickered ever so briefly to where Hank stood on the other side of the back door. "Hank knows—"

"A lot, apparently," I said.

The noise she made while she chewed was pretty much a harrumph.

Levi backstepped toward the door. "I'm going to see if Hank needs anything," he said. "That way, you two can talk."

It was code for *You can interrogate Chandra and ask if she killed Vivien* and I knew it, but there didn't seem to be much point in arguing. Once Levi was outside, I concentrated on my friend.

"You don't seem surprised," I told Chandra.

She wrinkled her nose. "Someone was bound to kill her sooner or later."

"Only I didn't say she was killed. I just said she was dead."

I didn't think it was possible for Chandra to get any more ashen. She proved me wrong. "That doesn't mean anything," she stammered. "It's just what people say. You know, when someone gets . . . when someone dies who no one likes. It's just the sort of thing people say about people they don't like."

"And you didn't like Vivien."

She took another chip out of the bowl, but she didn't dip it in the salsa, and she didn't eat it. She juggled the chip in nervous fingers. "Not one person on this island liked her."

"But you were the only one who was married to Bill Barone when Vivien came along."

Chandra tossed the chip down uneaten and brushed crumbs from her hands. "Hank's got a big mouth."

"He came to the crime scene. And it's his job to get all the facts straight."

She tried for a casual shrug, but it didn't fool me. "Then you two know everything there is to know."

I put a hand on Chandra's sleeve and felt her tremble at the touch. "I know you must have been very hurt when Bill left you for Vivien. And I can understand that. I also know that Bill was a lot older than Vivien and I suspect that had something to do with how she managed to dazzle him, right?"

She stuck out her lower lip. "It was twenty years ago, Bea. Twenty years this month. And Bill, he was a middle-aged guy with a wife and a job and a mortgage, and we weren't flashy, but we had a good life. Then she . . ." She cleared her throat. "Then Vivien came along, and I don't know who she'd been talking to, but someone told her Bill was a real catch, that he had money."

"Did he?"

Her shrug was barely perceptible. "Some. He was a smart guy and he made some good investments over the years. He was good-looking, too," she added, and her shoulders slumped. "At least I thought he was good-looking. I don't think Vivien cared about that. From what I heard, she'd made a mess of her life back on the mainland and she came here to get her head on straight. Estelle took her in, taught her the real estate business, but . . . well . . . Vivien never really fit in. She thought we were a bunch of hicks."

It wasn't a leap of faith, and I sure wasn't reading minds. It just made sense. "Vivien saw Bill's money as a way out," I said. "A chance to get away from the island."

Chandra nodded. "That girl set her sights on my husband and . . ." Her voice clogged. "It was a long time ago," she said, giving her shoulders a shake. "And it doesn't matter anymore."

"It does. Because I think it still hurts."

Chandra is nothing if not self-aware. She didn't need me to tell her. She brushed a tear from her cheeks. "It would have been our anniversary next week. I've been thinking about Bill a lot."

"Hank must realize that."

Chandra is not dumb; she knew exactly what I was getting at.

She knows I'm not dumb, either, and that I was bound to catch on. Which is precisely why she went over to the cupboard where she knew I always kept a bag of cookies and dragged out the Chips Ahoy!

She popped an entire cookie into her mouth and washed it down with coffee. "What you're saying—"

"Is that Hank has no choice but to consider you a suspect. At least until he has a chance to eliminate you. Obviously, that will be easy enough to do. All you have to do is tell him where you were this afternoon at the time of the murder."

Chandra grabbed two more cookies out of the bag and tipped it toward me, and when I waved off her generous offer of my own cookies, she rolled the bag shut and put it back where she'd found it.

"That's silly," she said. "What difference does it make where I was this afternoon? You know I didn't kill Vivien."

"Yes. I do." I finished my coffee and rinsed out the mug, and when I was done, I turned to Chandra and leaned back against the sink. "But you know how these things work, Chandra. You've been in on a couple of investigations with me. Hank has to get statements from everyone who might be involved."

"Except I'm not. Involved, that is."

"Then it will be quick, easy, and painless. But you might as well be ready for whatever it is he might ask. You know he's going to ask how you felt about Vivien."

"He knows how I felt."

"Maybe that's the problem?" I suggested.

Chandra finished her cookies in silence, and when she was done, I tried a different tack. "Hank might know how you felt about Vivien, but I don't. I mean, I knew you didn't like Vivien. But, were you still angry?"

"Of course not!"

"And you never confronted her or threatened her?"

"You mean any time in the last twenty years?" Chandra narrowed her gray eyes and choked back her anger. "I threatened her plenty back when she first set her sights on Bill. Is that what you mean, Bea? Because I'll tell you what, I threatened her plenty more once she married him and then a year later when Bill got really sick and those of us here on the island who had known him all his life wanted to do anything we could to help him and Vivien wouldn't let us near him. Is that what you're talking about? About all those months I tried to see Bill before he died and Vivien never let me? Did I threaten her then? You're darned right I did!"

I couldn't begin to act the tough interrogator, not when there were tears in Chandra's eyes. I closed in on my friend and pulled her into a hug. "I get it," I told her. "No one can fault you for any of that. Vivien—"

"Vivien stole what was mine." Chandra stepped away. "Bill was a little older than me, a lot older than her. And there she was, young and cute and chipper, and he fell for it, hook, line, and sinker. I forgave him long ago for being stupid. But I never forgave her, Bea. I never will."

"And Hank understands that." At least I hoped he did. "But he's still going to want to know where you were and what you were doing this afternoon."

Chandra's shoulders shot back and she raised her chin. "I was out, that's where I was. And what I was doing . . . well, that's not any of Hank's business, or yours, either! I was out. And if a friend can't take my word for that—"

I wanted to tell her that of course I could. It was Hank she'd need to satisfy.

But Chandra didn't give me a chance.

Before I could try to calm her down, she ran out of my kitchen, raced out to the porch, and banged the front door closed behind her.

❮❖ 7 ❖❯

That Friday night was quiet.

I ought to know—I didn't sleep a wink of it. Instead, I took a cup of tea and a stack of Chips Ahoy! into my private suite with me and locked the door behind me, taking comfort in the fact that Levi had thoroughly checked every suite and I had locked each one of them, and that the attic and the basement were shut up tight and locked, too.

None of which made it any easier for me to relax.

I heard every creak of every board in the old house and every whisper of the wind against the windows. I listened when a brief but heavy rain fell, pattering on the leaves of the tree outside my bedroom window. I watched as flashes of lightning lit up the night, throwing my bedroom into relief, and as much as I tried, I couldn't help myself—when I peered into the shadows, I wondered who might have gotten into the house, who might still be there, who might be looking back at me.

By the time the sun came up over the eastern end of the lake, it all seemed silly, of course. But that didn't make up for the hours I'd spent being nervous and worried.

I got up, got dressed, and, in an effort at thumbing my nose at the Fates and the boogeymen who had robbed me of my sleep, I made myself French toast for breakfast. I was just sopping up the last of the maple syrup on my plate with the final bite of cinnamon-sugar-coated bliss when my phone rang.

"You're up early."

"Hi, Hank." I would have bothered to mention that if he didn't think I'd be up yet, he shouldn't have called, but the French toast had sweetened my mood. "What's up?"

"I need a favor."

It wasn't often that he asked, so when he did, I paid attention. After I took a drink of coffee, that is.

I swallowed and smiled back at the sunbeam that peeked through the kitchen window. I'd been foolish to be afraid the night before. No one had gotten into my house and I'd already decided to upgrade my security system and have cameras installed at the doors. Life was good. So was the French toast. My coffee, as always, was superior.

"What can I do for you, Hank?" I asked the chief.

"It's Donahue. Zane Donahue."

For a second, the wonderful sweetness on my tongue soured along with my mood. "You don't mean something's happened to him, too?"

Hank didn't so much laugh as he snorted. "No, no. Nothing like that. It's just that with what happened over at Estelle's and then coming over to your place to take care of things there . . ." Something told me it was the first he remembered that in the name of being neighborly, he should ask. "Everything okay last night?"

"Fine. Everything's normal," I assured him, and added a little white lie. "I was fine last night here by myself. Snug as the proverbial bug."

"Good." I could tell he was glad to get the formalities out of the way. "So like I was saying, about yesterday."

"Did you talk to Chandra?" I asked him.

This time, the sound he made wasn't so much a snort as it was a snarl. "Tried. The woman is impossible."

"I'm afraid I upset her."

"You upset her. I upset her. Talking about Bill Barone upset her. Far as I can see, the only thing that didn't upset her was thinking about Vivien being strangled."

"You know that's not true!" Of course, I didn't. But it seemed like the right thing to say. "She didn't like it that you thought she could have—"

"Well, of course I didn't. Not really. Not seriously. But I have to cover all my bases. You know that, Bea. No stone unturned and that sort of thing. Chandra, she should understand that, too. She was married to me for three years. She knows what goes into this job. I wouldn't be doing it right, not if I didn't ask her what she was up to yesterday."

"So you did."

He grunted, and I imagined him nodding.

"And she told you . . ?"

The grunted morphed into a rumble. "Told me she was out."

"Out where?"

"Out taking a walk."

"The weather was perfect, it makes sense that she was out," I reminded Hank.

"Yeah, it makes sense, and she's just the type to go skipping through the fields picking dandelions. But heck, Bea . . ." He sniffed. "If that's what she was doing, that's all she needs to tell me. Where she went. What she did when she got there. Instead, she said she didn't remember where she was. She was out. Just 'out.' That's all she'll say."

It would have been odd. For some people. But Chandra had always been a little airy-fairy. I didn't need to remind Hank of that, though. "Did anyone see her?" I asked instead.

"She says she doesn't remember that, either. She might have been down at the state park. At least for a little while. And there could have been some people around there. And she may have made a stop over at the winery near the marina. But she says they were so busy, she didn't stick around and she didn't order anything and it was full of tourists and she didn't see anyone she knew. She claims she was just wandering."

"Other than the fact that she missed out on that appointment to read tarot cards for some tourists, it sounds like something she would do." I didn't need to remind him about that, either.

"Yeah, but . . ."

He didn't need to remind me what "Yeah, but" meant.

"I can try talking to her again," I suggested.

"Exactly what I was calling about."

My lack of sleep gave me an excuse for being confused. "I thought you said you were calling about Zane Donahue."

"I am calling about Zane Donahue." I heard a long slurp and knew Hank had decided he needed more coffee. I thought we both did, so I poured myself another cup. "That's great that you'd talk to Chandra again, Bea. I'd appreciate that. But Zane Donahue is the one I'd really like you to talk to."

"Me? I don't know the man."

"Exactly."

Any other day, I may have been able to follow what he was saying. That Saturday morning, things were a little hazy, and I was so not in the mood for games. "Explain."

He did. "Donahue showed up here on the island for the first time maybe five or six years ago. He used to rent the Albertson place over there on your side of the island, near the nature preserve. You know the house."

I did. It was big and splashy and pricey.

"It's not like Donahue was ever a real problem. He's never been arrested. But we had a few calls from the neighbors. You know, noisy parties, scantily clad women racing through the yard. That sort of thing."

I could only imagine, and it was way too early in the morning for that.

"Then, when he bought that property from Vivien Frisk . . ." Hank whistled low under his breath. "That's when all the real problems started, the two of them going at each other like Rocky and Apollo Creed. One of them would call me to complain, and no sooner would I hang up than the other would call me with a conflicting story. I'll tell you what, Bea, those two just about made me nuts."

From a seasoned law enforcement professional, this was tantamount to baring his soul. I sat down at the breakfast bar to hear more.

"I've refereed so many fights between those two, I can't even begin to tell you," Hank said. "There was the time at the park when she dumped lemonade on him and he claimed it was on purpose and she insisted he'd stuck out his foot to trip her and she was only defending herself. And the time at the Christmas in July festivities last year when she ran over the inflatable reindeer on his front lawn. He says he saw her aim her car right at Rudolph. She says a raccoon darted out into the road in front of her and she had no choice but to swerve or she would have flattened it. It was always something between those two, and it was never something good."

I got it. Or at least I think I did. "So you're thinking that if you go to talk to Zane—"

"Well, he's going to clam up the minute he sees me, of course. Too many bad memories associated with me, and too much bad blood. If you talk to him, Bea—"

"So what do you want to know?"

Hank chuckled; he knew he'd be able to convince me to help. But then, as I'd proved since moving to the island, there wasn't a mystery I could resist. "Just the usual. Where he was yesterday. What he was doing. When he saw Vivien Frisk last if it wasn't at that memorial service where he dumped that bucket of water on her. And if it really was him you saw over near Estelle's last night."

Yeah, I figured he'd come around to that.

I glanced out the kitchen window. Last night's rain had left the world looking fresh and shiny. The sun was out and it glinted against the petals of the zinnias planted in the bed outside the kitchen, intensifying their jewel colors. "It's a nice day," I reminded Hank. "He's probably out on the lake."

"Oh, come on, Bea!" His chuckle turned into a full-throated laugh. "We might be a small department, but we're not dumb! We kept an eye on Donahue all last night. Didn't like the idea of him slipping onto his boat and sailing off to Canada while we weren't looking."

"So you know he's home."

"As of right now . . ." Why did I have the feeling Hank glanced at his watch? "I just talked to Jenkins, who sat on the house all night. He's home, all right. If you get over there fast . . ."

I grabbed my jacket. If I was lucky, Zane Donahue would have a pot of coffee going when I got there. If I was really lucky, his coffee would be as good as mine.

What had Alex Canfield said about Zane Donahue buying this property, then finding one with a better view?

I couldn't imagine it.

Zane's house stood atop a bluff on the north side of the island, and there was nothing at all between him and the Canadian shoreline twenty-six nautical miles away except a glimpse of Middle Bass Island, a peek of tiny Sugar Island, and miles and miles of water that was a glorious blue that Saturday morning. Here, I knew the sunrises were sure to be breathtaking and the sunsets were spectacular.

Something told me that's why the Native Americans who'd buried their dead on the property had chosen the spot.

Yeah, I couldn't help myself—it was all so crazy, I had to smile when I waved to Officer Jenkins in his squad car and walked up the paving stone path to the front door of the charming Cape Cod.

An Indian burial mound. As they say in the cartoons, who would have thunk it?

Obviously not Zane Donahue.

It took three rings of the bell before he answered, but I guess I could understand that. It wasn't even nine, and when Donahue showed up, he was wrapped in a maroon satin smoking jacket. The robe actually might have given him a rakish look if there weren't smudges of sleeplessness under his eyes and if he wasn't wearing just one gray sock.

"I hope I didn't stop by too early," I said.

He blinked at me in silence for a few moments, then shook his head as if to clear it. "Who are you? Why have you stopped here at all? I don't want to buy it, whatever it is you're selling, and I don't want to be saved, either, if that's what you're looking to do. So why don't you—"

He'd already started to close the door when I put one hand on it. "I'm Bea Cartwright. Hank Florentine asked me to talk to you." Yeah, yeah, I know . . . Hank didn't exactly want his name bandied around, not in Zane's presence, but I could see where this was headed, and it was headed straight for *Go away and don't come back*. I had to risk a little name-dropping.

"Oh." I guess in the great scheme of things, the single syllable meant I was successful. Zane stepped back, opened the door a little wider, and waved me inside.

The house, storybook-pretty on the outside, had been remodeled within, and not that long before, if the smell of new wood and fresh paint meant anything. What I imagined had once been a living room and a dining room had been combined into a single great room with a timbered ceiling open to a second-floor loft and floor-to-ceiling windows on the back wall that looked out over the lake. I could understand the windows. Sunrises and sunsets, remember. The rest of the decorating was too modern for my taste. There were glass and stainless steel tables scattered throughout the great room, one of those sectionals that opens up into lounge chairs on either end, and a chair that was too low to the floor and with a back too pitched to look really comfortable. It was turquoise and it sat next to a table that had an open bottle of scotch on it.

Outside the windows was a patio with a strip of lawn beyond and then the edge of the bluff. From here, we looked as if we were floating above the water and I imagined the scene in the fall with the waves dancing and chopping or in the winter when the lake froze and mounds of ice pushed through the surface and created an Arctic landscape.

"So?" I turned away from the view to find Donahue watching me, his arms crossed over his chest. "What do you want to know?"

"Sorry." I'd always been told (and not just by Levi) that I had a nice smile. It didn't work its magic on Donahue, but I managed to keep it in place anyway, in the hopes of putting him at ease. "Your home is spectacular," I told him. "The view is—"

"Yeah. The view. That's what got me into trouble in the first place. I couldn't resist the view."

"You're talking about the burial mound." I was glad, because I wanted to bring the conversation around to it, anyway. I leaned a bit to my left in the hopes of seeing more of the yard. "Can I—"

"See it?" He snorted, slid open the patio door, and led the way. "Sure. You might as well. Everyone else has been here taking a look at it—the state archeological society, the local historical society, a whole bunch of newspaper report-ers." We rounded the corner from the backyard to the side, and he waved toward a grassy bump, maybe a foot high and twelve feet across, just where the driveway ended and the lawn began. "There you go."

"That's it?" I cringed, and hoped that was enough of an apology. "What I mean is—"

"Yeah, I know what you mean. You mean you expected

something more grand and mystical and tribal-looking. Hey, if this mound was a little more spectacular, maybe I would have noticed it when I bought the property. The way it is—"

"No one would ever know it was even here," I said, moving around to the northernmost end of the mound for a look at it from another angle "Not if they weren't looking."

"Exactly." Donahue turned and headed back into the house, and I followed him. "You can see why I was surprised."

"So how did you find out?"

"About the mound?" He reached for a box of orange Tic Tacs that was on the counter and tapped a few out of the pack, and the way he chomped on them told me oodles about how he felt about the topic. "Some college kid here for the summer and doing a paper on indigenous people. Indigenous people!" His snort pretty much said it all. "They're all long dead, so why should we care about them? What about the people who live here now?"

"The people who want swimming pools where ancient people are buried."

The sarcasm was lost on him. "Exactly." He grabbed a few more Tic Tacs. "Don't we count for anything? It was right after I moved in, and when that kid came to me all excited about what he had found and said he was going to call the state to verify that it was what he thought he was, I offered the little creep five thousand dollars to keep his mouth shut. And you know what he said to me?" I knew I didn't have to ask, and I was right, because Donahue went on. "He told me that history is more important than money. That we owe it to all the people who came before us to honor their memory. What a lot of crap!"

"So you were angry."

"You're darned right." He picked up that scotch bottle

and was all set to screw the cap back on when he paused and shot me a look. "I don't suppose it's any secret."

"On an island this size . . ." My shrug said it all. "And I suppose if it's true and if you didn't know a thing about that burial mound before you bought the property, you have every right to be angry. Except yesterday, I heard that it's not true. I heard that Vivien Frisk told you about the burial mound before you signed the papers on the house."

Donahue's dark eyes flashed. "Who told you that? Oh heck, what difference does it make?" He re-capped the bottle and took it over to the wide steel gray kitchen counter that bordered one side of the great room. "There's always gossip in a place like this. And it's not always true."

Rather than taking the risk of looking too eager, I took my time joining him in the kitchen. "What about this time?" I asked him. "Is it true?"

"That Vivien told me about the mound? Absolutely not." He grabbed a used wineglass from the counter and filled it with ice and water from the fridge. "Whoever told you that . . ." His fingers closed around the delicate stem of the glass and I waited for it to snap. "Well, I guess I can't blame anyone if they heard the story and repeated it. But I know for sure where the lie came from. Vivien." He bit his lower lip. "It must have been her. She was the only one who would dare to spread that sort of rumor."

"You didn't like her." I remembered saying something similar to Chandra and how it had caused her to melt into a puddle of emotion and painful memories, but if I expected the same from Donahue, I was wrong.

He laughed. "No one liked Vivien."

"And pouring that bucket of water over her at the memorial service the other day, that was your way of showing it."

He opened his mouth to respond, then snapped it shut again. "Look," he said, "I had kind of a rough night last night. I didn't get much sleep. If you're expecting me to make some sort of confession—"

"I'm not. Honest." I held up a hand, Boy Scout–style. "I'm only looking to fill in the blanks. That's all Hank asked me to do. One of the blanks definitely is not how you felt about Vivien. Everyone here on the island knows you two were enemies."

"Yeah. Enemies. Right." Donahue downed the water in his glass. "So what else is there for me to tell you? I was downtown last night at the bar in the hotel when I heard the news about what happened to Vivien. There were . . ." He pursed his lips, thinking. "There were maybe forty or fifty people there. Forty or fifty witnesses. I'm afraid I didn't catch all their names but Joe, the bartender, might know most of them in case you want to verify my alibi."

"Only it really wouldn't, would it?"

My gaze locked to his, I let him think about it for a moment. "You were at the bar when you heard the news, but Vivien was killed earlier in the evening, and earlier in the evening . . ." Oh so casually, I ran a finger over the countertop. "You were right across the street from Estelle Gregario's a little before seven thirty."

If he was surprised, he didn't show it, and I told myself it was exactly what I should have expected. A man like Zane Donahue doesn't get where he is and what he has—the money, the reputation, the women—by caving easily.

"So?" he asked.

"So from what I've heard, Hank told you not to go anywhere near Vivien."

He leaned forward, his eyebrows raised and his eyes

wide, and just to be sure I heard him loud and clear, he raised his voice enough for it to ping against the open ceiling. "Are you listening to yourself?" he asked. "Because maybe if you were, you wouldn't make stupid statements, Ms. Cartwright. After what happened at the yacht club on Thursday, you're right, Hank did tell me to stay away from Vivien. And I did."

"But Vivien—"

"Was at Estelle Gregario's. Yeah, I heard. I heard that's where she was . . ." He ran his tongue over his lips. "I heard that's where they found her body. Only since I hadn't seen Vivien, since I hadn't talked to her, and since I was staying far, far away from her just like I was told to do, I couldn't have had any way of knowing she was at her aunt's, could I?"

He had a point, but he didn't need me to tell him that. Even if there wasn't a burial mound in question, I could see why Vivien and Zane would never get along. Not in this universe or in any other.

Two such huge egos couldn't possibly coexist at one time and in one place.

"Then it was you I saw near the church yesterday." He didn't deny it, so I went right on. "What were you doing there?"

"What were you doing there?"

"Going to see Vivien."

"Then maybe you're the one who killed her."

"I didn't have any reason."

"And you think I did?" He lit a cigarette and didn't bother to turn aside when he blew a stream of smoke in my direction. "If you must know, I was enjoying the summer evening before I settled in with a few scotches over at the hotel. I had dinner at the Yardarm. Lobster bisque and a fish sandwich, and tell Hank that when he wants it I can provide him with the receipt. I'm sure there's a date stamp on it, and a time stamp, too. After dinner I went over to the Frosty Pirate and got an ice-cream cone. Chocolate peanut butter. Yeah, I know. It's not good for me." He slapped a hand to his pancake-flat stomach. "But it sure was delicious, and once in a while, I like to treat myself. After that, well, I told you, I was at the hotel bar when I heard the news about Vivien. Looks like I'm not your killer."

"I never said you were."

"But you wondered." Donahue moved through the kitchen and toward the front door, and I got the message: It was time for me to hit the road.

"Hank will probably have some follow-up questions," I told him on my way out, mostly because I knew it was true but also because I wanted to make him squirm just a little. "And you can be sure he'll be verifying your alibi."

"Verify away!"

As soon as I was outside, Zane slammed the door behind me.

I grumbled all the way back to my SUV, and grumbled some more when I got as far as town and found out there was a library-sponsored parade all set to start. Don't get me wrong, I love readers—especially ones like the kids who were lined up in DeRivera Park dressed as their favorite characters from books. But I was so not in the mood for the Cat in the Hat. Or Harry Potter. Or Winnie the Pooh. Just like I wasn't in the mood to find streets blocked for the parade and my trip home put on hold.

With a sigh, I grabbed the first parking place I could find and got out of the car. If nothing else, I could take care of some business while I was downtown. I grabbed a copy of the local newspaper to check to see how my latest ad looked and headed over to the Frosty Pirate.

Hey, I was obligated, right? I mean, Donahue had mentioned it, and it would be downright sloppy of me if I didn't check his alibi.

Besides, I had visions of sitting on the front porch that evening with an entire pint of ice cream, drowning my business woes and my detective troubles and my in-the-dumper love life in calories, chocolate, and peanut butter.

I headed past the shop that sold T-shirts and other island souvenirs, dodged a couple of people already coming out of one of the local drinking establishments a little tipsy, and made a right at the front door of the Frosty Pirate.

Where I stopped dead in my tracks.

Closed.

That's what the sign on the door said, in big red letters.

Refrigeration problems.

Below that was scrawled, *Sorry,* and the owner's signature, along with the date the sign had been hung.

Three days earlier.

Two thoughts hit simultaneously. The first was all about how I'd miss the chocolate peanut butter ice cream.

The second?

Bye-bye, Zane Donahue's alibi.

« 8 »

With no promise of ice cream to brighten my evening, I dragged through the morning and afternoon, wondering about Vivien. There was no question what happened to her down there in that laundry room, of course. That was clear from the get-go. So I spent my time thinking about the biggest part of the equation—the who.

Who was in the house with Vivien?

Who had the motive and the opportunity?

Who wanted her dead?

And I couldn't help but think that in other murders I'd investigated, I never seemed to have enough suspects.

This time, it was almost as if there were too many.

Cody Rayburn, Vivien's stalker.

Zane Donahue, the man who made no secret of hating Vivien and who'd lied about his alibi.

Alex Canfield, who didn't look like a suspect on the face of things because he claimed to actually like Vivien. In my book, that alone made him suspicious.

And then there was Chandra, of course. My mind always came back to Chandra. She of no alibi, no explanations, and a hatred for Vivien that had simmered for twenty years.

It was enough to make me crazy. And very sleepy.

I finally gave up and took a nap, and in an effort to thumb my nose at the Fates and my own way too overactive imagination, I left both the door to my bedroom and the door to my suite open. I woke just in time to hear the clock in the front hall strike six, and feeling more refreshed and more alert than I had all day, I uncorked a really good bottle of wine and settled on the front porch to look through the newspaper I'd picked up when I was downtown earlier in the day.

Or at least I would have if Jerry Garcia weren't in my favorite chair.

"Shoo!" I don't know why I bothered, since I knew there was no way the sassy tabby cared what I thought or what I wanted or that he was on my front porch instead being of over at Chandra's where he belonged, but I set down my glass and the bottle of wine and waved both hands in his direction.

He watched me with as much interest as a fat cat can muster—right before he yawned and went back to sleep.

"Come on, Jerry!" Since my hands were free, I scooped the feisty feline off my chair and deposited him onto the porch floor. "Go home where you belong."

Much to my surprise, he did. But not before he stopped to sniff the geraniums in the pots on the steps. I didn't watch to see if he used them as he usually did: as a bathroom stop. I didn't want to ruin my mood.

Instead, I settled down with my wine and looked over the front page of the newspaper and an article that talked about planned improvements at the marina. No, I'm not a boat owner, but boating and fishing are part of the lifeblood of the island. Anything that affects commerce and tourists affects me.

Especially when I have no commerce or tourists.

My sigh had just faded into the evening air when I noticed Kate coming across my front lawn.

"That better be a Wilder wine!"

"It's not," I called back to her. "But I bet I can talk you into a glass."

She sauntered up the steps two at a time and peered at the label on the wine bottle. "French white burgundy. You really know how to tempt me, don't you?"

"Get yourself a glass."

She ducked into the house and was back outside in a minute. She poured, swirled, sipped, and smiled. "I'll tell you what," Kate said, "we might be able to grow chardonnay grapes around here, but they'll never taste like they do when they come from the Côte de Beaune. This is one of the best perks of having a famous author for a friend. You can afford the really good stuff."

"It is nice, isn't it?" I sipped, too, letting the wine's aromas of soft white flowers, dried grasses, and fresh apple and pear mingle with the slightly mineral taste and dance along my tongue. "It's what the French call *vin de soif*," I told Kate. "Thirst wine. Nice for just sitting and sipping, no meal required."

"Except I'm starving." She pressed a hand to her stomach, over the black Wilder Winery T-shirt she wore with khaki-colored shorts. "You want to go into town for dinner?"

"On a Saturday night in June?" She should have known better. "I might have a pizza in the freezer."

"And I have a bag of salad greens."

We agreed on the menu without another word and settled back to drink our wine, and after a few moments of quiet, Kate glanced at the newspaper I'd tossed onto the wicker table in front of my chair. "Marina, huh? Changes down there should make Luella happy."

"And a lot of tourists, too." I reached for the paper and flipped the front page, and it was a good thing I'd put down my wineglass before I did, or I would have dropped it for sure.

"The Twins." I pointed one trembling finger at the picture that took up a good portion of the top of page two just so Kate couldn't miss it. "Another interview with the Twins, and the picture was taken at Tara."

Kate's lips twitched in a way that told me she didn't care. Ordinarily, I wouldn't have either. But . . .

I tapped my finger on the picture, right between Riva and Quentin. "That's it," I said. "That's my curly maple highboy!"

I'd been so excited about having the piece in my house, of course I'd told Kate about it, so of course she was perfectly justified in asking, "The one you bought from Estelle?"

"The one I couldn't buy from Estelle because it wasn't at Estelle's when I got there. Now I know why." In an effort to drown my outrage, I downed the rest of the wine in my glass. "They stole it out from under me!"

"Well, maybe not," Kate said, then decided she was being altogether too reasonable. "But they must have, right? I mean, Estelle told you—"

"That I could buy it."

"And Vivien told you—"

"To come pay for it yesterday and arrange to pick it up."

"And the Twins—"

"Never said a word to me about it, not even when I was standing there in Estelle's living room staring at the blank wall where the highboy used to be. That's not right!" To emphasize my point, I slapped the newspaper back on the table and stood. "I'm going to talk to them about it."

"Do you think that's a good idea?" Unlike Chandra, Kate is usually the voice of reason, and it was just like her to make the effort.

Only I was in no mood to be reasonable. "I don't care if it's a good idea or not, I want to know what happened and how my curly maple highboy ended up at Tara." I went inside for my purse and made sure (okay, double sure) both the front and back doors were secured before I went back out onto the porch. "You coming with me?" I asked Kate.

She looked at the bottle of white burgundy wistfully. "When we get back—"

I wound an arm through hers and pulled her down the steps and to my car with me. "I'm not planning on attacking the Twins and making off with the highboy. I swear, we won't get arrested and be gone for days and days," I promised her. "When we get back, we can finish the bottle."

My B and B is on the north side of the island. Tara is on the south side, not far from the western shore and the ferry dock. We went the long way around and managed to avoid the downtown crowds, but it was Saturday evening, the ferry ran into the wee hours, and people were still arriving in droves, looking to make the most of the perfect weather and the vibrant party atmosphere that gave the island the nickname "Key West of the Great Lakes."

It took longer than normal to get to Tara, and maybe that was a good thing.

At least by the time we pulled into the circular drive, my heartbeat had slowed, my temper had calmed, and I didn't feel like trouncing anyone. At least until the curly maple highboy was in sight.

I parked the car, laid my hands against the steering wheel, and studied the house. I'd been past it a million times, both before and after the Twins purchased the property, but it was set far back from the road, and though I had known it was being restored and transformed, I'd never gotten a close enough look to see what was really happening. Now, I saw that the Twins had done a ton of renovations and that they were, for the most part—

"Hellish!"

When I breathed out the single word, Kate laughed and looked where I was looking—at the huge house that spread out in either direction from a central portico. At the white pillars all along the front. At the trees that stood like sentinels on either side of the long drive. Oh, the trees themselves were real enough, but the Spanish moss hanging from them? I shook my head in amazement and jumped when a peacock strutting across the lawn let out a sound that was a combination of buzz saw and donkey hee-haw.

"People actually want to stay here?"

Another laugh from Kate was enough to warn me that I may have been a tad too critical. "It's fantasy," she said. "The way Revolutionary War reenacting is fantasy. Or Disney

World. People come here because they want a taste of what they think the Old South was like."

"I don't think it was anything like this." I was sure of it when a yellow Hummer with huge chrome wheels pulled behind us and stopped, its radio blaring a song with a beat that made my bones vibrate.

"People are fighting to get rooms here," I grumbled. "And my place—"

"Your place is prettier, quieter, and has a whole bunch more class." Kate opened her door and hopped out of the SUV. "Let's go prove it."

I knew what she meant: *Mind your temper, Bea. Keep your cool. Don't accuse anyone of anything because you never know the whole story until . . . well, until you know the whole story.*

Now all I had to do was not forget any of that.

The couple from the Hummer were already rolling suit-cases up to the front door, and we fell into step behind them. Inside, we walked into a wide entryway where there was a massive desk made from dark wood against one wall and a young girl in a gown with a plunging neckline and a wide skirt poised behind it with her fingers on a computer keyboard.

Since the Hummer folks were here first, I let them check in and took the time to look around.

The carpet was thick and plush and a shade that reminded me of watermelons. The walls were papered in dark green that was swirled with paisleys and accented with gold. The light fixture over our heads was made to look like a gas light, its bulbs flickering and casting soft, fluttering shadows. Ahead of us and beyond a pair of French doors was a sitting room complete with not two, but three red velvet fainting couches, a couple of chairs with stiff, uncomfortable-looking backs, and a grand piano that, at the moment, was being played by a three-year-old who I think it was safe to say was not the next Mozart.

Kate rolled her eyes.

I waited for the Hummers to step away from the desk and sashayed over there to ask for the proprietors.

I got the feeling this was something like arriving at the gates of Oz without the broomstick of the Wicked Witch. The girl behind the counter batted her eyelashes in Southern belle surprise. "I'd really have to check and see if they're indisposed." She said the last word as if it had taken a while to familiarize herself with it and, now that she had, she couldn't get enough of its delicious syllables. "They're super busy people."

"Aren't we all?" I pointed to the phone on the desk in front of her. "Call them and find out."

She did, and just a couple minutes later, Riva Champion swept down the stairway at the far end of the entryway like a cool breeze over a cotton field.

She caused as much of a commotion.

A ripple of excitement shivered through the crowd. Cell phones were produced. Pictures were taken. The moment of stunned exhilaration ended when someone breathed, "There she is," as if the words were a prayer, and all around me people moved toward the staircase, where Riva made the most of the moment, one hand elegantly draped over the banister. People begged for pictures and she obliged, and when her brother finally joined her (smelling faintly of cigars, I couldn't help but notice), they started all over again.

I will give the Twins credit. I knew enough about fans to

know the smiling and the posing and the autograph-giving could take its toll. Yet the Champion Twins handled it all like . . . well, sorry, but there's only one best way to say it—they handled it all like champions. They posed for picture after picture and signed everything from the receipts for people's rooms to copies of that day's newspaper.

Ah yes, that day's newspaper.

I told myself not to get caught up in the sweet tea atmosphere and to remember why I was there.

Once the last of the grovelers was gone (but not gone far away; plenty of them hung around the lobby positioning themselves so that their selfies included the Twins in the background), Riva hurried over, the tight, small smile on her face barely concealing the fact that she had no memory at all of who I was. "Delilah . . ." She glanced ever so briefly at the girl behind the desk, who I would have bet a bundle was not actually named Delilah. "She says you needed to see me. I do hope there's nothing wrong with your room."

I saw Kate's lips twitch and spoke up fast, because I was afraid of what she might say.

"I'm not a guest. I'm Bea Cartwright. We met last night. At Estelle Gregario's."

I'd think that two people who'd been that close to murder wouldn't have had to consider it for a few long seconds, but both Quentin and Riva did. The truth dawned on her first, and her expression cleared. "Of course! You're Bea! Of course I remember you. You have that little B and B over on the other side of the island."

"Well, it's certainly nothing like this." How's that for diplomatic? And just cutting enough to make me feel righteous?

"Oh! Oh, my gosh." Before I could say another thing, Riva turned as pale as the lily-soft hands on the most spoiled

Southern belle. "I heard what happened at your place last night. Quentin, did you hear?" Since her brother was standing just off to the side, sizing up Kate from the tips of her shoes to the top of her head, she had to raise her voice. "Someone broke into Bea's B and B last night."

"They didn't break in," I corrected her. "They tried to break in."

"Still." She fanned one hand in front of her face. "I would just never get a wink of sleep in a place that might be broken into at any minute. Would you get a wink of sleep, Quentin?"

I was fairly certain that Quentin wasn't thinking about sleep at that moment. Kate knew it, too. That would explain why she skewered him with a laser look and turned her back on him.

"Bea's place is safe and beautiful," Kate said, a little louder than necessary. "That's why people love to stay there."

"But not a whole lot of people. Not right now." Riva raised pencil-thin eyebrows. "Am I right?"

"So much to discuss at the next Chamber meeting in addition to all the details for the gala!" I managed to make this sound as if I actually would. Yeah, like it was anyone's business but my own. "For now, there's something else I'd like to talk to you about." I'd brought the newspaper with me, open and folded to the page that showed the picture of the Twins, and I flashed it in front of Riva. "Highboy," I said.

She had the nerve to smile. "It's way cool, isn't it?"

"It was supposed to be mine."

"Really?" She couldn't have been more surprised if I told her that I saw right away that her snakeskin ballet flats were knockoffs. "Come on." Riva led us through the parlor and into a room that must have been used for guests' breakfasts.

There were twenty tables there, all of them covered with

white linen cloths, each of them with a small vase filled with fabric flowers at the center of it. Since it was late, the settings were already out for the next morning: pink napkins, along with flatware that wasn't nearly as nice as the silver I put out for my guests. There was a sideboard opposite the door, and on the other side of the doorway . . .

I made a beeline for the highboy and Kate followed along.

It was just as beautiful as I remembered it from the time I saw it at Estelle's and told her how much I admired it. Top-notch workmanship. Gorgeous wood. Lovely hardware.

"Estelle told me I had first dibs on the highboy," I told Riva when she joined me.

"That's weird." She wrinkled her nose. "Because last week when I talked to Vivien, she said she didn't know what to do with it. She talked about donating it to Goodwill."

My heart nearly stopped, and something told me Riva realized it. She laughed. "I offered to take it off her hands. It reminds me of a piece of furniture my mom has in her house in Malibu. Or is it the house in Honolulu?" Apparently, she decided it didn't really matter because she shook her shoulders and laughed. "It looks perfect in here, doesn't it?"

It would look more perfect in my dining room, but rather than point that out I said, "There must have been some miscommunication."

"Must have been." She ran one finger lovingly down the side of the highboy. "I'm sure Vivien didn't know what her aunt told you. Otherwise, I mean, she never would have sold this piece of furniture to me, right? I've had it just about a week now. Long before . . ." Riva's eyes filled with tears. "Poor Vivien."

"You were there last night to pick up more of Estelle's things." Yes, a no-brainer, but I wanted to hear it from Riva.

She nodded. "There were some books I thought would look precious on the tables in the parlor, and a couple pictures, and . . ." She tipped her head, thinking. "I wonder what happens to all of it now."

"I suppose that all depends on if Vivien had a will."

"Well, it doesn't really matter as much as finding out who killed Vivien." Riva lifted her perfectly shaped chin. "Have the cops arrested anyone yet?"

"They're working on it," I assured her.

"I hope they've talked to that woman." Riva's golden brows dropped low over her eyes. "That what's-her-name." When we walked into the dining room, Quentin had stayed near the door to chat up a couple of sweet young things who couldn't control their giggles, and Riva had to call out to him. "Quentin, what's the name of that woman? The one we saw at Estelle's last night?"

Quentin pointed to me. "That's her."

Riva rolled eyes the color of a clear Georgia sky. "You'll have to forgive my brother," she said. "He's always had an eye for pretty ladies, and after what we went through during our terrible captivity . . ." She glanced away, swallowed hard, then turned her attention back to me. "He's making up for lost time, and who can blame him!" She tried again. "Not her, Quentin. I know she was there. I mean earlier. You see"—Riva glanced my way again—"you were already at the house when we got there last night. You and that good-looking guy." A smile touched her lips. "Somebody told me he owns a bar somewhere here on the island, but I never did catch the name of it."

I lied with a straight face. Yes, it was unworthy of me, but hey, there was nothing wrong with fighting fire with fire, and Riva had snatched the highboy out from under me. "I don't have a clue."

She was not deterred. "Well, I'm sure I'll run into him somewhere. But that's not what we were talking about, was it? I was telling you that Quentin and I, we were at the house earlier. You know, before anyone else got there."

"And you saw Vivien?" I asked her.

"Vivien? Oh, no. We knocked, but there was no answer. That's why we left and came back again later, and that's when you were there. But when we were there the first time . . ." Thinking about it, she hugged her arms around herself. "Well, I never thought about it. I mean, I should have. I know I should have. But the thought of Vivien being dead . . ." She sniffled. "I've had a pounding headache all day and I know I haven't been thinking straight. That's why I didn't remember, not until right now. We were already back in the car, see. That first time we stopped to see Vivien and she didn't answer the door. We were already back in the car, and that's when we saw her."

I was afraid to ask.

Almost as afraid as I was to not know the answer.

"Who?"

"Well, I don't know her name, but I've seen her around. Blond. Middle-aged. She wears these crazy clothes and usually all bright colors, but yesterday . . ." Thinking, she squeezed her eyes shut, and that gave Kate and me a chance to exchange glances. "She was dressed all in white, and just as we pulled away from the house, she walked around the front. You know, like she'd been in the backyard the whole time. She must have heard us when we were pounding on the door, don't you think? I wonder why she never let us know she was there."

Yeah, I wondered, too.

But I sure wasn't going to wonder out loud.

Instead, I thanked Riva for clearing up the confusion about the highboy, gave it a long, wistful look good-bye, and Kate and I headed back through the parlor.

My mood did not improve one bit when I saw that painted, potbellied lamp in there along with the silver candlesticks I'd planned to buy at Estelle's.

Back at the car, Kate leaned against her door. "Wow. You don't think—"

I knew what she was thinking. And it wasn't about my highboy. I yanked my car door open. "I don't know what to think," I admitted. "Chandra never mentioned that she'd been to Estelle's."

"Well, she wouldn't, would she? Not if she—"

"You can't really believe that!"

Kate spent a few moments considering the possibility. "There was a time I would have liked to," she confessed. "I mean, Chandra with her crazy drum circles and her bonfires and her customers who show up at all hours to commune with the Other Side. She drove me crazy for years."

"And now?"

"And now, she's my friend. She's your friend, too, and you don't think—"

"I don't think it. But there's something going on, and we need to get to the bottom of it."

I pulled out of the driveway, carefully making my way around not two, but three groups of people dressed in Civil War–era costumes. Either they were early for the gala or they always dressed that way. At least when they were under the spell of the Twins and Tara. "I wish there was some sort of proof that Riva and Quentin killed Vivien," I grumbled.

Kate had the nerve to laugh. "Why would they want to kill Vivien?"

"I don't know," I admitted. "But the more I get to know them, the more I'd like nothing better than to see them leave the island. At least if they were in prison, I might get some customers back. And maybe my highboy, too."

« 9 »

By the time we got back home, it was nearly dark and I was more than ready to pop that pizza in the oven, sit back, and finish the bottle of white burgundy.

I would have done it, too.

If there wasn't something weird going on at Chandra's.

Yes, yes, I know. Weird and Chandra go together like hot fudge sundaes and whipped cream.

Only this weird was an out-of-character sort of weird.

Kate and I both noticed. When I parked the car, we exchanged looks.

"If we're smart, we'll just keep walking and pretend nothing odd is going on," Kate said.

I knew she was right.

Which doesn't explain why I got out of the car and headed right next door.

Here's the thing about Chandra's house: Though we are next-door neighbors, our homes couldn't be any more different if she lived in an igloo and I pitched a Bedouin tent in the yard. My grand Victorian was built a little more than a hundred years earlier; Chandra's single-story ranch was a product of the fifties. From what she told me, it had once been the summer home of some banker from Cleveland who packed up the missus and the kids as soon as school was out and sent them to the island.

All that fresh air and sunshine.

All that fooling around he was doing back in Cleveland while his family whiled away the hours on South Bass.

Eventually, the house was sold and the profits were divided as part of the divorce settlement. Chandra's parents were the ones who'd bought it.

All told, Chandra had lived in the house for nearly fifty years, and since her parents had moved to Florida, she'd owned the house outright for more than twenty. In that time, she'd put her own stamp on it, and it should come as no surprise to learn the place was . . . well, let's just say *eclectic*. *Artistic* also fits the bill. The house had *Chandra* written all over it, from the four outside walls each painted a different color (turquoise, pink, purple, and orange on the side of the house that faced mine) to the sunshiny yellow doors. There was a patio out back that she surrounded with twinkling lights and plantings everywhere that included plenty of the herbs she used for teas and spells, a variety of flowers, and a veritable forest of wind chimes, fountains, and chubby gnomes.

Back when I moved to the island, my first encounter with Chandra was on the night of a full moon when she was burning what she called a *bonfire* and what I termed a *con-*

flagration in her yard, and I soon found out that those once-a-month fires were a bone of contention throughout the neighborhood.

Then again, the chanting and the drumming that went along with the fires might have had something to do with why they gave the neighbors fits.

Still, once a month. Full moon. We'd learned to cope, and a couple of times, some of us had even been coaxed into joining in. For the record, I'm a lousy chanter and a not-half-bad drummer.

Now, Kate and I closed in on Chandra, who stood with her back to us in front of a fire with little flame and a whole lot of smoke, and while we were at it, I glanced up at the sliver of moon just inching over the horizon.

The closer we got, the harder it was to breathe. The air was thick with smoke, and the smoke was ripe with . . .

I took a couple of careful sniffs and waved a tendril of heavy, gray smoke away from my face. "What's up?" I asked Chandra. "I think you've got your dates wrong."

She sucked in a screech of surprise and whirled to face us. Yes, the light of the fire was behind her but Kate had left a single lamp on in her house directly across the street, and its light revealed the tears that stained Chandra's cheeks.

"Uh, wrong? Oh, no, nothing's wrong." As if it weren't already too late, she dashed the back of one hand across her cheeks to wipe away the tears. "I'm just . . ." She stepped a bit to her right and that made it just a little harder for me to get a gander at the fire.

"Just cleaning up some stuff in the yard," Chandra said and sniffled. "You know, twigs and branches and such."

"Stinky twigs and branches." Kate waved a hand in front of her face. "It smells like burning hair."

It did, and, curious, I leaned to my left, hoping for a better look at the fire.

Chandra took another step to her right.

"So you two . . ." Chandra closed in on us and Kate and I had no choice but to step back. "You two were out."

"At Tara," Kate told her. "The Twins have Bea's highboy."

Since Chandra is so tenderhearted and since I'd made no secret of how much I was looking forward to owning the piece of furniture, I expected a little more from her than "Oh."

"We're back now." Not that I had to tell her, since she was looking right at us, but it never hurts to state the obvious in awkward situations. "And we're going to have pizza."

"And wine," Kate added.

I poked a thumb over my shoulder toward my house. "You want to—"

"I can't." Chandra tried for a smile but it was feeble and watery. "I've got things I have to do, and—"

"We could bring the pizza and wine over here," I suggested. "Pull up some chairs, sit in front of the fire. I might even have some marshmallows around."

Chandra loves roasted marshmallows—the crispier, the better.

She shook her head. "I'm really tired, and like I said, I've got things to do and . . ."

And we got the message.

Even if we didn't like it.

Kate put a hand on Chandra's arm. "You want to talk?" she asked, and while she did, I moved ever so casually a tad to my left to try for a better look at the fire.

It wasn't as big as Chandra's ritual bonfires, and though there were twigs and branches and a couple pieces of driftwood piled in the fire ring, not much of it had caught the flames. But then, there was something wadded up beneath the pile of wood, and that something was preventing the fire from really getting started. A lick of flame flared for a second against the object and a puff of smoke rose. The blaze erupted and just as quickly went out again, and a new, stinky cloud of smoke belched from the fire ring.

From here it was impossible to tell exactly what that object in the center of the fire was, but it looked soft, and though I knew the combination of night and fire and smoke was playing tricks on my eyes, I was pretty sure it was blue and white.

If I didn't know better, I would have said it was a sweater.

I slept with all the windows closed that night. But then, though the flames never shot up higher than we had seen them when we were over at Chandra's, that smell Kate had described as "burning hair" only intensified as we sat on my front porch and finished the wine. When the wind shifted and the smoke came our way, along with more of the odor, we finally gave up and went inside to eat our pizza, and when Kate left, I locked the front door behind her and thanked whatever angels watched over innkeepers—if I'd had guests that night, I would have had a heck of time explaining away the actions of my crazy neighbor and the smell that seeped through the neighborhood and lodged in everything from my hair to my clothes to my bed linens.

Fortunately, by the next morning, a fresh breeze from Canada had whisked the stink away, and when I got up just a little after the sun climbed over the lake, there was no sign of Chandra outside. Or of feeble flames or stinky smoke, either.

The good news? I had a call on my voicemail from two couples who were already on the island and had stayed at Tara Saturday night. They had assumed that with people heading back to the mainland at the end of the weekend, rooms would open up there on Sunday night, but much to their "dismay" (that was actually the word the woman who left the message used), Tara was booked solid and they weren't ready to go home.

Was it possible for them to book two rooms with me that Sunday night?

Let's pretend I didn't whoop and do a little happy dance there in the kitchen while my coffeepot worked its magic. That would be too pathetic for words.

I waited until I had my act together enough to sound professional rather than desperate, called and told them they could check in any time after three, and sat down to work out a menu for the next day's breakfast.

I was just trying to decide between quiche and shirred eggs when my front doorbell rang.

Hank Florentine didn't look any happier that Sunday morning than he looked any other time. In fact, there were bags under his eyes and his uniform was as wrinkled as if he'd slept in it.

"Coffee?" I suggested.

Without a word, he followed me into the kitchen.

I poured and I figured I didn't have to ask; as long as he was there and looking like what the cat dragged in after a rough night, I got out some eggs, cracked them in a bowl, and scrambled.

Hank held his coffee mug in both hands and breathed in deep. "You're a saint, Bea."

"I don't think so." I dumped the eggs into a frying pan. "But I know a hungry man when I see one."

He worked a kink out of his neck. "Saturday night drunks!" He grunted his opinion of them. "On top of this murder investigation, it was the last thing I needed. Spent the night at the station and haven't eaten since . . ." He checked the time on the microwave and made a face. "Called Chandra about six yesterday evening so I could ask her to stop somewhere and pick up some dinner for me, and I'll tell you what, I thought the woman was going to faint dead away on the other end of the phone."

"Because you asked for dinner?"

He shook his head and grunted while he took a drink of coffee. "I never even got as far as asking her. All I did was say that it was me and I was calling from the station and I swear, she started hyperventilating right then and there. I thought for sure she was going to pass out and I'd have to send EMS over to her place."

The eggs were done, and Hank watched with genuine reverence in his eyes while I loaded them onto plates. "I swear, Bea, she acted like I was going to accuse her of robbing tourists at the ATM."

"And after you told her you wanted her to bring you dinner?"

Hank scooped up a forkful of eggs. "That's the weird part, because after that, she was just fine. Right as rain. Or at least as right as she can ever be. Brought me soup and a sandwich, and she didn't even stop anywhere to pick them up. Made them for me herself." His gaze drifted in the direction of

Chandra's house. "She can be a dear woman." He snapped to and gave me a scowl. "But she can be a crazy lady, too. Don't ever forget that."

I wasn't sure if he was reminding me, or himself, but I didn't point it out. I thought about the bonfire, and the sweater I might—or might not have—seen smoldering in it. "You don't need to tell me." I'd popped some English muffins in the toaster, and when they were done, I went to retrieve them. "I know all about Chandra's crazy tendencies."

"Well, here's to her." Hank raised his mug. "I couldn't live with her, that's for sure. But I guess I can't live without her, either. And she does make a darned good bowl of chicken, lemon, and rice soup."

I clinked my coffee mug to his, finished my eggs and muffin, and refilled our coffee. "So what's up?" I asked Hank, because let's face it, I knew this wasn't a social call. Hank didn't make social calls. "What's happening with the case?"

"Vivien's murder?" Of course he knew that was what I was talking about, but for all I knew, he had plenty of other cases going on and he needed to make sure. When I nodded, his grumble pretty much said it all. "None of it makes any sense," he said.

I knew how he was feeling because that was exactly what I'd been thinking.

"Alex?" I asked.

"His friend John says they were together, all right. But I don't know, Bea—do you think he really can be as happy about the breakup with Vivien as he says he is?"

This, I didn't know. "What about his story about how Vivien didn't want his money? That she didn't need it?"

"Funny you should ask." Hank slipped a piece of folded paper out of his pocket. "I had a look at Vivien's finances.

Without giving too much away to a civilian . . ." His gaze held mine for the briefest of moments, sending a silent message. He knew I'd never talk about the details of a case to anyone who wasn't authorized, but he had to be sure. A lift of my coffee mug told him I was good to go.

"Truth is," Hank said, "Vivien didn't have two nickels to rub together."

I thought about this while I took a drink of coffee. "So why did she tell Alex he didn't have to pay for the tools?"

"Maybe she was trying to get back together with him," Hank suggested.

"Maybe. Though now that Alex has come out as gay, that doesn't seem likely."

"Unless she didn't know."

"Alex doesn't seem shy about telling anyone."

He agreed with a nod. "Then maybe Vivien didn't have money yet, but she knew she was getting some from somewhere."

"Did she have any big home sales pending?"

Hank bit his lower lip. "Nope. None that I can find."

"Then how about Estelle's estate? If Vivien stood to inherit—"

"She did," he told me. "But not the whole thing. Vivien got the house and the contents, but the bulk of Estelle's estate went to a food pantry over on the mainland. It was a lot of money but I'm not surprised. Estelle, she was a nice lady."

"She was." It was true, and I tried not to obsess about how Estelle could have been just the teeniest bit nicer and slipped a note in the highboy about who should buy it when she was gone. Estelle had been sick, I reminded myself; she had more important things to think about than my home decorating needs.

"Well, that would explain it," I said. "Vivien was selling the contents of Estelle's house and she eventually would have sold the house, too, I bet. So she knew she had money coming. Maybe that's what she meant when she told Alex she didn't need him to pay for the tools."

"Maybe," Hank conceded, and we both knew what it meant—the Alex line of the investigation was at a dead end.

"So who gets Vivien's estate?" I wondered.

Hank knew I'd ask. "Cousins," he said, and he was ready with the names. "Originally, of course, her will stated that Bill Barone would inherit, but after he died, Vivien had the will changed. She never had any children but there are cousins outside of Akron, six of them, and her will states that they'll split up her estate."

"Worth killing for?" I asked.

"I can't think of another woman I could have breakfast with who could ask that question with a straight face." Since Hank grinned, I knew he didn't hold this against me. "It's a nice amount and there will be more, of course, once Estelle's house and furniture are added in, but it's far from a fortune. Don't you worry, though, we've checked into all six of those cousins. Two of them are in Cancún at the moment and have been for at least a week, so they couldn't have killed Vivien. The other four . . ." He consulted another piece of paper he produced from his pocket. "A nurse who was on duty Friday all day. A butcher who was right where he was supposed to be at the grocery store where he works, and two elderly females . . ." He squinted at the paper to read his own writing. "They're both in nursing homes, and I talked to the directors, who assured me they're not going anywhere and they sure couldn't have been here on the island on Friday."

"So what about Cody?" I asked him, setting aside the idea of Vivien's family.

Hank made a face. "Cody Rayburn doesn't look like he's got the brains God gave a goat, but I'll tell you what, the whole time we looked into Vivien's allegations about Cody stalking her, there wasn't much we could prove. He's a sneaky little so-and-so, and clever, too, in a smarmy sort of way."

"So he could be covering up for a murder."

"It's possible."

"And the story about him only being at Estelle's because he was looking for his ring?"

Hank's mouth twisted. "What do you think? I don't believe a word that comes out of Cody. Like I said, sneaky."

"And looking guilty."

"Maybe."

I knew Hank wasn't being coy, just practical, but I couldn't help but puff out a breath of frustration. *Maybes* didn't do much for my mood. "Then what about Zane Donahue?"

"You tell me. You're the one who talked to the man."

"Who insists he had every right to be angry at Vivien because she never disclosed the burial mound," I told him. "He also admitted that it was him I saw near Estelle's on Friday evening. He says he was only there because he had a taste for ice cream and had just finished a cone."

Hank's eyebrows slid up his forehead. "The Frosty Pirate? It hasn't been open since last week."

I spared one wistful moment thinking about chocolate peanut butter. "I know."

"Interesting. What else you got for me?"

I was tempted to tell him that I was sure the Champion Twins were our killers, but Hank is nothing if not a professional. I knew he'd ask about the whys and the where-fores of my theory.

Because they have my curly maple highboy didn't seem to fit the bill.

Hank's phone rang and while he took a call from the station, I cleaned up the dishes, and when I was done, I grabbed some of the strawberries I had in the fridge and sliced them into little china bowls decorated with pink flowers and greenery. I knew better than to add extra calories to my diet, but all this thinking and getting nowhere led me to make excuses and my excuses led me to the container of heavy whipping cream.

I splashed cream over the berries, handed a bowl to Hank, and kept one for myself.

"I'm going to stop here every Sunday." He actually smiled.

"Anytime," I told him and glanced toward the phone he'd set on the counter. "Something you need to handle?"

"Nah. Boaters fighting over a berth. I sent a couple officers. You know, Bea, when I came to the island and joined the department, I never thought it would be anything like this."

It was as close as I'd ever heard him come to revealing personal thoughts. "What were you expecting?" I asked.

Hank shrugged. "Helping tourists find their way to Commodore Perry's monument. Assisting little old ladies across the street in weekend traffic. Watching over the kids at the park on the swings. You know, island stuff."

"And instead you got people fighting over berths at the marina."

"And murders." This time, he didn't shrug; he shook his shoulders as if he could get rid of the memories. "We've got to figure out what happened to Vivien, Bea. We can't let something like this go unpunished. It's wrong, and it's bad for the island, and dang, I like this place. It's home."

"Agreed." Done with my strawberries, I grabbed his empty bowl and mine, and when I was done rinsing them out, I sat on the stool next to Hank's at the breakfast bar. "What do you want me to do?"

"Well, if you're not too busy . . ." He realized what he had said after the words were already out of his mouth and the tips of his ears turned crimson. "What I mean is—"

"I know what you mean. I'm not too busy because I don't have any guests. But not to worry, I've got four people checking in this afternoon."

"Four. That's great, Bea."

It was not great, it was okay, and for now, okay would have to be enough. Since Hank was doing his best to be sincere, I didn't point this out to him.

"So maybe until this afternoon . . ." He finished the last of his coffee. "I'm going over to Vivien's. I was there on Saturday and took a look around, but I don't know, I think I must be missing something. Some idea of who might have been angry enough to kill her. Some sign that points us in the right direction. I wondered if you'd come along. You know, just to take a look. You're a writer. You've got a great imagination and a good eye. Maybe something will jump out at you."

I grabbed a light jacket and followed Hank to the door, and sure, I was eager to help.

Even if I didn't like the thought of something jumping out at me.

« 10 »

There is nothing quite so peaceful as South Bass Island on a Sunday morning.

When I first moved here, I had thought it was because after Friday and Saturday nights, all the tourists were partied out and hiding their heads under their pillows until long after the sun was up and they decided they had no choice but to get up, get out, and be human again.

The longer I live on the island, though, the more I learn that it's more than just that. Sure, that Sunday morning, like every Sunday morning, the partiers were recovering, and that definitely explains why the downtown sidewalks that teemed the night before were empty now and why the streets, packed with golf carts just a few short hours before, were deserted.

But that doesn't explain the way the light always looks a little softer on Sundays, or why that one day a week I always want to breathe a little deeper and walk a little slower. The tempo of island life ratchets back, at least until the brunch crowd starts in on their pitchers of Bloody Marys. The sound of the bells from Mother of Sorrow Church ride the air. And early—as early as Hank and I made our way to Vivien's in his squad car—there were lots of gulls squawking overhead, and, when he stopped the car to let a cat cross the road, I heard the gentle sounds of lake waves licking the rocky shore.

My house is near the narrow point on the island just outside of downtown, more on the eastern edge of South Bass than the west, and definitely more north than south. Vivien's place, Hank explained since I'd never been there, was off in the other direction, closer to Tara and the ferry dock and to the retreat center where, a few months before, I'd worked with a group of nuns to solve not one, but two murders. Since Hank knew where we were going and this was official business, I rode shotgun and sat up, curious, when he pulled into a driveway shaded by maple trees and bordered by a lawn that was shaggy and had enough brown patches in it to make me think that, from the air, it might actually look like a crop circle.

"Not what I expected," I commented, taking a look at the old stone farmhouse. It had two stories and a front porch that someone had made the unfortunate decision to close in. There were no flowers planted in the beds, and the one bird feeder that hung from a metal shepherd's crook from the nearest tree was empty.

When we made our way up to the front door, Hank gave me a sidelong glance. "You were expecting . . ."

"Showy, I guess. Flamboyant. You know, like Vivien.

Fountains. Maybe a pond with swans in it and water lilies, too. This place seems . . ." I climbed the stone steps. "Too solid. Too homey. Where are the pink roses climbing a trellis? And the white picket fence?"

Hank grunted. "Vivien was not the white picket fence type, and you know it. Besides, you haven't seen the inside of the house yet." He stuck a key in the lock of the front door and turned the handle. "She saved all the really outrageous stuff for—"

The rest of what Hank had to say was lost in his mumble of annoyance when the door slammed into something on the floor of the built-in porch and refused to move another inch.

"Son of a gun. Something must have fallen. There was nothing on the floor yesterday when I was here." He gave the door a no-nonsense push and once again I was reminded that there is only so long anyone—or anything—can resist Hank. Whatever was behind the door got pushed aside and the door opened enough for us to slip inside.

"Oh." The comment was mine, though it could just as well have come from Hank. Fists on hips and eyes narrowed, he glanced around the porch. There was a glass-topped table against the wall, a couple of chairs near it. The rest of the porch was covered with debris.

Archives boxes like the one on the floor that had made it hard to open the door were open and dumped and left on their sides.

Books with pages torn out were scattered around.

There were magazines everywhere, or at least what was left of them, their glossy pictures ripped to shreds.

"What the—" Hank stalked through the door and into

the main part of the house, and I followed along. Apparently he saw more of the same in there. At least that would explain his grumbling. My own attention was diverted for a moment.

Just like my own heartbeat started a sudden clatter inside my ribs.

But then, it's not like anyone could blame me.

Not when I saw the tiniest scrap of fabric that clung to the door frame between the porch and the living room.

It was white and gauzy, and I might not have noticed it at all except for the way the morning sun crawled through the windows on the porch and put it in the spotlight.

Looking back on the moment, I'd like to think that I at least considered the ethical implications of what I knew I was about to do. Truth is, I acted on impulse and impulse alone, and snatched the teensy piece of fabric away from where it was snagged without even thinking about it. I tucked it in my pocket and by the time Hank looked over his shoulder at me, I had already wiped any trace of guilt from my expression. To make sure it stayed away, I looked beyond him and to a living room that was just as much of a mess as the porch was.

The floral-print couch in shades of ecru, baby blue, and mauve that matched the color of the paint on the walls was overturned. The bookshelves, pretty little matching ones on either side of the painted-white fireplace, had been emptied. While Hank took it all in with the eye of a trained professional, I ducked around him and into the dining room with its Louis XIV–inspired white and gold table, chairs, and sideboard. That room was just as much of a mess as every other part of the house we'd seen—with the addition of broken dishes that looked like they'd been scooped off the shelves of the china cabinets built in on either side of the window seat and left to break wherever they landed.

Before I could even begin to take it all in, Hank had his phone out and was calling the station and asking for someone there to get ahold of the state bureau of criminal investigation so they could come by and examine the scene. By the time he had ended the call, his breaths were coming in short, heavy gasps that reminded me of the sound of a teakettle about to hit a boil.

"It wasn't like this yesterday when I was here," Hank rumbled. "Someone got into the house after I left."

I fingered the piece of fabric in my pocket, and even though I knew it was impossible, I thought about Hank, and X-ray vision, and a cop seeing right through my pocket—and the rush of guilt I suddenly felt for tampering with a crime scene.

I fought to look casual when I pulled my hand out of my pocket and said, "It wasn't someone who cared what kind of mess he left behind," and yes, I wondered if that someone could have been Chandra. I pictured her in her white, gauzy outfit, and my stomach soured.

As I reminded myself that plenty of people wore white in the summer, I peeked into the kitchen with retro fifties charm. Pink fridge, pink stove, funky gray Formica table. Not my style, but it actually would have been cute if not for more broken dishes and a pantry that had been emptied. When a five-pound sack of flour had hit the floor, it split, and there was a coating of white over a good portion of the black-and-white ceramic-tile floor.

"Footprints." I pointed, though I knew I didn't have to. Hank would never miss anything as obvious as that. "Man's shoes, I think. They look big enough." And not anything like the sandals Chandra usually wore, I told myself.

Hank muttered, nodded, then muttered some more when he bent closer for a better look. "They're too smudged to make out much of anything, but we'll see what the crime scene team has to say." He stood and sent a laser look around the kitchen. "See anything else?"

If spilled packages of crackers, a trampled loaf of bread, and a silverware drawer pulled out and the silverware scattered on the floor meant anything, I saw plenty. But not plenty that helped us figure out what happened, to the house or to Vivien. And nothing else—thank goodness—that pointed in Chandra's direction.

I shook away the thought. "You think word went out that Vivien was dead and the house was empty and someone took the time to come in here and burglarize it?" I asked Hank.

"Sure as heck looks that way. The murder has been the talk of the island and the locals all know where Vivien lived. Wouldn't be that hard for tourists to find out, either. Like I said, talk of the island." His forehead puckered. "Unless it was just some stupid thrill seekers. I don't understand this kind of stupidity or this kind of destruction. If it was someone who came to burglarize the house, why mess things up? And if it was kids just looking for some jollies . . ." Kicking his way through the Cheerios on the floor, he made a noise from deep in his throat and I couldn't help but pity those kids if Hank ever got ahold of them. Back in the dining room, he dodged a porcelain umbrella stand painted with pink and white mums that sat on its side and the peacock feathers that had spilled out of it, and he headed for the stairway.

I stood for a moment longer in the doorway between the dining room and the living room.

"What?" Already on the stairs, Hank turned to me. "What do you see?"

What I saw was a chair that had been knocked on its side and pushed up against the fireplace behind the couch. The seat of it was too low to the floor and the back too pitched to look really comfortable.

It was turquoise.

"The chair." I knew better than to touch anything—well, almost anything—before the crime scene techs arrived, so I just pointed. "Zane Donahue has one exactly like it in his house."

"Yeah, well, I guess even though Vivien and Zane hated each other, they did have one thing in common after all." It isn't often Hank laughs, and the sound reminded me of chains moving over a metal grate. "They both had lousy taste in furniture!"

He was right, and I laughed, too, and followed him up the stairs.

There were four nice-size rooms on the second floor, and though each of them was a mess—just like the rooms downstairs—there was no mistaking which of them was Vivien's bedroom. The plain room with the twin bed with the nondescript quilt that had been ripped off it and was lying on the floor—guest room. The one with the treadmill and the stair-climber knocked over on its side—exercise room. The one filled with racks of clothing—well, I guess that was her personal wardrobe room, and every piece of clothing in it had been ripped from its hanger and cast aside.

But the one with the vivid pink walls, a canopy bed

draped with lace, and the white wall-to-wall shag carpeting . . . Oh yes, we were in Vivien's inner sanctum.

For the record, it was as an even bigger mess than the other rooms in the house. Drawers had been pulled out; clothing was spilled. There was a vanity against the far wall, and various and sundry bottles of wrinkle cream, eye makeup remover, and nail polish lay around it like colorful petals that had fallen from a flower.

"If there are any clues here, we're not going to find them," I told Hank. Yeah, as if he didn't already know that.

"It's crazy." I got the feeling he would have sunk right down on the bed if not for the fact that the mattress was half off and the sheets and bedspread were stripped and laying in a heap. "Twenty-four hours. I'm telling you, Bea. I was here twenty-four hours ago. And I can't say Vivien was the most careful housekeeper I've ever seen, but the place sure didn't look like this."

"I believe you." Carefully, I made my way between a mound of skimpy underwear and a pile of slinky nightgowns. "If there was anything for us to find, someone got to it before us."

"Maybe. All I'm saying is that if they were looking for something and found it, the whole place wouldn't be turned upside down."

"Unless they found the something they were looking for in the last place they looked."

The single word he mumbled under his breath was all the reply I needed.

"So . . ." He glanced around. "I guess it's pretty much a waste of time to try and see if we can find anything here that will help us."

"Oh, I don't know." There was a small desk nearby with

delicate legs and a small writing surface. Its drawers, too, had been pulled out and emptied. "We know someone's looking for something."

"Agreed," Hank said, "because I'm thinking if this was done by kids, they wouldn't have been so thorough. Everything's been touched. Everything's been gone through, and—"

"We're here, Chief!"

From downstairs, someone called out from the front door and Hank got up and walked out of the room. "Going to have a couple officers stay here," he told me on his way down the steps. "Until the crime scene unit shows up."

As long as he was out of the room, I took the chance, tugged the sleeve of my long-sleeved gray T-shirt over my hand, and poked through some of the detritus on the floor. Clothing, costume jewelry, more makeup than I'd owned in my entire lifetime. It was all pretty unremarkable, and none of it told me what anyone might have been looking for.

Only—

A thought hit and I hurried downstairs to find Hank giving instructions to the two fresh-faced cops who'd arrived to watch the property. I waited until he was done, then closed in on him.

"Did you check out Vivien's office yesterday?" I asked him.

"Yeah, I was there, but—" I knew exactly when he thought what I was thinking, because he barked out to the two officers, "Stay here and don't move a muscle. Ms. Cartwright and I are going downtown."

It took a while for this New Yorker to get used to the fact that what everyone on the island refers to as downtown is, in reality, simply a small patch of land with a marina on one side of it and Perry's Victory and International Peace Memorial on the other. Oliver Hazard Perry of "We have met the enemy and they are ours" fame won the Battle of Lake Erie during the War of 1812 not far from the shores of South Bass. Downtown Put-in-Bay is also where most of the restaurants and bars are located, and they bring people to the island by the thousands. When we rolled through, there was a little more activity than there had been on our way to Vivien's, and Hank slowed just past the historic hotel and turned down a side street not far from Estelle's where residential houses were mixed with properties that had turned commercial.

Vivien's office was one of those.

Once a home, the building was small and neat: a white house with green shutters and a sign in the front window that said *Frisk Realty, Own a Piece of Paradise!* We parked and went to the door, and while Hank unlocked it, I held my breath.

Untouched.

Once inside, both Hank and I looked around and breathed sighs of relief.

"It looks just like it looked yesterday," he said. What had once been the living room of the house served as the office, and there was a desk over near the fireplace that had a nameplate on it. *Vivien Frisk*, it said in loopy gold lettering. There was a stack of manila file folders on the desk, all neat and tidy.

The other desk, closer to the front door, was completely naked. No nameplate. No folders. Not a scrap of paper.

It was no secret why. At least no secret to those of us who lived on the island.

Vivien went through receptionists like a buzz saw went through tree limbs. And with pretty much the same results. The latest in a long line of come-and-go assistants was a woman name Grace Monroe, who, from what I'd heard through the grapevine, lasted for exactly three weeks and six minutes—far longer than most. These days, Grace spent most of her time bellied up to the nearest bar, drowning a ferocious case of Post Vivien Stress Disorder in tall, frosty glasses of Long Island Iced Tea.

"There's nothing upstairs but storage," Hank said. "But I'll check up there, anyway." While he did, I peeked into the kitchen. There was a coffeemaker on the counter, right where it belonged. Boxes of printer paper, paper clips, pens, and other office supplies nearby hadn't been touched.

So whatever someone was looking for, they'd looked for it only at Vivien's home.

I was just about to mention this to Hank when he got back downstairs but his phone rang, and he answered, mumbled a curse, and headed for the door.

"Trouble over at the coffee shop." He held up a hand when I made to follow him. "Nothing serious but I've got to handle it. I'll pick you up in a couple minutes and you can . . ." He glanced around the office. "Take a look around. See what you see."

I agreed, and once the Hank's cruiser pulled away, I sat down behind Vivien's desk.

A dead woman's desk.

I shook off the little shiver that cascaded over my shoulders and tickled up my neck and, one by one, opened the desk drawers. There was nothing more remarkable than pencils and papers and standard real estate contracts in any of them, and nothing more interesting than a stack of pictures of homes currently for sale on South Bass and nearby Middle Bass, North Bass, and Kelleys Islands, along with lists of vital statistics like square footage, prices, and tax rates.

Done with the drawers, I glanced through the files on top of the desk.

"Not Vivien's," I told myself after a quick look. Estelle's old files.

It made perfect sense. Vivien had been charged with cleaning out and selling off the contents of Estelle's home, and Estelle had an office there. No doubt Vivien had brought the files here for storage. Her lack of administrative help— and now, of course, her murder—had prevented her from getting the files put away.

Curious, I flicked through and saw that each of the files was dated within the last three years and each was for a property for which Estelle had handled the sale.

Levi's Bar was among them.

Okay, sure, it had nothing to do with the case. And everything to do with personal curiosity. I slid the other files aside, spread out Levi's on the desk in front of me, and, one by one, went through the papers in it.

There was a picture of the bar with a "For Sale" sign in the front window, and more pictures of the inside taken from every angle—the long bar that ran the length of the first floor, the pool tables, the restrooms. There were photos of the apartment upstairs, and they'd obviously been taken before Levi moved in and did some major renovation. These days the apartment was comfortable and pleasant, sleek and decorated in a no-nonsense, manly sort of way, but back in the day . . .

I took a look at a photo of the kitchen with its prewar (pick a war, any war) appliances, pitted linoleum, and stained drop ceiling, and I cringed.

The rest of the file was filled with paperwork, and I glanced over it casually. Or at least I would have if I hadn't come to the page where Levi listed past employers.

Yeah, his own PI agency was listed. So while he'd lied to me, he'd never lied to Estelle or to his bank. I wasn't sure if this was a comfort or not.

According to the papers, he'd worked as an assistant at another private investigation firm prior to starting his own, and for a few years and right out of college (no big surprise, he listed his degree as criminal justice), he was a juvenile probation officer. In college . . .

I scanned the page, and it was a good thing I wasn't sitting too close to the desk, or my jaw would have broken when my mouth fell open.

"Chippen—!"

My blood heated and caught my imagination on fire. Levi had worked his way through college as a stripper!

Thank goodness Hank wasn't around. It would have been difficult to explain why I sputtered and grinned one minute then turned beet red the next.

Tell that to my brain. It glommed on to the picture that formed in my head (I refuse to go into details!) and refused to budge.

My hands trembling and my cheeks flaming, I shoved the photos and the papers back into the folder and slipped it to the bottom of the pile.

Yeah, like that would help me forget the juicy secret!

In an effort to at least try, I riffled through the rest of the file folders, looking for my own. Estelle had sold my house to me at about the same time Levi had bought his bar, so the papers were bound to be there. It would be interesting to take a look at the before photos of Bea & Bees. Maybe if I concentrated on peeling paint, I could forget the thoughts of clothes being peeled off.

I gave myself a mental slap and reached for my folder. Just like with Levi's, all the paperwork was there, but—

"No photos."

Disappointed, I chewed over the thought and briefly looked through a couple of the other files. Each and every one of them included pictures—insides of houses, outsides of houses.

But no pictures of any kind in Estelle's file on the crumbling Victorian I would eventually call home sweet home.

"She put them somewhere else," I mumbled to myself. "She dropped them."

I got up and looked under the desk, and when I didn't find anything there, I checked out the desk of Vivien's former assistants. Nothing on top of it, obviously. Nothing in the drawers. I knelt on the floor to peer underneath.

Looking back at the incident, I keep telling myself that's why I didn't realize someone had walked into the realty office without me knowing. I was on my hands and knees, poking around under the desk. I mean, that had to be the reason, right? It couldn't have had anything to do with those images of Levi that kept flitting through my head.

Levi in nice, tight pants and no shirt.

Levi with that chipped-from-granite chest of his sculpted even further by the artful use of stage lighting.

Levi stripping down to—

I finally realized I wasn't alone when something smacked

me in the back of my head and I *oof*ed out a breath of surprise. Stars burst behind my eyes as I tumbled forward and my nose hit the carpet.

I'd like to say it was the last thing I remember, but honestly, the last thing I remember was thinking about Levi in collar and cuffs.

❖ 11 ❖

C ollar and cuffs.
   And tight black pants that ripped away . . . zip . . .
like magic when Levi grooved to the grinding beat of music
with a punishing bass line.

The same music pulsed through my bloodstream and
pounded through my head, its tempo changing in an instant
from smooth and sizzling to stuttering and discordant, but
despite it, each of Levi's choreographed movements was as
smooth as silk and as hot as sin.

His muscles rippled in the same stage lights that added
blue fire to his eyes. His bare chest gleamed. The music
pulsated and—

"Bea!"

His bare chest gleamed and—

"Bea! Are you with us? Come on, Bea, answer me. Open
your eyes. Bea!"

His bare chest—

Disappeared from my imagination completely when my eyes fluttered open and I found Hank's nose just inches from mine.

"That's better." He must have been on his knees. I mean, that would explain how he was able to look at me up close, since I was lying on my back on the floor of Vivien's office. Hank sat back, and maybe I was still imagining things, because I could have sworn he let down his guard long enough to breathe a sigh of relief. "You had me worried there for a while. I thought we lost you."

"Lost. Stage lights and . . ." The music thumping in my ears wasn't music at all. It was the pulsing sound of a police siren outside the real estate office. Though it was still daylight, the emergency flashers strobed over the ceiling. Red and blue. Red and blue. Watching them, my stomach flipped, and I squeezed my eyes closed for a second. "There was music." Like it came from the far end of a long tunnel, I heard my own voice. It was fuzzy, floating. Kind of like my head felt.

The part of my head that didn't hurt like the dickens.

"Don't worry about talking." A young man in dark blue pants and a crisp white shirt put a hand on Hank's shoulder and, with a grunt, Hank pulled himself to his feet and the young man took his place. "I'm Jeremy," he said. He had a thin face and a pointed chin, and ever so gently, he put a latex-gloved hand to my forehead. "You just lie still and don't pay any attention at all to Chief Florentine. It's more important for us to take care of you than it is for you to talk to him."

"Except I have to talk to her." Hank was out of my line of vision—which was pretty much the ceiling most of the time, with Jeremy moving back and forth, into and out of sight. From the rumble of his voice, I knew the chief was standing somewhere to my right and behind me, near Vivien's assistants' desk. The place where I'd been looking around when—

When I gasped, Jeremy appeared, his eyes dark with concern. "I started an IV. Just fluids to help you come around. Did that hurt? I'm sorry."

I tried to shake my head to tell him I hadn't felt the pinch at all, but instinctively, I knew that was a bad idea. There were elephants inside my brain. They were taking a Zumba class.

And I'm pretty sure they were wearing football cleats, too.

"Files," I croaked, and when I did, Hank was right there looking down at me. "Looking at files."

"Yeah, well, files are something we've got plenty of." I couldn't tell what he was referring to, but I saw him flash a look around the room that was so angry, I expected flames to shoot out of his nostrils. "Whoever hit you," he told me, "ransacked the office once you were out like a light. Unless you left the place looking like the wreck of the *Hesperus*."

"No." I ran my tongue over my parched lips. "What—"

"Were they looking for?" Hank barked out a sound that wasn't a laugh. "I wish I knew, Bea. I wish I knew."

Jeremy listened to my heart, checked my blood pressure, and used a penlight to look into my eyes. "You might have a concussion," he told me when he was done. "We can transport you to the mainland and—"

"Hank." I wasn't sure I'd get the support I wanted but even in my scrambled-egg brain, I knew it was worth a try. "Can I . . . I just want . . . home."

"Figured you'd say that." Sometime while Jeremy was checking me out, Hank must have made a call, because when he walked back into my line of sight, he was just sliding his phone back in his pocket. "It's not up to me," he said. "If Jeremy says it's all right . . ."

"Jeremy says he'd be happier if she had someone to look after her," the paramedic said. "I know you live alone, Ms. Cartwright. And I won't release you from care without some assurance that someone can be with you for the next forty-eight hours."

"Kate. Luella. Chandra."

It made perfect sense for me to suggest the Ladies of the League, but even in my muddled mind, I could tell that Hank wasn't buying it. A second later, I found out why—and who he'd made that phone call to. The front door slapped open, then banged shut, and Levi stood over me, breathing hard, his face red, as if he'd run all the way from the bar.

He took one look at me looking back up at him and the panic in his eyes softened to concern. He dropped to his knees and took my hand.

"What happened?" He wasn't talking to me; he was talking to Hank. "How did somebody get in here and—"

"Looking at files," I managed to say, because maybe when I had said it the first time, Hank wasn't paying attention. "My pictures weren't there. And then someone came in and—"

"They're after something," I heard Hank grunt. "I left Bea here for an hour so I could go over to the coffee shop and found her knocked out cold when I came back. And the office . . ." I couldn't see him, not from where I lay, but I imagined Hank shaking his head in disgust. "They've been through every scrap of paper in the place."

"Just like . . ." I had a perfectly good point to make but I got that far and completely forgot what it was. How hanging on tight to Levi's hand was going to help me remember, I wasn't sure, but I did, and when he closed his fingers over mine, just like that, the idea popped out of the fog of confusion in my head.

"Just like at Vivien's," I said.

Hank's mumbled reply confirmed it. It also told me that with Jeremy and the other paramedics around (I heard them talking), he didn't think it was wise to discuss the details of the case.

Scrambled brain or not, I knew he was right.

"You should go to the hospital."

It wasn't like I had forgotten Levi was there; it was just that I thought it best to ignore the concern that glimmered in his eyes.

And the picture that formed in my head of him in those tight, tight black pants.

"What are you smiling about?" He leaned closer. "I just said I thought you should go to the hospital."

I wiped the expression from my face. It wasn't as easy to banish the picture inside my head. "I just want to go home."

"Then I'm going with you." He didn't wait for me to tell him it was a terrible idea. He stood up and talked to Jeremy and I heard words like "physical and mental rest" and "nausea" and "unusual behavior" and "headache and dizziness - and blurry vision" mentioned. I let it all float for a bit then settle. My eyes drifted shut then popped open when Jeremy said, "You'll need to wake her up every couple hours, just to make sure she's all right. If that's going to be a problem, I'd suggest the hospital."

"No problem," Levi said.

"Problem," I croaked.

The look Levi gave me was too sour to be a smile. "I think you can be pretty sure you'll be safe. I'm not going to try anything with a woman who's got a concussion."

There was probably a snappy comeback I could have thrown at him.

And I planned to do it, too.

As soon as I thought of one.

Instead, I listened to Jeremy give Levi last-minute instructions and heard him promise that I'd get to a doctor first thing the next day. The next thing I knew, Jeremy unhooked me from the IV and helped me sit up.

"Still okay?" he asked.

I wasn't going to risk a nod, so I told him I was good to go and braced a hand on the desk chair so I could get to my feet.

"Not a chance!" Levi didn't offer and he didn't give me a chance to protest; he scooped me off the floor and carried me out to Hank's squad car. He put me in the backseat, then slid in next to me.

"You really don't have to—"

"Yes, I do," he said, and when he closed the door, Hank started off for the B and B.

I can't say if we attracted any attention on our way out of downtown because I drifted off for a bit—not sleeping, exactly, but not fully awake, either. I gave myself over to the purr of the engine and the smooth feel of the car when it swayed around corners, and my head bobbed and landed on Levi's shoulder. When Hank stopped the car in my driveway, I opened my eyes and regretted that I didn't live farther from town.

"You're not carrying me into the house," I told Levi, who

said he wouldn't think of it, then wrapped his arms around me and carried me out of the car.

He set me down on the wicker couch on the front porch and ducked into the house, and just a minute later, he was back with my bed pillows, an ice pack, and a light blanket. Before he'd gone back down the steps to talk to Hank at the car, I was already asleep.

"Sorry. I promised I'd wake you every couple hours. I didn't want to do it, but it's important."

The feel of Levi's hand on my arm roused me from a sleep that was thankfully without any dreams. Waking up and looking into his eyes, the last thing I needed was the remnants of music and stage lights playing with my imagination. I burrowed deeper into the pillow and saw that the shadows were painted across the lawn from Chandra's house toward mine. It was afternoon.

"You want something to eat?" Levi asked. "Jeremy said you might be a little nauseous, but if you think you can keep something down, I'll get it."

"No thanks." I took the chance of shaking my head, and when it didn't explode, I swung my legs off the couch so I could sit up. "I'm not hungry."

"Good." He'd been crouched in front of the couch and he got to his feet. "I've got some soup on the stove. I'll go get you a bowl."

"But I said—" It didn't matter what I had said; he was already in the house.

And back in just a couple minutes with a tray. He set a bowl of tomato soup on the table near the couch, along with a glass of ice water and some crackers, instructed me to

"Start eating," and went back inside for his own lunch. Once he was settled in the chair across from the couch and I hadn't taken a bite yet, he urged me to get going and started in on his own soup.

I was two bites in when a memory slammed into me and I sat up like a shot. "I have guests coming this afternoon!"

"I'll handle them." With his spoon, Levi pointed toward my soup. "Eat."

"But—"

"The house looks great; the rooms are perfect. I saw the booking listed on your calendar and checked it all out while the soup was simmering. You're all set. I even took some chocolate chip cookies out of the freezer so when they get here, they can have tea and cookies. I figured that's what you'd do for guests."

"But how am I going to—"

"You heard what Jeremy said. No physical or mental exercise. At least not until you see a doctor, and probably not for a few more days after that. So you're not going to do anything. I'm going to do it. Whatever it is. Whatever you need me to do."

"Breakfast. And dinner recommendations. And—"

"I'll handle it."

There was only one thing I could say. "Thank you."

"Eat."

I did, and the soup was delicious. "You found the stuff to make this soup in my pantry?" I finished the last of the soup in the bowl and licked my spoon. "Maybe you should be a chef instead of a private investigator."

I knew it was a mistake the second the words left my lips. Not because neither of us knew the truth. We did, and nothing was going to change that. But because mentioning it put a damper on the afternoon, and Levi's kindness.

"I'm sorry," I said, because it was true and because he needed to hear it. "I didn't mean to—"

"Not a problem." He finished his own soup, cleaned up the dishes, and took them inside. When he came back outside, he brought me a chocolate chip cookie. "I figure your guests won't miss a couple."

"Perfect." The cookie was. So was the fact that he'd been that considerate.

He'd brought a cookie out for himself, too, and he chomped on it and sat down, but not in the chair where he'd eaten his lunch. On the couch, next to me.

"This *is* perfect," he said on the end of a long sigh.

It was. The blue waters of the lake across the street. The golden sunshine that glimmered through the trees. The gentle breeze from the west that sent fat clouds scuttling high up over the water and made me think of sheep gamboling in a meadow.

"There's nothing like summer on the island," I said.

"You're right. It's great, but when I talk about perfect, I'm not talking about the weather. Or the island, either."

When I turned—carefully—to give him a better look, I found Levi smiling. "It's perfect because I can sit right here and talk to you, and in your condition, you can't run away," he said.

I threw back the blanket he'd settled over me. "I can try."

"Oh, no!" Levi laughed and put a hand on my arm to keep me in place. "No quick movements, remember?"

"Going in the house doesn't count as a quick movement."

"Running away from me does."

I settled back against the pillow and thought about how right he was. Though the island had been my home for close to two years, and though I loved it like I'd never loved any other place I'd ever lived, it never felt complete until I got to know Levi. Now, the two were inseparable. The island wouldn't be the island without Levi. Home wouldn't be home.

If I needed any proof, I only had to think about how miserable I'd been since we had the set-to about how I'd kept my real identity a secret from him and he'd kept his background hidden from me. The sun hadn't been quite so bright all those weeks. Not like it was now. The breeze hadn't been as refreshing. Yeah, my head hurt, and if I moved it too quickly, the scene in front of my eyes got blurry around the edges, like an Impressionist painting.

But my heart was happy.

Happier than it had been since the day I revealed my secret, Levi confessed his, and I reacted with knee-jerk anger that I'd worn like a suit of armor ever since.

It would be nice to lower my defenses. It would take a load off my mind and lift my spirits.

All I had to do was find a way for Levi and me to make our peace.

I'm not sure where the idea came from. Maybe my bruised brain made it possible for me to think a little outside the box. I drew in a breath for courage, and gave it a try.

"There's something else Jeremy mentioned," I said. "He said that one of the symptoms of concussion is memory loss."

Levi nodded. "He did, but don't worry about it. For one thing, you remembered that you've got guests checking in this afternoon, so that's obviously not a problem. And even if it was, the memory loss from a concussion doesn't last. I mean, not permanently. It usually clears up in just a couple days."

"Then maybe . . ." I fingered the satin edge of the blanket. "Maybe before a couple days is over . . . What I mean is . . . Say that I had a terrible concussion. It's possible, right? I did get whacked over the head pretty hard. And say I wasn't thinking straight, that I did have memory loss. I mean it would be like I didn't even know you, right? Like we've never met."

I knew he was trying to work his way through to what I was up to, because he went perfectly still, every muscle tensed as if he was afraid that if he moved, the moment and the place we found ourselves in might dissolve. "You mean like—"

"I mean like . . ." I grabbed his hand and shook it. "I'm Bea Cartwright. It's really nice to meet you. I used to live in New York City and I'm an author. I write under the name of FX O'Grady. You may have heard of me. I'm kind of famous."

A smile played around his lips. "More than kind of famous, as it happens, and for very good reason. You write some crazy, whacked-out stuff."

"But I'm not a crazy, whacked-out person. I'm just sort of . . ." I shrugged. "Just looking to get by, day by day. Looking for some peace and quiet. That's why I came to the island. That's why I bought this place. I'd just like to be a regular person and to make a success of my business. And you . . ?"

For a heartbeat, I thought he might not play along. Maybe he just wasn't sure this was heading where I hoped it was heading. "I'm Levi Kozlov, a private investigator, and I'll admit, I never read your stuff. Saw a couple of the movies," he added quickly, as if he was afraid I might be offended. "But I never read the books until I got a call from your attorney about taking a job to keep an eye on you here on the island. He told me about the stalker back in New York and yeah, the guy's in jail, but your attorney, he just wanted to make sure you got settled, that you were safe. That's what he wanted me to take care of. That's when I read your books, and I'll tell you what, I was blown away. Then I saw you and . . ." I didn't even realize we were still holding hands until his fingers closed over mine. "Then I saw you and I lost my head and my heart," he said. "And I guess my common sense, too, or I would have told you who I was right from the start."

I wrinkled my nose and pretended to be confused. "Start? What are you talking about? Isn't this where we start?"

Levi smiled. "You mean, me telling you the truth and you telling me the truth?"

Sure, I have an overactive imagination. I mean, that's what being a writer is all about, right? Still, it didn't take a bestselling novelist to conjure up the images that popped into my head. They were the same ones that had been plaguing my brain and heating my blood ever since I'd read through Levi's file back in Vivien's office.

I gave him a probing look that might have been more effective if my eyes weren't so blurry that I saw two of him.

"Are you telling me the truth?" I asked. "The whole truth and nothing but?"

"You mean the PI thing? Absolutely!"

"And there's nothing else? Nothing else in your past that I should know about?"

He scratched a finger behind his ear. "Like . . ?"

I was tempted to put him on the spot, to tell him I knew his secret and suggest that a demonstration of his moves might actually be the perfect cure for my concussion, but at the last second, I swallowed the words. I was too woozy to appreciate a demonstration, and anyway, something told me that playing this card close to my chest might have more benefits in the long run.

"You're not still worried about the Vivien thing?" Levi groaned, and I was glad I had kept my mouth shut. "I told you, Bea, it was nothing. And if you're looking for the truth, there it is. She was pushy, and I was happy to get away from her. But not nearly as happy as I am"—he leaned nearer—"to get close to you again. And that is the truth."

"And the truth is important. Right from the beginning." I looped my arms around his neck. "You know, so it doesn't get in the way later. What do you say?"

As it turned out, he didn't say anything at all. But then, he was pretty busy kissing me.

"Hey, you two! Break it up! We heard what happened. Bea's not supposed to have any physical exertion!"

The voice was Luella's, and Levi and I came up for air and found her and Kate at the bottom of the stairs, both of them grinning ear to ear.

Kate spoke up first. "The way we heard it, you're supposed to be taking it easy, Bea." She shot a withering look in Levi's direction, and sure, she was only kidding, but Kate's withering looks can drop a grown man at ten paces. "That's not taking it easy, mister!"

He sat back, his hands in the air. "Just comforting the patient."

"Yeah, well . . ." Kate bounded up the stairs and Luella followed. Kate took the chair where Levi had eaten his lunch and Luella stood, her hands tucked into the bib of her Carhartt overalls.

"We know you're not supposed to get upset or anything, too," Kate said, her cheeks as pink as the T-shirt she was wearing with black shorts. "But we've got to talk to you, Bea."

"And you're not going to like it," Luella added.

My heart started up a clatter. "I already don't like it. What's wrong?" Automatically, my gaze shot next door. "It's not Chandra, is it?"

"No, no. Nothing like that." Luella stepped forward and she and Kate exchanged looks. "We were just in town. I had a charter today and I just finished up and—"

"And I met Luella at the boat and told her what happened to you. It's all over town. The news, I mean. About how you got attacked and knocked out." Kate's ginger brows puckered. "You're all right, aren't you, Bea? You look all right, but it must have been really scary. If there's anything you need—"

"I need you two to stop beating around the bush." I looked from one of them to the other. Slowly and carefully, so my head didn't spin. "What am I not going to like?"

Luella is as tough as the lake where she makes her living as a fishing charter captain—a seventy-something grandmother with the personality of a lion and the heart of a lamb. She made a face. "There's something else they're talking about in town today, too. I mean, something other than you getting waylaid. We figured it's better if you hear it from us."

"It would be. If I heard it from you. Either one of you."

Kate cleared her throat. "There's a rumor around town, Bea. And we know it's not true and I bet just about everybody who hears it knows it's not true, but something got it started and people are talking and . . ." A rush of bright red colored her cheeks.

Luella pulled in a breath. "Word is, you've got bedbugs."

I was up out of my seat and on my feet before Levi could stop me. "What?"

"We shouldn't have told you." Kate wrung her hands. "I knew it was going to upset you. We shouldn't have said a word."

"And let me hear it somewhere on my own?" I plunked back down on the couch, but only because Levi had ahold of my arm and tugged. "I can't believe this. How . . . ? Who . . . ?"

"We'll get to the bottom of it," he promised me. "For now, the best thing you can do is just ignore it. You heard what Kate said—nobody believes it."

"But they're saying it. They're talking about it." Outrage blocked my throat and pounded through my bloodstream. "What's going to happen to my business?"

"Not one single thing." Levi patted my hand. "You'll see. Your guests will check in this afternoon, they'll see how wonderful your place is, and they'll tell everyone they know. If you ignore a rumor this crazy, I guarantee you, it will just fade away."

"Fade away. Sure." I didn't bother to add, "Just like my business," because that seemed a bit overdramatic. Even if it was what I feared. I pressed a hand to my heart. "You're right. We'll let these new people check in and—"

"And we'll help." Kate jumped out of her chair. "Whatever you need, Bea, you know we'll help. We'll make sure they know this is the finest B and B on the island."

"And pretty soon, everyone will know it." Luella's face is as wrinkled as an old blanket, and it split in a smile. "It's going to be fine, Bea. You'll see. Everything's going to be all right."

I wanted to believe them. I *would* believe them, I told myself, because if I didn't, my splitting headache and queasy stomach would be the least of my worries.

The phone rang inside the house and Levi went to answer it, and I looked at my friends. "You had to tell me. Don't feel bad about it."

"I don't feel bad about telling you." Kate's hands curled into fists. "I do feel plenty bad for whoever started that stupid rumor if I ever get ahold of them."

It was as much as I could ask. I settled back. "You're right, when my guests get here this afternoon—"

Levi came back outside, his face a thundercloud. "That was them," he growled. "The people who were checking in today. They heard about the bedbugs. They just canceled."

« 12 »

Just for the record, Levi claimed he'd be fine sleeping on the couch in the parlor that night but I was having none of it. Hey, it wasn't like the place was packed and there was no room at the inn! I insisted he stay upstairs in Suite 4, where I knew he'd be comfortable, and he made the trip downstairs three times during the night. In theory, he was supposed to wake me to be sure I wasn't unconscious due to the concussion, but really, he shouldn't have bothered.

"There's no way I can sleep," I told him on his third visit. The clock out in the hallway had just chimed five and he found me sitting with my elbows propped against my desk, my head in my hands. "I can't believe it, Levi. Bedbugs!"

"I haven't met one in my room yet." He tried to coax a smile out of me with one of his own, but there was no way that was going to work. I was too worried. Too angry.

"Who starts that kind of rumor?" Yeah, I know, rhetorical question, but I'm a fiction writer, remember. In the back of my mind, there's always hope that the answers to all my questions will come to me in some mystical, magical way, and if they don't (because let's face it, they hardly ever do), just hearing my own voice speak the words will shake loose some bit of logic from my brain and give me the answer.

This time it didn't work, and I sighed. "Why would anybody do something like that?"

"I wouldn't be surprised if somebody just heard something wrong and made some bad assumptions."

"You heard what Kate and Luella said. People were talking specifics. Specifically my place. I need to find out what's going on."

I guess he thought I was going to pop up right then and there and head out on my quest, because he put a hand on my arm. "Can we at least wait until the sun comes up?"

He got his way. I realized how silly I sounded and smiled. "It's just so—"

"Yeah, I know."

"Then what are we going to do?"

"Coffee?" he suggested.

I had to admit, it was the best idea I'd heard all night.

By the time we'd finished a pot of coffee and I had taken a shower and gotten dressed, I felt a little more human. The fact that I walked into the kitchen and found the table laid with my china dishes decorated with bright red cherries helped. Cheery dishes, the sun skimming the horizon, and omelets done to perfection just finishing on the stove.

I looked them over, sniffed, and smiled my approval. "Maybe you're the one who should be running a bed-and-breakfast," I suggested to Levi.

He dismissed the thought with a shake of his head and put the omelets on our plates. "Too refined and genteel for me. The bar, pool tables, beer on tap. That's more my speed."

"Well, you should start offering Sunday brunch at the bar." I took a bite and sat back, content, and when we were finished, he grabbed the dishes and took them over to the sink.

I wasn't nearly as woozy as I had been the day before, and when I stood, the room didn't tip. To me, this was a sign that I was good to go. "I'm heading into town."

"You are, but not for the reason you think you are. You've got a doctor's appointment."

I glanced at the time on the microwave. "But how—"

"Don't worry about it. Hank's got an in with a doc who's got a summer house over near Kate's winery and he agreed to see you first thing."

"But I'm fine."

"We'll wait for him to tell us that."

I crossed my arms over my chest. "And if he doesn't?"

"Then you're coming home and going right back to bed. Agreed?"

I puffed out a breath of annoyance and hoped Levi didn't notice when I crossed my fingers. "Agreed."

The doctor was a young guy with a wife and three little boys who were already up and running through the house like madmen when we got there. He checked me out and said I was fine but suggested I take it easy for a few days.

I promised I would, but by the time I got back into the car, I already had a plan in mind.

"Downtown," I said.

From behind the wheel, Levi slid me a look. "Why?"

"Because we have to find out who's behind the bedbug story."

"And you're going to do that . . . how?"

"The same way I investigate murders," I told him. "I'm going to talk to people. I'm going to ask questions. Talking to people isn't exactly strenuous so I'll still be taking it easy, but I'm going to get to the bottom of this."

"I'll tell you what"—he backed out of the doc's driveway—"if you go home and promise to rest, I'll go into town and ask questions."

"But—"

"But nothing. You heard what the doctor said. Getting in and out of the car, talking to people, getting annoyed and upset . . . that's not taking it easy. Going home and sitting down is."

He was right, and I promised I would. But sitting down isn't the same as doing nothing, is it? Once Levi settled me on the couch on the front porch with a blanket, a pot of tea, and a stack of magazines I had no intention of reading, I called both Kate and Luella and got each of their detailed versions of the bedbug story. That gave me a place to start, and I called the person they'd heard the rumor from, who said she'd heard it from someone else, who, when I called, swore he'd heard it from some tourist he'd never seen before.

I am smart enough to realize I could have gone on like that all morning, making calls and getting more frustrated by the moment, but a couple things happened:

My phone rang and the nice lady named Dara who handles the admin work at the Chamber of Commerce informed me that the meeting at Tara that was supposed to take place the next day had to be canceled. The Twins, it seems, were getting a visit from the producer who was making their harrowing kidnaping story into a major motion picture, and Dara could barely contain her excitement at the thought.

That was all I needed to hear.

Not about the movie or the producer or Dara's utter conviction that she would be chosen as an extra for the film, but the part about the meeting being canceled.

In a flash, I had a plan.

By the time Levi arrived just before noon with corned beef sandwiches and the bad news that he'd learned nothing that could help us determine who'd started the bedbug rumor, I was knee-deep in preparations.

He glanced at the handwritten list I had out on the couch next to my phone, ducked inside for plates, and set a sandwich down on the table in front of me. "What's up?" he asked.

I checked the time. "An inspector from the health department will be on the two o'clock ferry," I told him. "If you could pick him up, it would save him renting a golf cart. The Chamber of Commerce will be here tomorrow. Seven sharp."

He had just sat down and was about to bite into a dill pickle, and he froze, the pickle at his mouth. "I had a message at the bar. The Twins canceled the meeting at Tara. Something about their producer being in town. How did you—"

"Don't you see? This is perfect! The inspector will give my place a clean bill of health today, and I'll host the meeting tomorrow. I'm thinking we'll offer tours of the inn after the business part of the meeting is over. You know, sort of the icing on the cake. Some of the Chamber members have been here for one thing or another, but not all of them. This way, they can look over the place and see that there's nothing wrong with it, and that will be an end of the bad rumors."

"You were supposed to be taking it easy."

"I have been. Honest." I crossed a finger over my heart. "Sitting right here and taking it easy."

"And hosting all those people tomorrow?"

I picked up the list and waved it. "I've already called all of them and told them the meeting is here. Except for you. I didn't call you because I knew you'd be here. And I talked to Luella's daughter, Meg. She was all excited, she figured I had guests again and she'd be back to doing my baking. She got over her disappointment fast enough, though, when I told her about the meeting and we've come up with a menu for tomorrow night. Nothing elaborate. Some finger foods, bottles of Kate's wine. Tracy from the fudge shop will be here and she says they have new flavors—cinnamon pumpkin, chocolate and banana cheesecake, and coconut rum— and she offered to bring samples, so that means we won't need dessert. So I've gotten a lot done, and I swear, I haven't moved a muscle, and since Kate and Luella said they'll be happy to help, I won't have anything to do tomorrow, either."

"And Chandra?"

Automatically, my gaze traveled to her place. "She's not home. Or she's not answering her phone. But I'll talk to her later. Book discussion group is here tonight."

"Here?" Since Levi had just taken a bite of corned beef sandwich, he talked with his mouth full. "You can't—"

"There's nothing for me to do," I assured him. "We'll sit here on the front porch and talk about *Gone with the Wind*. What could possibly go wrong?"

God bless the county health department!

When the inspector left, he handed me an official certificate that said Bea & Bees was as perfect as an inn could be.

No health violations.

No code problems.

And certainly no bedbugs.

By the time the members of the island Chamber of Commerce arrived the next day, I planned to have copies of that certificate framed and hanging in very conspicuous places of honor. Between that and offering tours, I was confident that I could turn around the unwarranted bad publicity.

We were on the front porch and I'd just finished telling Kate and Luella about my plans when we heard a door smack closed in the distance and saw Chandra heading across her yard, then mine, to join us for the latest meeting of the League of Literary Ladies.

"I wondered if she'd come," Luella said below her breath. "She's been acting—"

"Weird." Kate made a face. "I mean, weirder than usual. Which, when you think about it, is pretty weird."

"Shh!" As if we were talking about nothing at all, I smiled when Chandra got to the steps and waved her up to the porch to sit down. "We were just about to start," I told her.

"I brought cookies." She set a plate on the table and stepped back, and Kate, Luella, and I eyed what looked like chocolate chip cookies—green chocolate chip cookies.

"There's matcha in the recipe," Chandra sniffed when she saw the looks of wariness on our faces. Or maybe the fact that we were all sitting on our hands, staring instead of reaching for cookies, sent the message loud and clear. "Matcha is dried green tea leaves that have been ground up, so it's full of antioxidants and fiber and chlorophyll. Go ahead, try one." Still no one moved, and Chandra shot a look all around. "Unless you all think I'm trying to kill you with poison. You know, the way you all think I killed Vivien."

"Nobody said that!" I blurted out.

"We never would," Luella insisted.

"Where did you hear something as dumb as that?" Kate demanded.

Chandra dropped into the nearest chair. "I suppose you all think I'm the one who knocked Bea over the head, too."

"No one ever even dreamed that." Now that Chandra had made me feel nice and guilty, I reached for one of the cookies and took a bite. It tasted like grass. I smiled and chewed and smiled some more, and thankfully, Levi had made a pitcher of iced tea for the Ladies, so I washed it all down with a big gulp. "I know you'd never do a thing like that, Chandra."

She crossed her arms over her purple top studded with green and gold sequins. "Well, that's good, because I haven't done anything wrong."

"Well, good!" Anxious to get off an uncomfortable subject and onto one that was bound to take Chandra's mind off the murder, I grabbed my copy of *Gone with the Wind* from the table in front of the couch and plunked the book down on my knees. "Now that we've got that out of the way, we can talk about what we're supposed to be talking about."

"The book." Of all of us (even me, and I am a writer), Luella was the one who loved reading the most. Kate, I was sure, put up with our group because she didn't want to miss out on any gossip. Chandra liked to daydream about plots and heroes and immerse herself in story and setting. I admit it, it was the words of any book that got to me, some of them delicious and evocative, others like the ping of BB shot against the page.

But Luella . . . one look at the way she clutched her copy of the book in both hands, and anyone who saw her knew how much reading meant to her. "It's a hokey story," she said, then, for Chandra's sake, added quickly, "but that doesn't make it any less riveting. It's a classic, isn't it? We all know what happens, so there are no surprises. And yet, I don't know about all of you, but I couldn't help but keep turning the pages."

"I wonder what it was like to read it back when it was first published." I tipped my head back (well, a little, anyway, since I still wasn't 100 percent sure of what would happen when I moved too quickly) and thought about this. "Before the book and the movie were cultural icons. I wonder what it was like coming to the book without any preconceived notions."

"It must have really been something." I noticed that Kate took a look at Chandra when she said this. She paused, too, giving Chandra the perfect opening for throwing in a *fiddle-dee-dee* or two.

When she didn't—when Chandra didn't say a word— Kate cleared her throat. "We're all going to the gala on Saturday night, aren't we?"

Both Luella and I assured her we were, and when Chandra still didn't speak, we all turned her way.

"You're more excited than anyone on the island about the gala." I knew I didn't have to remind her. "Don't tell me you're not going to go."

"I haven't decided." Chandra bit her lip. "If I go and anyone says anything about how I'm a murderer . . ."

"That's not going to happen," I assured her. "Because nobody thinks it's true. Besides"—I could be devious in the name of a good cause—"that's not the way Scarlett would have handled things."

Chandra perked right up. "You mean—"

"Think of the scene when those women find her with

Ashley and assume the worst." I tapped the book with one finger. "Scarlett didn't stay home and hide her head. She went to Ashley's birthday party and she never backed down."

Chandra's chin quivered. "I can do that."

"And we'll be there with you, every minute," I promised her. "Now, Chandra"—I leaned forward in my chair—"what are you wearing?" This, too, of course, was a cleverly devised question. I knew nothing would get Chandra's mind off murder like the thought of playing the role of the Southern belle. "Hoop skirt? Big picture hat?"

A smile tickled Chandra's lips. "You think I'm going as Scarlett."

"I think every woman on the island's going as Scarlett," Kate said. "I know I am. I had a seamstress on the mainland come up with a perfect little picnic dress."

"And I was thinking of something more refined," Luella put in. "Wasn't going to bother making something or having something made. That kind of fuss is for you young girls. But I've put together a long black skirt and a top that would be perfectly appropriate for the widow of a Southern warrior. What about you, Bea?"

What about me?

I thought it best to downplay the fact that I'd contacted one of the costuming wizards who'd worked on the wardrobe for the movie made from one of my books and had him come up with a confection sure to turn the heads of every Ashley and Rhett in the room. Of course, that was before things between Levi and me were back on an even keel and his was the only head I was worried about.

"I've got something that will work," I assured them. "It should be an interesting evening. If only . . ."

"You're hoping that the case gets solved before then," Chandra said, and let out a long breath. "You and me both."

"Actually, I was going to say that I wish we weren't going to Tara for the party," I admitted. "But I guess that's the whole point. A *Gone with the Wind* gala wouldn't be right without Tara. It's just that those Twins . . ." I swallowed the rest of what I was going to say. The Ladies knew that Tara's gain had been my loss, business-wise. There was no use pointing it out and looking like a sore loser.

"I wouldn't be surprised if they were the ones who started that rumor." Chandra grabbed a cookie and bit it in two. "You know, about the bedbugs. Maybe they're trying to sabotage your business."

I reminded myself about the health department certificate and took heart. "That lie will all be cleared up by tomorrow," I told them—and reminded myself. "And why would the Twins want to do something like that, anyway? They don't need to hurt my business. Not when theirs is going gangbusters."

"Maybe it's someone who doesn't like you poking around in Vivien's murder," Kate suggested, and I had to admit, though I hadn't thought of it before, the theory did have merit. "If someone wants to discredit you—"

"Making you look bad would be a good place to start," Luella added.

"Maybe that means I'm actually getting too close to finding out the secret." Yeah, brave words, but I knew they didn't mean squat. "It sure doesn't feel like it."

"How about the business of Vivien's house being all messed up?" Kate asked, then, for Chandra's benefit, added, "Hank and Bea were there and it was turned upside down."

"Really?" As if this didn't jibe with reality as she knew it, Chandra puckered her brow. "It wasn't like that when I was—" She caught herself and shoved the other half of her cookie in her mouth.

Luella and Kate exchanged looks but I didn't dare join in. I was afraid my expression might give something away. Something about that scrap of gauzy white fabric I'd found at Vivien's. "You and Vivien weren't exactly friends," I said, playing the innocent. "Everybody knows that. When were you at her house?"

"Me?" Chandra asked this with her mouth full, pointing to herself. She swallowed and washed down the cookie with some iced tea. "Years ago." She waved away my question. "We were collecting canned goods for the local food bank. You remember that, Kate. We went from house to house, asking for donations."

"And you asked Vivien for a donation?" Considering their history, it seemed out of character, but if there was one thing I knew about Chandra, it was that in the name of a good cause, she just might knock on Vivien's door.

Chandra nodded, and her dangling earrings (orange and purple balls) glimmered in the evening light. Her lips thinned. "The way I remember it, she tossed three cans of tuna into the box I was carrying. Three cans of tuna! She could have afforded a whole lot more than that."

"Maybe not," I told them. "Hank says her finances weren't all that great."

"Which probably means someone didn't kill her for her money," Kate said.

"It could have been anyone," Chandra added. "No one liked Vivien."

"Especially you." When Chandra flinched, I held up a

hand. "Come on, it's no secret. And I'm just saying. Which actually brings up a point, Chandra." I thought about the white scrap of fabric I'd found at Vivien's. "Are you sure the last time you were at Vivien's was when you collected that canned food a couple years ago?"

Chandra lifted her chin. "I told you. I was there once. Why would I want to go to Vivien's?"

Why, indeed.

"So . . ." Since that was a dead end, I edged the conversation the other way. "That walk you went on Friday. Was one of the places you walked Estelle's backyard?"

Chandra's jaw dropped and she glanced around at the circle of friends on my porch. "Do you really believe that?"

"I really believe someone saw you, and that means it's something we need to talk about," I told her.

"Good. Fine. Believe somebody else, not me. That's just fine. That's how friends treat each other." Her face red and her eyes moist, Chandra popped out of her chair. "If that's how you're all going to be, I'm leaving. Let me know when you decide that I'm the murderer. It will be nice to know I have that kind of support from my so-called friends."

Before any of us could say anything or stop her, she raced down the steps and across the lawn.

I hated to say it, so I kept my mouth shut, but it was pretty obvious that Chandra was gone with the wind.

❖ 13 ❖

If I weren't so exhausted from not sleeping on Sunday night, I would have spent that Monday night pacing the floor and worrying about Chandra.

She was up to something.

She was involved in something.

And whatever it was, she wasn't talking.

That in itself was plenty suspicious. Chandra talks about everything. All the time.

The way it was, though, I slept like a log. Well, except for the times Levi came in and woke me up to make sure all was well. According to the doctor, this was the last night he'd need to do that, and to tell the truth, I was glad. The longer Levi stayed at Bea & Bees taking care of me, the guiltier I felt for keeping him from his own business. Not to mention the fact that the longer he stayed with me, the better I felt, and the better I felt, the more I was tempted to ignore that ban on physical exertion.

I reminded myself that we might get there again, Levi and I. But even an author with an overactive imagination and an overpowering attraction to a certain bar owner/PI knew that after all we'd been through, we needed to find our way there slowly.

I kept that in mind on Tuesday morning when he zipped through the kitchen dressed in worn jeans and a black T-shirt with a green and white cotton plaid shirt open over it. The island Chamber of Commerce was set to descend on the inn in a few hours and Levi had been up long before me taking care of the details.

"I've got your usual cleaning people coming in an hour to do a quick once-over on everything," he told me, checking that item off the list he was carrying. "And when I was outside this morning, I noticed that one of the slate tiles on your roof is loose. I don't think it's any big deal, and it doesn't have to be done today, but I called Chuck over at the hardware store anyway and he'll come by when he has a chance to take a look. I dragged that big extension ladder out and put it in back of the garage so if he shows up, he can use it. Oh, and Meg says she'll be here at three with the food."

"And you really should sit down." I caught his sleeve so he couldn't escape. "I should be taking care of all that."

"You should be taking it easy."

There was no use arguing, and as it turned out, I didn't have a chance, anyway. The front doorbell rang, and just to prove how much better I was feeling, I popped out of my chair and went to answer it. It was a delivery. All the way from Hollywood.

Levi leaned over my shoulder and checked out the box. "What's that?"

"A surprise." When I tried to get around him so I could carry the box into my suite, he plucked it out of my hands and took it there himself. "I'm not an invalid!" I called out after him.

"Yes, you are. For one more day." He returned with the stack of health department certificates that I'd copied on the printer in my little office and, together, we put them in the frames he'd picked up for me in the grocery/variety store that was an island mainstay.

Cheap, quick, and easy—and when we were done, he put one certificate in each guest room and I put one on the fireplace mantel in the parlor and the last one in the dining room where the food would be set out that evening. Not exactly subtle but that wasn't the point.

"So now that you're feeling better"—the final framed certificate leaned against the back of the mahogany sideboard in the dining room, and Levi stepped away, looked it over, then straightened it a bit—"you'll get back to investigating?"

"Are you going to tell me it's too dangerous?"

"You did get bashed over the head."

"Only because I was in the wrong place at the wrong time. Obviously, whoever ransacked Vivien's house didn't find what they were looking for and figured they might have better luck at her office. A Sunday morning, they probably figured they were home free. But there I was."

"And you never saw a thing?"

I thought back to my visit to the real estate office. "I was looking through files." With everything that had happened since the time I walked into the real estate office, I couldn't remember if I told Levi this piece of the story. "Estelle's files were there, and that makes sense. Estelle probably kept them at home and Vivien was cleaning everything out of the house. The files were all piled up on Vivien's desk."

"Mine, too?"

It wasn't my imagination; he actually looked worried I might have taken a peek.

"Estelle handled the sale on the bar," he said, explaining away his interest. "I just wondered—"

"Your file was there. So was mine."

"Makes sense. Like you said, Vivien was taking care of wrapping things up as far as Estelle's business was concerned." I can't imagine there was anything all that interesting in the sky outside the dining room window, but that's what Levi was concentrating on. Was that a little case of the nerves I saw reflected in his rigid shoulders and his too-steady chin? I had no doubt of it and I had to give him credit—he did his best to make it sound like there was nothing but natural curiosity (and not worry) that I might have seen more in his file than I should have when he asked, "The pictures of my place, were they there?"

It wasn't until he asked that I realized I'd really stepped in it. Darn, with all we'd said to each other about always telling the truth, I had to put up or shut up. "There were pictures of your bar there, all right," I told him, deftly sidestepping the advice of my conscience. "From before you bought it. Your apartment was a mess back then."

"So was the bar. It took a lot of work to get that place in shape. But then, you know all about that. I remember seeing this place before you started the renovations. It was a wreck."

I could have changed the subject. Or at least deflected it to the investigation and kept it firmly there.

But there was that whole thing about the truth.

"What?" Levi glanced over in time to see me squinch up my face. "What's the problem?"

"It's not a problem. It's a moral dilemma."

"We're talking about photographs in real estate files. The same photographs Estelle took, then posted on her website when she listed a property. How much moral dilemma can there be?"

"It all depends on if the person who saw the photographs maybe saw something else in someone's file."

"Something that has to do with the murder?" There was so much hope in Levi's question, I couldn't help but feel shamefaced when the truth hit and his eyes got wide and his mouth fell open. That would be right before he flushed a color that reminded me of a summer sunset.

"It's nothing to be ashamed of," I told him, because it was true and because I felt awful for outing him like this. "I'm sure you needed the money and you worked very hard and—"

There was only so much empathizing I could manage before I burst out laughing and had to brace a hand against the nearest chair to stay upright.

Levi groaned. "All right, I get it. We said we'd tell each other the truth. I should have told you."

I fought to control my laughter. "And I should have told you I knew. Sorry! Really. I was waiting for the right moment."

He scraped both his hands through his hair. "And when would that have been?"

I did my best to look the picture of innocence. "Oh, I don't know. Like maybe when you could demonstrate?"

Both our smiles dissolved at the same time and my gaze locked with his.

"Now would be a really good time," I suggested.

"Oh, no!" As if I was on fire, Levi backed away. "You heard what the paramedic said. And the doc, too. No physical exertion. Not for a few days."

"They were talking about me, not you."

The tips of his ears turned red. "I guarantee you, if I demonstrate, there will be physical exertion involved. For both of us."

"Is that a promise?"

He didn't have to say a word—he just gave me a wink.

And I needed to change the subject fast or I was going to ignore the paramedic's advice and the doctor's warning and then who knew what would happen to my head!

I shook away the feeling that my veins had filled with lava and led Levi into the kitchen. "So here's the strange thing about looking through your file," I told him. "I mean, the other strange thing." I made it look as casual as can be when I went to the fridge and got a glass of nice, cold water. Not exactly the cold shower I needed but it would have to do. "See, in addition to looking through your file, I glanced through all the other files, too. And they all had pictures in them. Every one except mine."

Considering this, Levi pursed his lips. "What do you think it means?"

"Well, I can't imagine anyone would want to take the pictures out of the file and keep them for any reason. Unless they wanted to prove what a total and complete mess this place was, and everybody already knows that. I know Estelle took pictures. I saw them online, and the first time I talked to her on the phone and mentioned the house, she told me I should look at them again long and hard before I flew from New York to Ohio to check out the property. She was sure the pictures would scare me away. She wanted the pictures to scare me away. She was afraid I'd get in over my head and have this albatross of a disastrous house on my hands."

Levi shrugged. "It's been a couple years. Maybe Estelle lost the pictures. Maybe she tossed them out."

"But why mine and no one else's?" I reminded myself that I could go on asking that question all day long and it would only frustrate me. Rather than think about it, I went over to the counter and started rolling silverware in the linen napkins I'd put on the buffet table that evening.

"You don't suppose whoever was in the office was looking for those pictures, do you?" I asked.

"I don't see why." Levi moved to the other side of the kitchen island, grabbed a stack of napkins, and started rolling silverware, too. "What would those pictures show that anybody doesn't already know about the place? Hey!" An idea struck and his hands stilled over his task. "You weren't in any of them, were you? You think someone's onto the fact that a famous author is on the island and they want to prove it?"

"I hope not!" I shivered. "The last thing I want is publicity and people coming over here to ogle me. Besides, I know Estelle didn't take any pictures the day I finally got here to look over the house. It was a gray, rainy, miserable day and the electricity in the house wasn't working, so she wouldn't have gotten any good pictures, anyway."

"You don't suppose those pictures are the reason someone killed Vivien, do you?" he asked, then immediately answered the question for himself. "That's just too weird to even be possible."

"There's a lot weird about this case." I weighed the wisdom of saying more and decided I had to. After all, we had promised to tell each other the truth. "I think Chandra was at Vivien's the day Vivien was killed." I went to the cupboard where I'd tucked an envelope with that little piece of gauzy fabric in it and showed it to Levi. "Chandra was wearing white that day, and this was caught on the doorjamb at Vivien's."

"Well, that's great, right? I mean, if Chandra was at Vivien's, then she couldn't have been at Estelle's killing Vivien."

"Unless she was at Vivien's looking for Vivien and when she didn't find her there . . ."

"Yeah." His hopeful expression melted. "You going to tell Hank?"

I always knew I would show him what I'd found, I just didn't want to admit it. I put the envelope back. "He'll take it the wrong way."

"Or he'll take it the right way, which is the way you're not taking it."

"Maybe." I rolled a half dozen more sets of silverware. "She's up to something."

He knew who I was talking about. "She had a good excuse for hating Vivien."

"Yeah. That's what worries me."

There was a lot to talk about at the Chamber meeting that night, so I wasn't surprised when most of the members showed. Then again, that was the whole point, wasn't it? They ate my food. They drank the wine Kate brought over from her winery. I saw more than a couple of them read over those health department certificates we'd framed, and I sent up a silent, "Hallelujah!" Now if only they'd spread the word (and more than a few of them were friends, so I knew they would), we could squash (sorry, couldn't resist!) the bedbug issue once and for all.

Once the fudge samples were passed around, we got down to business and talked about things like the renovation at the marina and a stop sign in a far corner of the island that been knocked down by a granny in a golf cart and had yet to be replaced. The last item on the agenda was Saturday's gala.

"The high school band from the mainland will be joining our kids over at the ferry dock at six." Andrew Gray, who was spearheading the Civil War gala on behalf of the historical society, had the floor. "They'll play and march from the ferry all the way to Tara."

"Oh, it's going to be something, isn't it?" Joan Battera from the grocery store could barely sit still on the couch in my parlor. "With the Twins hosting the event, I knew we'd draw a crowd. We've already sold all the tickets, and there are thirty people on the waiting list. Oh, and I've got everything arranged with Chief Florentine regarding the no-cars rule." Joan didn't have to explain. The Chamber had talked long (and sometimes loud) about trying to make the event more authentic by banning the driving of cars on the island Saturday night. Hank was not convinced it was necessary, but he'd finally capitulated. Except for emergency vehicles, it would be golf-carts-only on Saturday from five until midnight.

"The news coverage is going to be terrific." Al Marks, from our local newspaper, stood near the fireplace and he rubbed his hands together. "I've had inquiries from the TV stations on the mainland. Everything those Twins do is news. And the whole no-cars thing is causing a sensation. We're going to get a lot of good publicity out of this."

"They'll be wishing they added more rooms to Tara!" Gil Lester, who owned one of the biggest bars on the island didn't have the sense to blush or look embarrassed to say this in front of me. "The more people who see Tara, the more people will want to stay there!"

"And speaking of seeing things . . ." I'd been standing back in the corner near the bookcases I'd had built to accommodate my collection of antique books, and I stepped forward. "Since some of you have never been here, I thought we could finish the evening with tours of the inn. You're welcome to bring your wine or your coffee and—"

"Oh my gosh, it's them!"

Joan's shrilled pronouncement cut me off, and when she popped out of her chair and pointed out the front windows, every Chamber member in the room sat up and paid attention.

We were just in time to see the Twins walk up to my front door.

They didn't need to ring the bell. Both Joan and Al darted out of the parlor and into the hallway. Joan got there first, opened the front door, and beamed the Twins a smile. I was surprised she didn't curtsy.

"Hey, everyone!" Like she was on the runway in Milan, Riva sauntered in, resplendent that evening in a royal blue sleeveless dress cut up to here and down to there. Her radiant smile made up for the sullen expression on her brother's face, which (I couldn't help but notice) brightened the moment he set eyes on Kate.

"We just thought we'd pop in," Riva said. "You know, while our producer gets settled in back at Tara. Our producer!" She clapped both her hands to her heart. "There's so much we need to tell you all about the movie. We want to share every last detail with all of you. But not until all the i's are dotted and the t's are crossed." She wagged a finger and added this last bit like it was all some big secret and we were all foaming at the mouth to get the juicy details. From the looks on the faces of the people gathered around me, a lot of them were.

"Then, Mark"—since he was standing nearby, Riva had the perfect opportunity to wind an arm through that of the local newspaperman's and he blushed like a prom queen— "we'll give you the exclusive story so you can tell the world. So . . ." She took us all in with one gleaming glance. "Does anyone have any questions about Saturday?"

"That gala's going to be the biggest thing to hit the island since the blizzard of seventy-eight," Gil Lester said.

"And you know we're all going to be there." Joan squeezed back into the room. "You're sure you don't need help with anything? We'd all . . ." She was so sure of herself, Joan didn't bother to consult with the rest of us. "We'd all be more than willing to take time away from our own businesses and do whatever needs to be done over at Tara."

"That's so nice. Isn't that nice, Quentin?" Riva asked her brother. He'd been lounging in the doorway between the hallway and the parlor, and at the sound of his name, he winced and looked as if he hoped he hadn't been asked a question that he was actually expected to answer. "We've got everything under control and we're so looking forward to hosting the event. All our rooms are booked for the night, of course, and that's a pity, because we were thinking that if there was at least one room open, we could have people go up and have a look at it. You know, just to give everyone a peek at what our rooms are like. There have been so many poor people"—she sighed—"who we've had to turn away because we just don't have any openings."

"Speaking of that . . ." Levi stepped forward, effectively cutting Riva off at the knees. "We were just about to let everyone have a look around here at Bea's. Ladies and gentlemen"—he motioned toward the double doors that led into the front hallway—"let's start upstairs in groups of five or six. When you're finished looking around, you can go out to the garden. It's a perfect night to be on the patio, and I hear Wilder Winery is pouring ice wine as a nightcap." He stepped back and waved toward the door. "Let's get started!"

From my spot in the corner, I sent him a silent look of thanks, and Levi led the first group out the parlor and up the stairs. I couldn't help but notice that Riva tagged along.

"Well, that little girl is about as subtle as a brick thrown in a greenhouse." Her lips pressed into a thin line, Luella joined me, and together we watched the first group leave the room. "You think she could be any ruder?"

"I think she's lived a life of privilege and she doesn't even realize how she tramples everyone in her path," I said—quietly, of course, so the people gathering in the doorway to go upstairs couldn't hear me.

"That gala is going to be a nonstop orgy of Twins adoration." Kate had been at my side throughout the meeting and she finished the wine in her glass. "Maybe we should all stay home."

I pretended like I hadn't thought of this myself a time or two. Or three. "And miss the excitement? Come on . . ." I excused my way through the crowd and, with Kate and Luella tagging along, went through to the kitchen and out to the patio to get things ready when our first group of people were done with their tour.

Ice wine, for the uninitiated, is something of a specialty in these parts, and one of the true benefits of having a winery in the snowbelt. The wine is made from grapes harvested when the weather is at or below seventeen degrees. Yes, the grapes are frozen when they're picked, and because of that, the sugars, the flavor, and the aroma are concentrated and a very sweet dessert wine results.

Kate poured tiny glasses and as our guests came outside we handed them around.

"The inn looks wonderful." Okay, so Luella hadn't been on the tour with the rest of them, but that didn't stop her from putting in a good word on my behalf. And just loud enough for everyone to hear, too. "You've got a great eye for decorating, Bea."

"And it's so wonderfully quiet here." Kate made sure she added a sigh that rippled the still evening air. "I can't imagine a more relaxing place on the island."

"Unless Chandra's burning and chanting, of course," Luella added under her breath.

Not for the first time that day, I looked toward Chandra's and wondered what she was up to. There wasn't a light on in the house and she hadn't responded to my invitation to the meeting.

Thankfully, I didn't have much of a chance to brood or to worry. The groups who'd toured the house came out to the patio and each and every person stopped to thank me and tell me how wonderful the inn was. Now all I could do was hope they spread the word.

They sipped their ice wine and gathered in little groups

on the patio and in the garden, chatting and enjoying the perfect evening.

Except . . .

I am not a big fan of sweet wines but I'd had a tiny sip of the ice wine so as not to offend Kate, and I set down my glass. "Have the Twins come back out yet?" I asked.

No one could tell me.

I went back into the house, and though he'd been up front saying good-bye to a fellow bar owner who had to leave, Levi noticed and joined me just as I got to the stairway that led to the second floor.

"Twins," I said without any preamble, and headed upstairs.

As soon as I got to the top of the stairs, I saw that the door to Suite 6 was closed and I scrambled to get there before Levi, but I should have known he'd beat me to it. He swung open the door, I walked in right behind him, and we found the Twins, all right—Quentin near the window and Riva in front of the door that led to the attic.

"Hi!" She smiled and waved.

And yeah, okay, call me suspicious, but I automatically darted a look around to make sure every book, lamp, and lace doily was right where it was supposed to be.

Certain that nothing had been touched, I turned my attention to the Twins. "The door was closed," I said.

"Well . . ." Riva raised her slim shoulders and rolled her blue eyes heavenward. "Quentin and I were having a little argument. You know, about how quiet a place like this could actually be. And he said"—she looked his way—"he said he bet that even if the door was closed, we'd hear everybody downstairs. And I said . . ." Really, it wasn't like she had to point a finger at herself; we knew who she was talking about. "I said, I bet we wouldn't hear a peep. And I was right!" Her chin raised, she marched out of the room, and Quentin followed behind.

"That was weird," I told Levi once they were gone.

"They're weird," he said.

"Why would they want to . . ." I looked around the room again, and sure that nothing had been touched, Levi and I checked out the other rooms, too, and now that the tours were over, locked each door before we went back downstairs.

We were just in time to hear Riva call out a jaunty "Ciao!" to anyone who was listening—which turned out to be everyone, of course. "We've got to get back and talk about our movie!" She kissed the tips of her fingers and waved, and she and Quentin left.

I wasn't about to let that break up the party. I signaled to Kate, she gave me the thumbs-up and refilled tiny wine glasses, and I strolled from group to group, joining in the casual conversations and doing my best not to gloat (well, at least not too much) when people mentioned that they saw now that the rumors they heard about the inn weren't true and they should have known better than to even listen.

A small, triumphant smile on my face, I came up behind the group chatting just where the corner of the garage met the small herb garden Chandra had planted for me so I could include the freshest ingredients in the breakfasts I served at the inn. Before I could say a word and let these folks know I was there, Paul Witkowski from the marina piped up, "Well, that's what I heard, and I don't know if it's true or not, but it makes sense, doesn't it?"

Christie Norman from the bait and tackle shop nodded. "You're right. Nobody knows anything about her background, do they? She says she came from New York. Well, that's not telling us very much."

I swallowed hard and stepped farther back into the shadows. Had word gone out that I was FX O'Grady? And if so, who had spilled the beans?

As it turned out, the possibility of being discovered as FX O'Grady was the least of my worries. I found that out when Doug McMann from the coffee shop lowered his voice. "Well, when you know what I know, you'll see why no one wants to stay in this place. Yeah, it looks great and the food is wonderful. But Bea? My sources tell me we don't know where she came from because it was either prison or a mental hospital."

"I hope everyone's having a great time!"

Oh yes, I had a smile on my face when I bolted into the center of that group of gossipers. "I appreciate you all stopping by this evening. And Doug . . ." When I turned to him, Doug McMann refused to meet my eyes. Too bad because he missed the wink I gave him. "Just so you know, sources aren't always right. Prison? Mental hospital?" I laughed, as if the anger that was building inside me like lava in Etna didn't matter at all. "I've got news for you . . . for all of you . . ." My smile outshone the moon overhead and I bestowed it on each of them, one at a time. "If you knew the truth, you'd see that my secret past is way more interesting than that."

Not one of them managed a reply. But then, what did I expect? One by one (and pretty quickly, too), the group broke up and headed for the street where they'd left their cars, and when Levi found me, I had my fists on my hips and a look on my face that must have been thunderous.

Otherwise, he wouldn't have taken a gander at me and stepped back.

"Trouble?"

I bit my lower lip. It was better than letting the words on

my tongue escape. "Not if I can help it," I said instead, and before he could ask what was up, I breezed past him and said good night to my other guests.

It didn't matter.

The words pounded through my bloodstream to the furious beating of my heart.

Stupid stories and stupid rumors didn't matter.

Doug McMann didn't matter.

I had lived on the island for more than a year and I knew that island residents were mature, sensible, logical.

No one would believe the sort of garbage Doug spouted.

And it didn't matter, anyway.

« 14 »

As of the next day, Wednesday, I officially had a clean bill of health and the doctor's permission to resume normal activity—and believe me, I planned to take full of advantage of it.

The first thing I did was shoo Levi out of the house, but not before I told him how much I appreciated all he'd done for me, and not before we'd made Saturday night's gala an official date. (There might have been a long good-bye involved, too, but I am not a girl who kisses and tells.) He would pick me up at five thirty so we'd have plenty of time to find a good vantage point to watch the band march over to Tara.

That done, I headed out. I had some shopping to do, and while I was at it, I wanted to touch base with some of the folks who'd been at the meeting the night before. Doug McMann's crazy stories might not matter, but that didn't mean I wasn't going to make sure the rumor hadn't spread farther than that little knot of visitors in my garden.

First stop, the bait and tackle shop. No, I wasn't taking up fishing. But I knew that, like every day, Christie Norman would be behind the front counter.

She was, and as soon as I walked in, her face paled and her eyes went wide. "I'll be there to help you in just a minute," she called out and disappeared into the back room of the shop.

I didn't wait a minute.

I waited five.

No sign of Christie and I left in a huff.

One of the island gift shops was next on my list. It was the kind of place that catered to the tourist crowd with T-shirts and key chains and shot glasses but also carried an assortment of home goods aimed at the cottagers. I knew what I was looking for would be over near a display marked *Just In*, and I looked past beaded evening bags made to look like seashells and signs that said things like *Welcome to the Beach!* and *Relax, You're at the Cottage Now* until I found the sparkly things I'd had in mind. I had my costume for the gala on Saturday and some jewelry to wear with it, but I wanted something for my hair, and I knew the shop carried barrettes decorated with ribbons and faux jewels like the ones on the wooden picture frames nearby. I found one I liked and would have bought it, too, if the shop owner hadn't kept fussing over two other shoppers and pretended I was invisible.

The same sort of thing happened at the grocery store.

And the walk-up sandwich place where I stopped for lunch and left as hungry as ever because no one would wait on me—and really, I would have attributed the whole thing to just some crazy mojo in the air if it weren't for the sly looks I was getting from people. And the pitying glances. And the way a couple of them backed off, just a little, when they saw me headed their way.

By the time I was just about to hop into the car and head home and I saw Luella coming back from a morning charter, I was ready to spit nails.

She squinted at me. "You all right?"

"Apparently I'm a leper."

Luella is as clearheaded as she is hardworking, but I couldn't blame her for being confused.

I got behind the wheel and motioned her to jump in. "I'm a pariah," I told her.

She lowered her silvery brows. "Because . . ."

"Because word has gone out that I'm some kind of . . ." I was so angry, the words choked me. I turned the key to start up the SUV, then changed my mind and turned it off again. "People think I'm an ex-con. Or that I've got some sort of dark and dangerous past and I was in a mental institution. I heard them talking last night at my place, and now, apparently, the rumor's all over town. Everyone's treating me like I have the cooties."

It was warm and Luella was in the tan Carhartt overalls she wore on her boat. She unhooked the straps and pushed the top of the overalls down around the gray T-shirt she wore underneath. "That's—"

"Crazy? I'll say it's crazy." To emphasize my point, I slapped the steering wheel. "I'm going to—"

"Breathe deep, that's what you're going to do." Luella put a hand on my arm. "We both know none of that nonsense is true."

"We know it, sure. But everyone else—"

"Everyone else can go dunk their heads in the lake." It was as simple as that. At least to Luella. She sat back. "But it seems really odd, don't you think?" she asked.

"That people think I'm crazy?" The words sputtered out of me. "It's more than odd. It's terrible. It's horrible. It's—"

"Plenty suspicious."

This was one word I hadn't thought of and, curious, I cocked my head.

"First it was the bad reviews of your B and B and the service and the food," Luella said. "Then it was the bedbugs. And now this? It doesn't take a boat captain to know fishy when she sees it."

She was right, and there was only one conclusion. "It *is* fishy. In a somebody's-out-to-get-me sort of way."

"You got that right." Luella smelled faintly like fish and water and sunshine and those red and white peppermints she liked to suck on when she was out on the lake. She crossed her arms over her chest. "What are you going to do about it, New York?"

"Find out who's behind the rumors."

She nodded. "I have no doubt you'll do it, too, but that might take a while."

"Then I'll . . ." I pressed my lips together, thinking hard, and when that didn't work, I let out a screech of frustration. "I don't know what I'll do! Someone's out to destroy my business, and from the looks of things, it just might work!"

"Let's not get ahead of ourselves." Like I said, when it comes to common sense, Luella is always right on the money. "If you act fast, whoever this nasty person is behind these rumors won't have a chance to hurt your business."

I wrung my hands. Yes, it was incredibly dramatic, but that's exactly how I felt, and if anyone criticized me, I could always blame my behavior on my brain injury. "Except I don't know what to do!" I wailed.

Except I did.

I froze when the thought hit and I guess Luella must have known that things were finally clear to me. That would explain why she grinned.

"I need to forget all these crazy rumors and figure out who killed Vivien Frisk once and for all," I announced. "If I can do that, people will see that I'm not some nutcase. Or some sort of criminal."

"Good thinking, New York!"

Luella hopped out of the car.

"Aren't you coming with me?" I asked her.

She waved when I started up car. "I've got another charter in a couple hours. And you . . ." She smiled. "You've got a murder to solve!"

There wasn't much question about where I needed to start. It was Wednesday and the traffic was light. It took me no time at all to get to Estelle's.

Yes, the house was locked up tight, just the way the police had left it, but that didn't matter to me. I didn't want to get in the house, anyway.

Instead, I started at the far left corner of the front yard and worked my way around the house, through one rhododendron, a couple of prickly rosebushes, and a lilac bush, all the way to the back porch. There, I sat in the sun for a minute, reminding myself that I was only halfway done and that what I found—or didn't find—might change the course of the investigation.

Revitalized, and with more enthusiasm than I'd had for

the case since I'd been whacked over the head, I did a slow, careful search around the rest of the house.

I poked through a couple of boxwoods that needed trimming badly. I pushed through a stand of pampas grass that should have been cut back in the fall and was now brittle, its leaves as sharp as razors. By the time I got back to the right front corner of the house, I was sweaty and grumbling.

But I wasn't done.

I slipped behind the rhododendron where we'd found Cody Rayburn the evening of Vivien's murder.

Truth be told, it wasn't a bad hiding place. If, indeed, Cody had been hiding. It was shady there next to the house, cooler than it had been out in the afternoon sunshine, and from there, I could easily see the street—who came and who went and who drove by. The rhododendron itself was years old and huge. I had plenty of room to maneuver, and I didn't waste any time. Sure, I could have kicked through the dirt, but heck, it was just easier to get on my hands and knees. It wasn't like I had any guests to impress, and half the island already thought I was crazy; I would deal with the mud later.

And mud there was.

This side of the house was shady, and thanks to that brief rainstorm a couple nights before and a nearby gutter that still drip, drip, dripped in a lazy sort of way, the ground was as mushy as a marsh. This was bad news, because within a few minutes, the knees of my jeans were soaked through and my fingers were caked with mud.

But it was good news, too.

See, all that rain dribbling in one spot had churned up the soil, and the churned-up soil revealed its secrets in just a few minutes.

I saw the glint of metal in the mud and poked my fingers in the dirt to scoop the ring up in my hand.

It was a gold band with a silver skull in the center of it, and I knew right away what I'd found—the present Cody's pregnant old lady had given him for Christmas.

"He was telling the truth."

To Hank's everlasting credit, he didn't cringe (at least not too much) when I walked into his office looking like I'd just gone a couple rounds in a mud-wrestling bout. But then, he was pretty busy sitting up and aiming a look at the ring I put on his desk.

His lips pursed and his eyes narrowed, he looked from the ring to me.

"At Estelle's?" he asked.

"Under the rhododendron, right where Cody said he was looking for it the night Vivien was killed."

"Which doesn't mean he isn't our killer."

"Not for certain, no. But it does mean at least part of his story has merit."

His nod was curt, begrudging. "It does." Hank drummed his fingers against his gray metal desk. "Dang, I sure wanted Cody to be our man."

"You and me both." I hadn't been invited to, but I sat down in the chair across from Hank's desk. It was old and uncomfortable: gray metal that matched his desk, with a gray plastic seat that had seen better days. Then again, I imagined that being face-to-face with the island police chief was never meant to be a pleasant experience. "We've still got Alex," I reminded him.

The way Hank shook his head spoke volumes. "His story checks out. He was with his boyfriend, John, all right. One of the neighbors saw them together early on the morning Vivien was killed and then later in the day. Alex isn't our man."

Did I groan? I didn't mean to, but heck, it was the only appropriate response. "Alex didn't do it. Cody didn't do it. That leaves Zane Donahue."

"And Chandra."

"You can't think—" But of course, he did, and in all honesty, I couldn't blame him. I slapped the arms of the metal chair (and yes, I did leave a little mud behind) and stood. "I'm going to talk to Chandra," I told Hank in no uncertain terms. "It's about time we set the record straight."

He didn't even try to argue. Or maybe he did and I just didn't wait long enough to hear it. The island police station is in the basement of the town hall building, and I climbed the steps and was outside in the parking lot in minutes.

In just a few more minutes, I was back home.

Deep breaths and firm resolve and a quick washup and a change of jeans, and I headed right over to Chandra's.

And really, after the way she'd been acting, I was surprised and ridiculously relieved when she answered the door.

She stepped back to let me inside, and instantly, I was enveloped in the scent of patchouli.

Chandra's home is pretty basic, though her decorating scheme is anything but. Just inside the front door was a small entryway and against the wall there was a skinny table where a stick of incense smoked in a burner. There were candles on either side of the incense burner, flickering in multicolored glass holders.

To our left was a doorway that led into the living room, where the walls were painted a shade of purple that matched the pillows on the orange couch. One of those little electric fountains gurgled on the table in front of the window, its babble far more soothing than the furious beat of my pulse.

Since I had stepped into the living room uninvited, I had to turn to see Chandra, who was still standing out in the entryway.

"You're not going to turn your lights off and hide?" I asked her.

Her chin rose a fraction of an inch. "Why would I do something like that?"

I was in no mood for games. "You've been dodging me for days. Ever since—"

"You told me I might have killed Vivien."

"You know no one believes that. Not really."

"Well, I *really* don't appreciate it when my friends think I'm a murderer."

Try as I might, I couldn't control my screech of frustration. "Don't you get it, Chandra? You're the reason I keep digging into this thing further and further. Not to prove that you killed Vivien, but to prove that you didn't. But I can't do that without your help."

Her bottom lip quivered, but I had to give Chandra credit. In true Scarlett O'Hara style, her shoulders shot back and her jaw tensed. "Would you like some tea? I'm brewing peppermint and lemon balm. It's good for the nerves."

My nerves needed it.

I let Chandra lead the way through the living room and into the dining room, but when she ducked into the kitchen, I stayed put. Then again, it was hard not to be fascinated by the display on the antique buffet (painted a yellow that reminded me of bananas, just in case there is any question about Chandra's appreciation of old furniture).

Candles, dozens of them, were scattered over the top of the buffet, winking in the early afternoon light. They were placed around pictures—I counted quickly and came up with fifteen—in frames. Pictures of a smiling man with a rugged face and a woman who was certainly Chandra twenty years before.

Her hair was dark then, and long enough to brush her shoulders, but there was no mistaking the panache. In one picture, she stood at the man's side dressed in an orange and green muumuu. In another, she was wearing an eighties-style party dress with puffed sleeves and a sweetheart neckline.

In each and every one of those pictures, she had a grin on her face wide enough to light up the world.

And so did the man at her side.

"Bill Barone." I touched a finger to the frame of the photograph closest to me. "He was a good-looking guy."

I hadn't realized Chandra had left the kitchen and was standing right behind me. "Yeah, he was. And he was the sweetest guy to ever walk the earth. At least until Vivien got ahold of him and messed with his head."

I examined another one of the pictures. This one was in a frame studded with fake gemstones. "He was older than you," I said.

Chandra didn't so much agree with me as she grunted. "I guess that was one of the reasons he lost his mind when Vivien came on to him. Middlelife crisis. That's what we used to call it. I was six years younger than Bill. Vivien was fifteen years younger. Imagine any middle-aged guy resisting when this sweet young thing—" She choked over her words and cleared her throat.

I allowed her time to compose herself, looking over the

rest of the pictures as I did. Bill at the marina. Bill standing outside Perry's Victory and International Peace Memorial. Bill eating sweet corn at a party in the park.

Knowing what I knew about everything that had happened after these happy pictures were taken, my heart squeezed.

And a question popped out of my mouth. "Didn't Hank mind that you had all these pictures of Bill around?"

"Well, you know they weren't always here." Chandra went back into the kitchen and came out carrying two steaming mugs of tea. "You've never seen them before, right?"

"Yes, of course." I sipped my tea. Carefully. Chandra was known for herbal concoctions that often tasted as bad as they smelled. Peppermint and lemon balm, it turned out, was a pleasant combination. "Then why—"

She lifted one shoulder. "It would have been our anniversary. Twenty. I just thought . . . oh, I don't know. I was just feeling sentimental. You know, with what happened to Vivien and with the anniversary, it all just kind of came back at me. I thought it would be nice to pay a little tribute to Bill. He might have gone loco when Vivien got her claws into him, but deep down, he was a sweetheart. And no, I didn't have the pictures out when I lived here with Hank. They've been packed away for years." She took a glug of her tea. "So, what did you stop over for?"

Don't worry, I knew she'd be bound to ask sooner or later, and I had an excuse all planned. "I was just wondering about the gala on Saturday night. What do you think I should do about my hair?"

Chandra stepped back and cocked her head from side to side, sizing me up. "Up," she said. "But you've probably seen enough Civil War movies to know that." She set down her mug and scooped my hair into what could have been a ponytail, except that she left out a section over each of my ears. While she worked, I watched our reflection in a nearby mirror framed in wood that was studded with bits and pieces of colored glass. "You'll twist the back of your hair into a bun like this." Quickly, Chandra demonstrated. "But you'll leave these front sections loose for now. When you're done with the bun, you'll twist each of these sections . . ." Again, she demonstrated. "Then wrap the twists around the bun. Simple—and it'll look great."

I looked at her standing behind me in the mirror. "What were you doing at Vivien's on Friday?" I asked her.

Chandra stepped away and my hair fell back around my shoulders. "Why do you—"

"Come on, Chandra!" I spun to face her. "Remember what I said. I'm not looking to jam you up on murder charges, that's for sure. But if I'm going to prove that you didn't do it, I need answers."

Her lower lip trembled. "What makes you think I was there at all?"

"Because you left a piece of yourself behind." I pinned her with a look. "You were dressed all in white that day, Chandra, and there was a piece of white fabric caught on Vivien's doorframe. And don't tell me a lot of people wear white. You were there. And I need to know why."

She looked up at the ceiling. "I can't tell you."

I set down my tea on the dining room table, the better to be sure it didn't slosh over the side of the mug when I stomped my foot. "Then you admit you were there?"

She pursed her lips. "Maybe."

"Then you've got to tell me why."

"I wasn't there killing Vivien, I can tell you that."

"Obviously, because she wasn't killed at home. But speaking of that, you were seen at Estelle's, too."

"I told Hank, I was out taking a walk."

"That's your story and you're sticking to it?"

Her lower lip protruded.

"Fine." I raised my arms and let them flop back to my side. "If that's how you're going to be, then there's nothing I can do to help you. But I've got a little advice for you, Chandra. If Hank comes around, he's not going be so easy on you. You need a better answer than 'I can't tell you.'"

Her gaze flickered over to the candles and the pictures and the happy memories of her life with Bill. "I wish I could," she said. "But I'd have to say the same thing to Hank that I did to you. I really can't tell."

It was beyond frustrating, and I couldn't stand it another minute. I headed out the door, determined to leave the aroma of patchouli, the bittersweet memories of Bill Barone, and the most maddening friend in the world behind me until I could regain my composure and, hopefully, some sort of perspective.

Good thing I picked that moment to do it, too, or I wouldn't have seen the Twins just leaving my front door.

They caught sight of me and waved, and we met halfway on my front lawn.

That day, the Twins looked like they were all set for lunch at a Hollywood country club, Riva in a pink sundress and platform sandals and her brother in white pants and an equally blinding white shirt.

"We thought you'd be home," Riva said. "Not that you have any guests or anything, but . . ."

She was the one who brought it up, so I was perfectly

justified to ask, "How would you know if I have guests or not? Unless you're keeping an eye on me."

Quentin paled. Riva, I couldn't help but notice, didn't bat an eyelash. "Don't be silly." She giggled as if I actually were. "We have too much on our plates to think about you. We're being interviewed on *Nightline*, you know. And then there's our movie."

I guess I was supposed to be impressed. The way my day was going, it was going to take a lot more than Hollywood faux congeniality and a perky smile to bring me around.

I cut to the chase. "What do you want?"

Riva's laugh rang like crystal. "The real question is what do *you* want? Or I should say, how much do you want? We're here to make you an offer, darling. We're going to do you a favor and buy your inn."

❖ 15 ❖

The call came in about four the next afternoon, and to tell the truth, I almost didn't answer it. I mean, that's why caller ID was invented, right? To dodge the people we don't want to talk to.

Then again, after what happened the evening before with the Twins and all I realized it meant, I'm pretty sure curiosity spurred me to pick up my phone from the kitchen counter next to where I was chopping vegetables for the salad that would be my dinner. I think anger had something to do with it, too. Then again . . . I stabbed the knife I was using into a zucchini and left it there as a sort of emblem of my mood . . . there was also a perverse sort of pleasure in realizing that maybe I'd have a chance to prove I wasn't nearly as dumb as certain people obviously thought I was.

I not only answered the call—I agreed to a meeting with the person on the other end of the phone.

This, of course, is all by way of providing an explanation for what I was doing at Tara at eight o'clock that Thursday evening.

Unlike the last time I'd visited, the inn was relatively quiet. But then, it was late. The gentle *tick, tick, tick* of the clock on the wall and the chirruping of feminine voices washed over me the moment I stepped foot in the lobby. The women in question were lined up at the main desk, where a young man in a Confederate uniform dutifully checked them into their rooms. There were six of them, each with a ball gown on a hanger slung over her shoulder, and they were obviously anxious to get their Civil War weekend started. At least if the way two of the women harmonized on "The Battle Hymn of the Republic" meant anything.

I stood back and patiently waited my turn, but just as he was starting with woman number three, the young man spied me and pointed toward the parlor.

I was expected.

I thanked him with a nod and stepped into the parlor but there was no one around. A second later, I heard the clink of glasses from the direction of the room where the Twins served breakfast to their guests. The person waiting for me at one of the tables wasn't the one I expected.

I stopped just inside the doorway. "Riva was the one who called."

Quentin, looking like the cover model from a romance novel that evening in black pants and a crisp white shirt with its three top buttons left undone, had been pouring champagne into two tall flutes, and he looked my way and flashed a boyish grin. "I thought if I called, you wouldn't come."

"I'm surprised you thought I'd come at all. I told you last night—both of you—I told you I'm not selling Bea and Bees."

He nestled the champagne bottle in a gleaming chrome bucket filled with ice and held up one hand, palm out, as if he'd expected that's exactly what I would say.

"I get it. I do. You have every right to be angry at us. My sister is a . . ." He hauled in a sigh and let it out slowly. "You might have noticed that Riva is a little spoiled. She thinks she can always have whatever she wants."

"Just her?"

He waved me toward the chair across from where he stood. Like the other tables in the room, it was laid for the next day's breakfast: white linen cloths, small bouquets of fake flowers, gray napkins on the tables on one side of the room, blue on the tables on the other side. No doubt, Tara was drawing its own lines for the next day's breakfast, North versus South.

Quentin sat down at the gray-napkin table where, in addition to the flutes and the champagne, there was one candle glowing from a glass holder.

He ignored my question. "I'm not going to try and change your mind about selling your inn, if that's what you're worried about," he said and laughed in a way that made me think of country club cocktail parties. "Though I can guarantee you, you'll hear from Riva about it again. Like I said, spoiled, and she doesn't take no for an answer."

"She hasn't heard no from me before."

Since I hadn't moved, he tried another wave, and this time when I didn't budge, he pulled in a breath and let it out in what might have been a huff from a less godly young man. Quentin, with his aquiline nose, trim body, and three-hundred-dollar haircut, made it sound as if being frustrated by my stubbornness was his natural right.

"I think maybe we got off on the wrong foot," he said.

It was exactly the opening I'd been waiting for. I smiled and sashayed just a little closer. "If you're talking about the bad reviews online for my inn, the bedbug story, and the fact that half the population of the island now thinks I'm an ex-con, you're absolutely right."

Of course I had no proof that the Twins were the ones who spread the rumors, but if I'm good at anything, it's putting two and two together. No business? A bad reputation? Rumors of my instability?

And then out of nowhere, a lowball offer to buy the inn?

One look at the way a muscle jumped at the base of Quentin's jaw and I knew I was on the right track, so I allowed myself a smile. "Just because we live on an island doesn't mean we're country bumpkins," I told him. "I've had my suspicions for a while, but as soon as you made your offer on the inn, the pieces fell into place. With business down and my rooms empty, you figured I'd be more likely to sell."

"There's only so long anyone can hold out."

"True." I took one step back toward to the doorway and was rewarded when he winced. Quentin was used to having the upper hand with women; he didn't expect me to cut and run so quickly. Or with so little interest in anything he had to say.

That made it all the more delicious when I added, "When it comes to the inn, though, you need to know that I can hold out forever."

I would have said his smile was repentant if I didn't know it was also practiced. "How about when it comes to the curly maple highboy?"

It was my turn to wince, and darn it, he noticed.

This time, his smile was genuine.

I tried not to do it. Really. But I just couldn't help myself.

My gaze flickered to the highboy on the other side of the room, its warm wood and polished hardware glowing in the hushed lighting, silently beckoning. This time when Quentin motioned toward the empty chair across from where he stood, I walked over and sat down.

"How much?" I asked.

"Wow, you don't waste any time!" He sat down, too, and handed me the champagne flute. "Come on, let's at least pretend to follow the formalities. Besides . . ." He tipped his glass in my direction. "It's Dom Pérignon. Courtesy of our producer."

I was supposed to be impressed. I wasn't, but I wasn't one to waste perfectly good champagne, either. I sipped. "And the curly maple highboy?" I asked.

He drank down half his glass and refilled it. "I told you, Riva is spoiled. The first time she saw the highboy, she fell in love with it, but Vivien told her that her aunt had already promised it to you. That was all Riva needed to hear. What anyone else has, Riva wants. And what Riva wants, Riva always gets."

"And you don't."

He sat back. "What I want . . ." Call me a sucker for nice champagne and the siren's call of maybe getting the high-boy; this time when he sighed, it didn't hit me like finger-nails on a blackboard. I think there might have been a tiny thread of sincerity hidden away beneath the Hollywood-heritage and I'm-so-cool exterior.

"There's something about you, Bea," Quentin said. "You're open. Friendly. I haven't gotten to know anyone well here on the island yet because we've been so busy with interviews and our book, and the movie, of course." He glanced my way long enough to see if I was salivating yet, and when he saw that I wasn't, he coughed and went right on. "We haven't made any friends, either. Not really good friends. I mean, except for Vivien, and now . . ."

He washed down what he might have said with another sip of champagne. "Everyone else we've met on the island, they're all so . . ." Did he really have to search for the word? I doubted it, but at least he tried to make a show of it. "All they see is the wealth and the fame and our reputations. All they think about is the stories they've read about us and everything they heard in those awful months when we were gone. They look at us . . . they look at me . . . and they think of all the media reports and the scandal and the sensation!" He twitched his shoulders. "But somehow, you're different. And I don't think it's because you're not impressed. I think it's because you know that there's more to a person than what's just on the outside. That's why I think I can be honest with you."

Oh, how I like a good spot of sarcasm! "You mean despite the fact that I'm a mentally deranged ex-con!"

He laughed. "Don't worry about that. We'll clear up that little rumor in no time at all. It was just a ploy. Just business. You understand that, don't you? All those rumors, we had to spread them. This has always been just about business."

"The business of buying my inn."

He screwed up his face. "Like I said, what Riva wants, Riva gets. She fell in love with your little place the moment she saw it."

The way to butter me up was not to call my home a "little place." I managed not to point this out, but then, I was busy being surprised when Quentin went on.

"See, here's the thing," he said. "This place . . ." He glanced around the breakfast room. It was big and at this time of the evening, shadows were gathering in the corners and outside the window that looked out over a fountain, a rose garden, and . . . I couldn't quite believe my eyes, so I squinted and leaned forward . . . cotton plants?

"This is not exactly the kind of place I ever pictured myself living," Quentin said.

I set aside thoughts of how the Twins must have had the cotton plants shipped in and how they would surely not live through an Ohio winter so I could look at him levelly. "Yet here you are."

His nod was barely noticeable. "Like I said—"

"Riva is spoiled."

"And Riva gets what she wants. And she's the one who wants to live on this island," Quentin said. "I'm more the Malibu type. Or maybe Anguilla. Anguilla, it's an island in the—"

"Yeah. I know." I did not point out that I had a home there that I didn't visit often enough, and at the same time I wondered what Levi would think about a Caribbean getaway, I took another tiny taste of the champagne and pointed out, "Maybe after a while you'll change your mind. There's a lot to like about the island. I love it here."

His mouth twisted. "Well, yeah, but you—"

I sat up, my elbows on the table. "I'm what, a hayseed like the rest of them? Unsophisticated? Easily amused?"

His laugh didn't fool me. "That's not what I said. It's not what I meant. I meant that we're used to a different life, me and Riva. Glamour. Excitement."

"And now you're hosting Civil War galas."

His shoulders dropped. "She's making me wear a uniform."

Just seeing him looking that despondent cheered me right

up, and I guess he knew it because Quentin caught himself, sat up, and inched back his shoulders. "The point is—"

"The point is, you say you crave peace and quiet, but you take every opportunity you have to put yourself in the spotlight."

Like my criticism was raindrops, he shook his shoulders. "That's Riva. She says we have to tell our story. She says we have to get the word out. You know, so people can understand what we went through. So they pay more attention when people go missing."

If it was true, I had to give the Twins credit.

But I wasn't convinced.

"You could do that and give yourself some peace. You could work behind the scenes with missing persons organizations."

When he shook his head, his golden hair glittered in the light of the candle that flickered between us and cast angular shadows against his high cheekbones. "I don't think so. We've got a platform. We've got a presence. People listen to us."

"They'd listen to you just as well if you were back in Malibu."

It was his turn to smile a knowing smile. "You'd love to get rid of us, wouldn't you? Then you wouldn't have any competition."

And my turn to be miffed. "I'm not the only B and B on the island," I reminded him. "I've got plenty of competition. I have had since the day I moved here. It's never discouraged me. There's plenty of room for all of us."

"But no one's ever given you the kind of run for your money we have. No one else has done a B and B here on the island as well as we have." As if he had to remind himself, he glanced around the dining room. "Or with as much panache."

"I'll give you credit for that." I lifted my champagne flute in a silent toast. "You've been clever with your marketing."

"And the gala on Saturday will seal the deal. You know"— he leaned forward—"our offer was genuine, and generous. Things will only get worse for your business after this weekend."

"I thought we were here to talk about the highboy."

"You're right." He gave up with good grace, but when I put down my glass and he refilled it again, I didn't take another sip. "The highboy . . ." As if he were doing the math in his head and it wasn't an easy process, he made a face. "Fifty thousand ought to do it."

I couldn't help but laugh. "You remember what I said about not being a country bumpkin, right? I could buy two eighteenth-century highboys for that price. So if you're done wasting my time . . ." I pushed back my chair and made to stand up.

"Don't go!"

I don't know what surprised me more, the sincerity in Quentin's voice or the fact that he reached across the table and put a hand on my arm.

I shook off his hold and my gaze shifted over his shoulder to the highboy. "You're willing to negotiate?"

He groaned. "I'm willing to admit the truth."

I settled down in my chair. "You mean—"

"I mean that I didn't want you to come over here tonight to talk about the highboy."

"But you said—"

"Yeah, I did, and maybe Riva will have a moment of weakness and you can buy it one of these days. Don't tell her I told you so but she doesn't have much of an attention span. She'll lose interest in the highboy just like she loses interest in everything else: men and cars and homes and clothes. She'll find something else she likes better, something flashier and more expensive, and she'll get rid of the highboy. It might take a while, but I guarantee you it will happen sooner or later. The highboy isn't the reason I asked you to stop over. I talked Riva into calling you and inviting you here so I could tell you that I'm fascinated. There. You got it out of me!"

Only I was pretty sure I hadn't.

"Fascinated by . . . ?"

Again he leaned forward and put a hand on my arm. "Fascinated by you, of course."

His look was soulful. His eyes were searching. His aftershave . . . well, I didn't need to put a name to it to know it was pricey. So yeah, it was the wrong time to laugh. "You're telling me that you're attracted to me?"

He stood just long enough to scoot his chair around to my side of the table so that we were sitting side by side. "I know it's not how women like to be romanced. I mean, I know most women like to take things slow and easy, to get to know a guy before—"

"Before what?"

I was glad he skirted the question. "I just wanted you to know that ever since we came to the island, ever since I met you, I can't stop thinking about you."

"That's funny, because every time I see you, you're staring at Kate Wilder."

"Well, sure." He had the good sense to blush, and I wondered how he called up the color on demand. "Kate is a beautiful woman and any guy would stare. But she's pretty much an ice queen, isn't she? She's got that whole stand-back vibe going on. You . . . you've got fire and passion and good looks and intelligence. You're far more interesting."

"And you . . ." I leaned forward just a tad so that I could trade him look for look. "You don't know a thing about me, so you can't even begin to know how interesting I might or might not be, and you certainly don't know anything about my fire and passion." This time when I scraped my chair back, I stood. "I think you've been cooped up on this island too long. You need to get back to Hollywood."

"I do." Quentin stood, too, but lucky for him, he had the sense to keep his distance. I didn't want to show off the skills I'd learned in a series of self-defense classes. As Levi had once learned when he followed me down a dark street and I didn't know it was him, I could manage a decent right hook to the nose when the situation called for it. "But don't you get it? I can't leave."

I marched to the door. "There's a ferry," I reminded him. "There's an airport. Heck, with the money you're making on your movie, you could buy a boat, sail back to the mainland and leave the boat at the dock in Sandusky, and never look back."

"But that wouldn't work!" I heard his voice—a little whiny now—right behind me, but I never turned back to him, not until we got out to the lobby, where those middle-aged ladies were gathered in a knot discussing dinner options and gasped at the sight of him.

They were the only reason Quentin kept his voice down. "Don't you get it?" he asked. "Don't you see why I can't leave? Why I can never leave? Because Riva gets what she wants, and Riva wants to stay here. If I left, I'd just be me. And that would never work. No one would pay any attention. We wouldn't be the Twins anymore."

The evening wasn't a total waste.

It was good for a few laughs, a few sips of nice champagne, and the fact that I'd learned what I'd set out to learn—that the Twins were behind the rumors about me so they could ruin me financially and scoop the inn out from under me.

And then there was the highboy.

Was Quentin telling the truth? Might Riva someday want to sell it?

I didn't know but if she ever did, I knew I'd be first in line, checkbook in hand.

As long as she didn't expect me to pay fifty thousand dollars for it.

As for Quentin's lame come-on . . .

The very idea that he was attracted to me was preposterous and obviously aimed at softening me up so the Twins could make another offer. It wouldn't work, but thinking about it sure made me smile. Oh, not because I was interested, but because it was pretty darned funny.

I was still grinning when I pulled into the yard and saw that the extension ladder Levi had stored behind my garage had been moved. That could only mean that Chuck from the hardware store had stopped by and taken a look at that loose slate shingle on the roof. He might not have been able to fix it, seeing as it was already evening by the time I left the house and he'd come by, but the fact that the ladder hadn't been put away proved he'd be back to finish the job.

Considering how the rest of the week had gone—what with Vivien's murder, the rumors about me, and Chandra acting like she'd lost her mind—things were actually looking up.

❖ 16 ❖

The next day was Friday, and despite the fact that I was dangerous/felonious/recently infested, I actually had three couples show up at the door and ask if I had open rooms. Maybe they hadn't heard the rumors. Maybe they had and they were made of sterner stuff than the folks who believed such baloney without proof.

Or maybe, with Tara packed to the gills and the other inns on the island doing a brisk business because of the gala, they simply had no choice.

Ask me if I cared.

I welcomed them, told them tea would be served at four, and, once I got them settled (they were thrilled with the rooms, by the way, and announced they couldn't have found a prettier place to stay), got down to some serious work. After all, I had a murder to solve.

I started at the most logical place with the most logical suspect.

No, that wasn't Chandra. It was, in fact, Zane Donahue, the man with hatred in his heart and buckets of water at the ready in case he ever wanted to ambush his nemesis.

"Buckets of water."

I was sitting at the breakfast counter in the kitchen finishing the last of the turkey and avocado sandwich I'd made for lunch, and, thinking, I tapped my fingers against the counter.

What was it about the incident at the memorial service that tickled something in my brain?

I thought some more, got nowhere, and gave up with a sound that was more of a huff than a sigh.

That's when I called Kate.

She was in a meeting, her administrative assistant told me, but due to finish in another thirty minutes or so.

I didn't wait for an invitation. I knew Kate well enough to know I didn't need one. I got in my car and went over to Wilder Winery.

It is never a hardship to stop in at the winery. For one thing, I could chat with Kate, and hopefully, talking through the investigation would shake loose some nugget of wisdom that would lead us in the right direction. For another . . . well, I am always eager to try any new wines Wilder produces, and while I was at it, I knew I'd order a case to have around for when friends dropped in. I remembered that back in the day when we were talking and not fighting, Levi had complimented Kate's old vine Zinfandel, and, hoping I'd have a chance to share a bottle of it with him one of these evenings soon, I reminded myself to include it in my order.

It was Friday.

It was June.

I knew that, like every place else on the island, the winery was bound to be a zoo.

Only I never expected anything like this.

I slowed at the entrance to the parking lot, which was packed to the gills and blocked by a string of yellow tape, and when the young man stationed there waved me over to the empty field on the far side of the property, I waved to let him know I got the message. There in an empty field that bordered the vineyard, I found a place to park along with a few dozen other outliers. Since the weather was gorgeous, I refused the offer of a golf cart ride from a youngster wearing a Wilder T-shirt whose job it was to ferry people back and forth and so keep them un-footsore and happy enough to taste and buy.

I preferred to walk. It gave me time to think, and besides, the setting was perfect. From what I'd been told by Luella, Chandra, and Kate, who had all spent their entire lives on the island, the winery had stood on this same spot since the late 1800s. At the time, it had been a monstrosity of an Old World building, complete with timbers and stucco and a gigantic cuckoo clock in a tower above the main door.

That had all changed just as Kate took over operation of the winery from her parents, who retired to Florida. An electrical fire leveled the place, but never one to be deterred, Kate rebuilt with her usual determination. Not to mention her good taste.

These days, Wilder Winery was housed in a building that reminded me of a charming slate blue farmhouse, complete with gables and enough white trim that, no matter the weather, it always looked cheery and welcoming. There was a peaked roof above the entryway and huge planters on either side of it that, this time of year, held red geraniums, purple stock, and marigolds in every shade of yellow, gold, and orange.

I stepped into the wide, open entryway and waved to Donna, the woman who managed (and did it very well) the gift shop, Wilder Ware, a little store that had a growing reputation for featuring the work of the finest artists on the island, along with an array of wine-themed merchandise. From there I stopped to say hello to Matt, who was behind the tasting bar and knee-deep in people waiting to be served.

"Ms. Wilder swung through here a minute ago and told me to keep an eye out for you," he called out to me. "She's in the fermenting room. You can go right on in."

The fermenting room was right off the tasting area, and I pushed through the door and stepped from the polished hardwood floor that guests saw to the cement floor here where the real work was done. This was where the newly fermented grape juice was stored in rows of gigantic stainless steel tanks, and I saw Kate across the room talking to Bud Granger, who supervised the area. I waited until they were done with business, and when they were, Kate came over and looped an arm through mine.

"I'll have some coffee brought up to my office," she said, and led the way.

Like the rest of the winery, Kate's private office was orderly and nicely designed. But my favorite part of it wasn't the plush carpeting, the sleek furniture, or the state-of-the-art computer equipment that kept sales statistics and production schedules right at Kate's fingertips. It was the wide window that looked out over the Wilder vineyards and the old-fashioned oil lamp that Kate put near the window every time she was in the office, just as her great-grandmother,

Carrie Wilder, had always done when she was in the winery. In fact, the old oil lamp had figured into our investigation of a murder the autumn before, and seeing it filled me with renewed hope.

I'd solved a murder then, and I could do it now, I reminded myself.

"So what's up?" When Martha, Kate's assistant, came in with a tray with two cups of coffee on it, we thanked her, and Kate handed me a cup, then plunked down behind her desk.

I sipped and smiled my appreciation. "I was thinking about Estelle's memorial service," I told her. "I know it was only a little over a week ago, but—"

"Feels like a thousand years, doesn't it?" Kate's phone rang. She checked the caller ID and ignored the call. "Call me crazy"—she gave me time to do just that, even though she knew I never would—"but I think I know what you're up to. You must be investigating. So what does the memorial service—"

"Have to do with Vivien's murder?" I set my coffee on her desk. "I wish I knew. I just can't get it out of my head. And thinking about the memorial service makes me think about Zane Donahue."

"Aha!" Kate's eyes lit with excitement. "I figured you'd come around to him eventually. You've talked to the man?"

"And found out nothing very useful," I admitted. "But that's not what I'm wondering about. I'm wondering about that stunt he pulled at the memorial service. What do you remember about it?"

She pursed her lips, but it didn't take her long to think. "We were outside waiting for Vivien to slap cement on the stone with Estelle's name on it and Zane showed up out of nowhere and then . . . *whoosh*!" She fluttered her fingers to simulate the splashing of the water. "What a stupid thing for the man to do on such a solemn occasion. You think he could have at least waited until Vivien was leaving and ambushed her out on the sidewalk."

"Yeah. You'd think." I considered this for a moment before I asked Kate, "Where do you suppose he got that bucket of water?"

She leaned forward, the better to peer at me across the desk. "Hello! Water? We are on an island, Bea."

"We are, but . . ." I thought back to the event and to the aftermath and how I'd gone home and showered to get the smell of chlorine out of my hair. "There's no swimming pool at the yacht club," I reminded her.

"And that water—"

"Definitely chlorinated."

"So how . . ."

"I just realized it, and it's got me stumped," I admitted. "If there was chlorine in the water, that means Zane had to bring that water from somewhere. But why would he leave, fill a bucket of water from a swimming pool, then come back with it? Of course, the whole thing with swimming pool water might have been a message. You know, because he wasn't able to build his swimming pool thanks to Vivien. But still, it all seems pretty silly."

"Yeah, leaving and coming back with a bucket of water does seem nuts. But not as nuts as if he were actually carrying around the bucket of water in his car with him," Kate said. "You know, just waiting for the right time to waylay Vivien."

She was right, and I told her so. "It just strikes me as odd, and odd makes me wonder. What else do we know about Zane and Vivien?"

"You mean aside from the fact that they hated each other?"

"That's a given," I said, then realized that maybe it wasn't. "Do we know that for a fact?" I asked Kate and myself. "Or is just what we've heard?"

"Well, we saw him dump the bucket of water on her."

This was true; I nodded.

"And we know they've taken each other to court umpteen times."

Another fact there was no denying.

"The rest—"

"Is kind of like the rumors that have been spreading around town about me," I pointed out. "And like those stories about me, I would hope people wouldn't just accept what they hear as gospel truth."

"People have seen them fighting."

Yes, but had someone walked into Levi's bar the afternoon I confessed who I was and he told me who he really was, they would have seen us fighting, too. Or at least they would have seen me assault him with the business end of a wet mop. "Maybe we can't always believe what we see," I told Kate and hopped out of my chair.

"Where are you going?" she called after me when I made for the door, but she didn't wait to find out. Like the true friend she was, she told Martha she'd be back and was just a phone call away if she was needed, and she came along.

I think Kate was a little disappointed when I got in the car and didn't go tearing out of my parking space hell-bent on the next step of the investigation.

In fact, she sat quietly (if not patiently) in the passenger seat and watched as my fingers danced over the screen on my cell phone.

"Something I need to know about?" she asked, and when I held up a finger because I was onto something and didn't want to be interrupted, she drummed her fingers against the passenger door.

"Aha!" I found what I was looking for and turned my phone so she could see the screen.

Kate sat up and squinched up her eyes for a better look at the chair pictured there. It had a seat that was too close to the floor for my liking and a back that was too pitched to ever be comfortable.

"That's the ugliest chair I've ever seen," she said.

I checked the next screen. "Comes in orange, yellow, and turquoise," I told her. "I've seen the turquoise number. In two places, as a matter of fact. Once at Zane's and once at Vivien's."

"So we know they both like ugly chairs."

I shook my head and poked my finger against the words on the screen. "We know something else, too. We know these chairs are sold by a place on the mainland. That they're pretty pricey and"—the print on the screen was small and I knew Kate couldn't read it from where she sat, but I turned my phone to her anyway—"we know they're only sold in pairs."

Kate took a few minutes to think about what I had said, and by the time she did, I was already driving away from the winery. "What do you suppose it means?" she asked.

I slanted her a knowing look.

"Oh." Her ginger brows slipped over her eyes, then shot up. "Oh! You think Zane and Vivien—"

"I think it's a possibility."

"But they hated each other!"

"Or they pretended to hate each other."

She thought this over for a second or two. "Or they started out hating each other and—"

"Realized they had a whole lot in common."

"Or realized that their hate stoked a whole lot of passion." Kate made a face and shivered. "Ick, Vivien and Zane."

"Vivien and anybody." I did not include Levi in the picture that flashed through my head. After all, when it came to Levi and Vivien, it was only coffee.

"Why would they pretend they hated each other?"

When she asked the question, it was a good thing Kate had just turned a bit in the passenger seat so she could see me better. That way, she didn't miss my shrug. "Who knows how people think. Maybe they liked the attention."

"They were the talk of the island," she admitted.

"And they did each have one of a pair of chairs," I reminded her.

"How are we going to find out for sure what was really going on?"

Ah, that was the question. And though I didn't have an answer, I knew where I had to go to start finding it. I drove downtown, worming my way through Friday traffic and over to Vivien's office. I'd called Hank on the way and he was waiting for us and already had the door unlocked.

He tossed me the key. "Lock up when you're done. And Bea"—he stomped down the stairs and over to his patrol car—"don't get conked on the head."

It was Hank humor, and since it made an appearance so seldom, I gave him a smile to let him know I appreciated it. That smile dissolved like chocolate peanut butter ice cream in the summer sun when I stepped into the office.

I hadn't forgotten that the place had been ransacked after I was knocked unconscious, but when the paramedics brought me around, I hadn't had time to take a good look. Now inside the door, Kate and I assessed the mess and exchanged looks. The office hadn't been cleaned up, and there were still files strewn everywhere. Kate's mouth thinned, and I knew what she was thinking just like she knew what I was thinking—this wasn't just looking like a difficult job; it was looking like an impossible one.

Never one to let that stop me, I tiptoed my way through the file folders on the floor and went over to Vivien's desk.

Kate plunked down at the desk once occupied by Vivien's host of assistants. "What are we looking for?"

I riffled my hands through the files scattered over Vivien's desk. "I wish I knew. But you'd think if there was something up between Zane and Vivien, there would be some indication of it somewhere. In a date book . . ." I pulled open the desk drawers, one after another, and didn't see hide nor hair of a calendar of any kind. "Or something scrawled on a piece of paper."

Kate got the message. Never one to shirk work, she went through the garbage can next to Vivien's desk and another one out in the kitchen where the office supplies were kept.

When she was done, she stuck her head out of the kitchen doorway. "Nothing."

I was just going through the files closest to me and separating them into piles, the ones for Vivien's clients on my right, the ones for Estelle's clients on my left. (And just for the record, I did not look through Levi's file again. I didn't want to take the chance of Kate finding out his secret.)

When she was done in the kitchen, she joined me. "You're sorting."

"I'm not sure it will help, but it's a place to start."

That's all Kate needed to hear. One by one, she went through files, too, making two piles, one for Vivien's real estate deals, one for Estelle's.

When we were finished, she stacked the piles on Vivien's desk along with mine and stepped back.

"So what does it tell us?" Kate asked.

"For one thing, that Estelle closed more sales in the last few years than Vivien did," I pointed out; the Estelle pile of files towered over Vivien's. "But I guess that's not news, and it sure doesn't tell us anything about why anyone would want to kill Vivien or if she and Zane might have been involved in some way no one knew anything about."

"That's for sure."

My sigh and Kate's overlapped. Neither of them was loud enough to drown out the sound when someone rapped on the front door.

It was a woman in white shorts and a peach-colored T-shirt, and I waved her inside.

"I hate to bother you." She stuck out a hand to both me and Kate. "Marie Brisbane. I've got a . . . that is, Vivien was . . . Oh, my." Marie sniffled. "I live in Cleveland, I haven't been up here for a couple weeks and I just got here for the weekend and heard what happened to Vivien."

"You were friends?" I asked her.

Marie pulled a tissue out of a tote bag that smelled of coconut sunscreen. She dabbed her nose. "Not exactly friends. I didn't know her all that well. But we own property over on Middle Bass." She waved in the general direction of the small island that is a half mile north and west of South Bass. "It was my parents' place and we used to go there all the time when we were kids, but these days, everyone's so busy, we hardly ever get up here. When we decided to sell, we listed the house with Vivien. I'm sure our keys are somewhere over there."

Marie pointed across the room to a row of hooks in the wall. Each hook had a set of keys on it, and each set of keys had an address label attached to it.

"I'm not sure how this works," she admitted. "I mean, your real estate agent dying when she's supposed to be selling your house. But I figure I'll need to list it with someone else, and . . ."

She didn't need to finish. I knew what she was thinking. "I'm sorry, I can't give you the keys," I told her. "I don't have the authority. But if you go over to the police station and talk to Chief Florentine and produce the proper documents to prove ownership, I'm sure he'll help."

Marie said she understood and told us she'd be back with the chief.

After she was gone, I stood for a while staring at all those keys.

"It would be easy, wouldn't it?" I asked, and I was talking more to myself than I was to Kate.

Which didn't stop her from replying. "What would be easy?"

"For a real estate agent to get into a whole lot of houses."

"Well, sure." Kate shrugged. "That's what real estate agents do."

"And if that real estate agent wanted to meet somebody and didn't want to be seen around town with that person?"

Kate's face lit up. "Then she could use those keys to come and go and have a whole lot of privacy." Just as quickly, her expression fell. "But look at all these folders." She pointed to the pile we'd made for Vivien's clients. "How are we going to narrow down the possibilities?"

"We don't have to," I told Kate, and I grabbed one set of keys from the hooks.

❦ 17 ❧

The place was furnished. The shelves next to the fireplace were piled with books, and from the quick tour I took of the kitchen, I could see that the cupboards were stocked with dishes and pots and pans.

Still, it felt empty there in the house with the *Own a Piece of Paradise!* sign out front.

"So?" Kate whispered the single word—it must have been an automatic reaction to the pressing silence. "Why here? Why do you think—"

"I saw him here." I spread my arms to indicate the house in general. "Well, not here, exactly, but I saw him outside. The evening of the murder. And Zane Donahue said he was just out to get ice cream, but we know it's not true. So if he wasn't out for ice cream, maybe he was here. Maybe this is one of the places he and Vivien met."

Kate nodded. "What are we looking for?"

"I'm not sure," I admitted, and because I didn't whisper, my voice pinged back at us from the beige walls decorated with pictures of fishing boats and seashells and sunsets over water. From outside, I could still hear the faint buzz of weekend traffic, but here in the house next door to Estelle's, the windows were closed and the air was summer-heavy and starting to smell musty. "I guess I just wanted to be sure Zane and Vivien could come and go."

"Just like we came. So now let's go." Kate hugged her arms around herself. She's not usually squeamish when it comes to the kind of snooping that always goes hand in hand with a murder investigation, but I couldn't blame her for feeling a little nervous. I'd called Hank before we came over just to be sure there was no official objection to what I had in mind, and still I felt like a trespasser.

"We'll go," I promised Kate. "But not until we've had a chance to look around."

She glanced at a closed doorway on the other side of the kitchen. "I'm not going in the basement."

"That's good, because I'm not going in the basement, either." I laughed. "Come on, use your imagination. If you were Zane and Vivien and you were looking for a place where you could get together for a little tryst, you think it would be the basement?"

She made a face and, with one finger, pointed up to the ceiling. "How about . . ?"

I knew she was onto something. With her right behind me, I made my way back through the living room and up the steps to the second floor. Like the rest of the house, these rooms had been left furnished no doubt because a house that looked homey was more appealing to potential buyers than one that was empty and cavernous. There was a kids' room decorated in a jungle theme, a small but tidy bath-room, a room that contained a desk and a guest bed, and a master bedroom, where there was a flower-print quilt on the bed in shades of green and blue, a dresser with a mirror above it, and a single wing chair in a color that didn't quite match the green in the quilt or the blue of the carpeting, either.

"Well, this would have to be a better place for a little rendezvous than the basement," Kate admitted. "But every-thing's neat and tidy. There's no way to know if Zane and Vivien were ever here together. There's no way of telling who's ever been here."

She was right, and I had no choice but to admit it.

I don't know what I was expecting—*I love you, Zane* written on the mirror in Vivien's lipstick?

The thought sitting heavy on my shoulders, I did a turn around the room, hoping for inspiration, and when it didn't come, I plunked down on the bed. "I'm not sure what I thought we'd find," I admitted. "Maybe just some . . ." Some-thing poked my butt and I shifted against the mattress. "I guess I was just . . ." I still couldn't get comfortable, and I slid off the bed and looked down at the flowered quilt where I'd been sitting.

"It's just like 'The Princess and the Pea'!" I shouted, and before Kate could ask what in the world I was talking about and why I was suddenly smiling like a loon, I plucked what had been poking me off the bed, cupped it in my hand, and hurried down the stairs and out the door.

From what I'd heard around town (back in the day when folks were still talking to me and not backing away like I had cooties), Zane Donahue had every intention of showing up at the gala at Tara the next day. But that was Saturday and today was Friday, and a glorious one at that. Blue skies, sunshine, calm waters.

If I were Zane Donahue, I know where I would be, so I didn't waste a minute. As soon as Kate hopped into the passenger seat of my SUV, I drove over to the yacht club.

No, I wasn't a member, and for that matter, neither was Kate. But though a newcomer like me might have been easy to turn away at the door, a powerhouse like Kate wasn't anyone to mess with. Her family was legendary on the island, and legendary goes a long way in a small town.

We sashayed into the yacht club and no one questioned us when we took a quick look around the bar.

There was no sign of Zane Donahue in there, but I didn't lose heart. Following the path we'd walked the day Vivien led us outside to lay the stone in honor of her aunt, I pushed through the back door and headed for the club's private marina.

"That's it," Kate said, pointing to a twenty-five-foot Catalina sailboat with the words *Ladies' Man* painted on the back of it. "That's Zane's boat."

Zane's boat—and Zane was on it, his back to the dock, busy stowing life jackets under a built-in bench.

I didn't wait for an invitation.

The moment my tennis shoes slapped the teak deck, Zane looked up. "What are you doing here?"

So it wasn't the most gracious greeting, but I could hardly blame him.

I did have a self-satisfied smile on my face.

I waited for Kate to catch up, climb aboard, and stand by my side before I crossed the deck. There was a table near where Zane stood with his fists on his hips and, I noted, an open bottle of scotch and a glass filled with ice on it, and I took the prize I'd plucked off the bedspread and set it down next to the liquor bottle where Zane couldn't fail to see it.

He looked from the table to me, totally confused, and honestly, I couldn't help myself—I thought of all the fictional detectives I'd seen in all the old black-and-white movies on TV and how they would handle this particular *Aha!* moment. With a little swagger. With a whole bunch of panache. Maybe even with a big dose of self-congratulations.

I came to my senses in an instant. None of that seemed as important as getting right down to the truth.

I pointed at the table. "You do know what that is, don't you?"

Since I'd never told Kate what I'd found in the bedroom of the house that was for sale, she peered over my shoulder for a look just as a *V* of confusion settled between Zane's dark brows.

"It's an orange Tic Tac," they said in unison.

"Exactly!" Okay, yeah, so I shot a finger into the air in what I imagined was a very Hercule Poirot manner. There is only so long I can control myself when it comes to these sorts of things. "You and Vivien . . ." I used that same finger to point to Zane. "You were meeting in the empty houses Vivien was selling."

It was a sunny afternoon and Zane was dressed in white shorts and a navy T-shirt with the word *Captain* embroidered over the heart. His inky hair gleamed in the light. His arms were bronzed from hours in the sun.

His face, though, was a little green.

"How do you . . ? How could you . . ?" He shook away his surprise. "That's crazy. What are you talking about?"

I pointed down at the candy I'd left on the table. "I'm

talking about two people each having one of a matching pair of chairs. And I'm talking about that candy. At Estelle's neighbor's. On the bed."

Zane's shoulders didn't so much droop as they deflated. There was a boat berthed in the slip next to his and no one on deck, but he looked that way anyway, as if to make sure there was no one who could overhear. A muscle jumped at the base of his jaw. "Maybe we better go down below," he said.

With Zane leading the way, we went down to the boat's galley. It wasn't big, but it was neat and looked to make an efficient use of space. There was a built-in bench along one side of the boat and Zane motioned us to sit down, then went to the half-pint fridge and got out three bottles of water and handed them around. He twisted the cap on his own bottle and took a long swig.

"You think Vivien and I were involved? Why do you care? What difference does it make?" he asked.

"It makes a difference because it means you've been lying all along. To me. To the police."

He took another drink. "Like I said, what difference does it make?"

"What difference did it make if people knew you and Vivien were seeing each other?" I asked him.

He dropped down in a chair across from where Kate and I sat, then popped up again and walked over to the other side of the boat. (Port? Starboard? I could never keep them straight.) His back to us, he propped his hands against the sink, his arms rigid. From this angle, I couldn't fail to catch the way his shoulders rose and fell.

"We hated each other," he said, then turned so he could see us and gauge our reaction. "Everyone on the island knew that. Vivien and I, we hated each other."

"Because of the Indian burial mound."

"She didn't disclose it when I bought the property." He bit through the words.

"So you took her to court."

At Kate's comment, he gave a begrudging nod. "And then she took me to court about some silly something. And then I countersued. And on and on and on."

My hands on the table, I leaned forward. I knew this wasn't the end of the story. "But . . ."

The expression that crossed Zane's face was half smile, half I-can't-believe-it-ever-happened. "But then one day, something clicked. Something . . ." He searched for the word. "Powerful. Impossible to resist. You're right." He looked my way. "Vivien and I were having an affair."

"She broke up with Alex because of you."

"Yes," he told me. "Not that they were all that serious to begin with, but they'd been seeing each other for a while. After we got . . . involved . . . she knew it wasn't fair to string him along. As for me, I haven't even looked at another woman since the day I realized that Vivien and I . . . well, we were soul mates. I know that sounds weird and old-fashioned, but it's true. It was like we were two pieces of the same person, like we weren't complete when we weren't together."

That much I suspected was true. There were no two other egos on this or any other island that were as big, or as self-absorbed. In a lot of ways, Zane and Vivien were a match made in heaven.

But I couldn't help but think that sort of overpowering attraction was bound to come along with baggage.

"So how did you feel about Vivien then?"

"You mean after we started seeing each other?" Zane

grabbed a box of orange Tic Tacs on the counter and flipped it open, then thought better of it and set the box down. "There were times we actually got along. Can you believe it? And I'm not just talking about in bed. Once, Vivien had me meet her at a place she was selling over on Middle Bass."

"Marie Brisbane's house." I took the chance of mentioning the name of the lady who'd stopped in at Vivien's office when Kate and I were there and got lucky; Zane sucked in a breath, surprised I knew so much.

"Vivien made dinner," he said, his expression settling and his eyes taking on a faraway look. "Candles and flowers on the table. Dinner on the stove. She could be that way, you know." Zane shifted his gaze to me and Kate, eager for us to understand. "There was a side to Vivien that most people never saw."

"And she liked it that way." Again I took a chance, and again, when Zane nodded, I knew I'd hit the nail on the head. "She wanted to appear tough and strong and intractable. That's why she didn't want anyone to know that you two were seeing each other."

"Yes, that's right."

"You could have been angry about that," Kate suggested.

Zane's smile was thin and quick. "I could be. I guess I was at first." He puffed out a laugh. "That gave us something else to fight about. Like we needed it! But I decided . . ." He twitched his broad shoulders. "I couldn't live without her. It was as simple as that. I didn't want to, but I knew I had to play by Vivien's rules or I was going to lose her. And her rule was that no one could know we were seeing each other. It was a secret. Our secret. I suppose in a lot of ways, that made the whole thing more delicious."

"And the evening of the murder?" I asked him. "You

weren't out to get an ice-cream cone, were you? You were at Estelle's with Vivien."

"No," he said. "Not at Estelle's. Vivien and I . . . We met at that house next door to her aunt's that afternoon. Vivien told me she had some people coming over to pay for furniture in the evening and she knew she couldn't stick around, but I fell asleep after she left. I was just leaving there when you arrived."

"What time did Vivien leave?" I asked him.

He thought about it for a moment. "Three. Maybe four."

"And she went right to Estelle's?"

"That's what she told me she was going to do."

"And you didn't see anyone else around?"

He scraped both his hands through his hair. "Don't you think I haven't asked myself the same question a thousand times? If only I hadn't fallen asleep! Maybe I would have seen something. Maybe I could have done something. Something—" His voice broke. "Something to save her."

"Did she talk about anyone who would want to hurt her?" Yeah, I knew it wasn't fair to keep peppering Zane with questions when he was so emotional, but that's exactly why I did it. If he was upset, his guard might be down, and if his guard was down, maybe I could get some answers.

"There was that Cody fellow," Zane said. "You know about him? The police do. They say he didn't do it, but I'm not convinced. Vivien had a restraining order against him."

"Cody says he's the one who should have taken an order of protection out against Vivien. He says she was obsessed with him."

"Right!" The single word packed a powerful dose of sarcasm. "He's nuts. He's always been nuts. It has to have been Cody."

"But there were other men, right?" Another sensitive question asked at a vulnerable time. Hey, no one ever said investigating a murder was pretty. "Was there someone else she might have broken up with?" I asked Zane. "Someone other than Alex? He doesn't hold a grudge against her but somebody else might. Or how about someone she might have mentioned in connection with another real estate deal gone wrong?"

I don't think it was a trick of the light there below deck; Zane's cheeks really did get red. "You act like I knew her really well, but to tell you the truth, Vivien and I, we didn't do a whole lot of talking. I think that's why that dinner on Middle Bass was so special, why I'll always remember it. It was one of the few times we actually tried to get to know each other."

There didn't seem to be a whole lot more to say. I looked Kate's way, and she got the message. She went to the steps and I followed her.

Up on deck, I squinted against the brightness. "I'm sorry for your loss," I told him.

Zane tipped his face to the sun. "I think that's one of the hardest parts of this whole thing," he admitted. "She's gone and I feel like hell, and no one knows it. I'm supposed to just be getting on with my life like nothing happened. There are even a couple people who've congratulated me and told me how happy I must be now that Vivien's not around to make my life difficult. I want to tell them—" He bit back whatever else he might have said.

"You really did care about Vivien, didn't you?" I asked.

"In spite of the Indian burial mound!" Zane's smile was lopsided. "In a way, I have that mound to thank for the most incredible months of my life. If Vivien and I had never fought about it in the first place . . ." He let his memories trail away.

Kate hopped off the boat and onto the dock, and I was all set to follow her when I thought of one more thing. I turned back to Zane.

"What about the bucket of water?" I asked him.

"Oh, that." He waved away the question. "It was just a prank."

"A prank that you arranged ahead of time."

His eyebrows twitched. "How do you know?"

"Chlorine," I told him. "The water didn't come from the lake and there aren't any pools very close to the club. You brought the water with you."

He didn't confirm or deny. He didn't have to. "Vivien liked to be the center of attention," he said. "I guess that's not a big surprise to anyone who ever met her. She honestly believed that the world revolved around her, and she was afraid . . ." He sucked in a breath and let it out slowly. "She knew the Twins were bound to come to the memorial service. Vivien sold Tara to them and they were on good terms. Not exactly best friends, but they had drinks together once in a while. Vivien was afraid that when they arrived at the memorial service, all attention would turn to them. And she right, wasn't she?"

"So it was her idea? She's the one who asked you to bring the bucket of water?"

This time, Zane's smile was wide and dazzling. "You bet she did! And she made me promise I'd dump it right on top of her at exactly the right moment when it would cause the biggest sensation!"

❮❖ 18 ❖❯

To say that South Bass Island was buzzing the next day was putting it mildly. The gala would begin at six, the ban on driving would go into effect an hour before that, and people were psyched like I hadn't seen them psyched before, not even the previous summer when the entire island celebrated Bastille Day and murder, mayhem, and art theft ensued.

My guests (they didn't have tickets to the gala but planned to hang around outside to see the costumes and the decorations and—they hoped—the Twins) were just as excited as everyone else, and after a breakfast of quiche, fresh fruit, and yogurt, they were eager to get out and check on all the other activities planned for the day.

"Hey, look at this!" Brad Newcomb, a big guy with a big voice and a big appetite for quiche (he and his friends had gone through four), waved his newspaper over the breakfast table. "There's a party in the park this afternoon. A special reunion for the alumni of Put-in-Bay High School."

His wife, Shelley, was as quiet as her husband was loud. She chinked her coffee cup down on its china saucer. "You have a high school here?" I was just gathering the breakfast dishes and she looked my way. "On such a small island?"

"Eight graduated this year," I told her. "From what I understand, it's one of the biggest classes in years."

"How nice! The kids must get a lot of individual attention." Kim Huntley, who sat across from Shelley, had mentioned earlier that she was a teacher in the suburb of Toledo where the six friends lived. It was no wonder she was interested in the island school. "It must be hard, though, getting enough kids to participate in things like sports and other extracurriculars. Isn't a band supposed to be playing this evening? There can't be enough kids in a school that size to make up a band."

"There's a school over on the mainland that's joining them." Kim's husband, Grant, pointed to an article in the newspaper open next to his coffee cup. "That's what it says here. And alumni are going to join with the band tonight, too. The whole thing is going to be great fun. What time does that reunion start?"

Brad consulted his newspaper. "Looks like noon. We might as well go, what do you say?" Apparently, he knew his friends well enough to know they'd fall into line. Just like Brad did, they pushed back their chairs. "We've got a couple hours. We can tour around the island, then head over to the park for lunch and see what's up."

I wished them well and reminded them that I'd serve a light snack at four before I got ready for the gala, and once they were gone, I cleaned up the dishes and took a cup of coffee out to the front porch.

Since it was sure to be one of the busiest weekends on the island all summer, we were fortunate to have continued good weather, and I sat for a while and watched the waves gently slap the shore at the little park across the street, glad to see that things were going well not just for the gala, but for all the extra activities that had been scheduled, too, like that school reunion.

"School." Automatically, my gaze slid toward Chandra's house. There was no sign of her that day, but I couldn't help thinking that she was an alumnus of the school, just like Bill had been, and that made me wonder if Chandra would attend the reunion.

I was on my feet before my coffee was finished. After all, now that I knew that Zane Donahue and Vivien Frisk had been carrying on an affair, it made Zane look less like a suspect.

And that left only one.

DeRivera Park is a lovely oasis of green in the center of bustling Put-in-Bay. The park is named after Jose de Rivera St. Jurgo, a Spaniard who bought what is now South Bass and Middle Bass Islands back in the mid-1800s. These days, it's a play center for kids, a place where visitors can eat at picnic tables, and often, the center of island festivities. It's right across the street from the marina so it's a natural place to see residents and tourists alike come and go.

Trying to do just that, I stood on tiptoe and did my best to look over the heads of the people who were gathered in the park, and when that didn't work (I'm not very tall), I climbed up onto the bench of a picnic table and looked around. It was a little past noon and after a reciting of the Pledge of Allegiance and the singing of both the US and Canadian national anthems by a woman who had more enthusiasm than talent, the Put-in-Bay school reunion was in full swing. No, I had not gone to school on the island. Back when I was in school, I'd never even heard of South Bass Island. But islanders aren't picky about things like that, and I was greeted by people I knew and didn't know and only a couple backed away or looked right through me as if I weren't there. When it came to dangling the possibility of getting the curly maple highboy (not to mention his lame attempt at picking me up), Quentin Champion might be a loser, but he'd apparently been true to his word about putting a stop to the rumor that I was a criminal nutcase. As the years went by and I thought longingly of the highboy, maybe that would be enough to soothe my soul.

Or not.

Maple highboy aside, I bought a hot dog from a stand run by the school athletic boosters, and while I chomped it down, I did my best to keep an eye out for Chandra and tried to get into the swing of the reunion. In honor of the occasion, the park gazebo was draped in blue and white, the school colors, the alumni committee sold raffle tickets, and next year's senior class (all four of them) acted as hosts. I saw Kate at one of the picnic tables with ferryboat captain Jayce Martin, but they were deep in conversation and I didn't interrupt. Jayce had had a thing for Kate for as long as I could remember and their relationship was inching along. Far be it from me to interrupt the snail's pace of love.

I did see Luella, though, near a vendor who was selling

ice cream out of a cart, and I caught her eye and waved, then hopped off the bench and went over to see her.

She'd just bitten into a chocolate-coated ice-cream bar, and she motioned to the vendor for another one and handed it to me.

"I've got a ball gown to get into tonight," I reminded her, but hey, I'm never one to refuse ice cream. I ripped off the paper and took a bite and wiped chocolate off my chin.

"Pretty nice party, huh?" Licking at the dripping ice cream, Luella glanced around at the knots of people chatting around us. On the far side of the park, a woman spied a man she'd apparently gone to school with and hadn't seen in a long time; she threw open her arms and squealed and the two of them hugged.

"Not too many from my class left," Luella said, and her smile was bittersweet. "Used to be we all thought we'd be here forever. You know how it is when you're young!" She shook her shoulders and glanced around the crowd while she finished up the last of her ice cream. "Still plenty of people I know here, and it's good to see them."

The sun was hot and my ice cream was melting fast. I made a valiant effort to wolf it down before it dripped all over me, and when I was done, I tossed the stick in the nearest trash can and reached for one of the napkins on the ice-cream cart so I could wipe my hands. "You haven't seen Chandra, have you?"

Luella slid me a look. "I talked to Kate. I know you two had a chat with Zane Donahue yesterday. You don't think he did it, do you? That's why you're looking for Chandra. You can't really think Chandra—"

I wanted to defend Chandra, honest. But the only sound that came out of me was a screech of frustration. "I'm trying to prove she didn't do it," I wailed. "And she's blocking me at every turn. What's she up to, Luella?"

She shook her head. "I wish I knew. The woman can be as crazy as a loon, that's for sure. And she can be stubborn, too, when she puts her mind to it." Thinking, she scratched a hand behind her ear. "She's not cooperating, huh?"

"Every time I talk to her, I'm left with more questions. The last time I went to her house—"

I didn't have time to finish the story and tell Luella about the flickering candles and the pictures of Bill Barone, because a silver-haired man ran up and scooped Luella into a hug, then lifted her off her feet and twirled her around. When he set her down, he grinned, and so did Luella. The man had a face creased with laugh lines and eyes as blue as the sky above our heads, and he was wearing a white cardigan sweater with a big blue letter *P* on it, for the Put-in-Bay Panthers.

"Frank Tolliver!" Luella's smile lit up the park. "How many years has it been? You didn't make it to the last reunion."

"Cathy, my wife, she was sick," Frank said and his smile faded just a bit. "She passed about a year and a half ago. So here I am, and I'm planning on going to that silly gala tonight, too." He gave her a broad wink. "You're going to save a dance for me, aren't you?"

Luella promised she would and, still smiling, she watched Frank walk away.

"Oh, what a crush I had on Frank when we were in school together!" she said. "He left the island right after we graduated. Joined the military, I think, and he's been back a time or two. I always liked Frank."

I made a noise that I hoped made it sound as if I was listening.

"I said . . ." Luella poked me in the ribs with her elbow. "I said I liked Frank, but from that look on your face, I might as well have said I like Frankenstein. Are you paying any attention to me? You've got that faraway look in your eye, like you're thinking about something else."

I shook away my temporary paralysis and kept an eye on Frank, too, who was going around the park, shaking hands and talking to people. "I'm thinking about letter sweaters," I said.

"You think schools have letter sweaters any more?" Luella wondered.

"Did they when Bill Barone went to school here?"

Her eyebrows rose. "Do you mean—"

"Was Bill an athlete?" I asked her.

Luella thought about it for a moment. "Bill was younger than me by a whole lot of years. By the time he was in school, I was already married and had kids to worry about. I didn't pay a whole lot of attention to that sort of thing." She glanced around and caught sight of a woman in an orange sundress. "Hey, Helen!" Luella waved her over. "You went to school with Bill Barone, didn't you?"

"Bill!" The woman had pudgy cheeks and her lipstick matched her dress. "He was one year ahead of me. Every girl in school was in love with Bill. Such a handsome kid!"

"Do you remember if he played sports?" I asked her.

"It's not easy to field a team in a school the size of ours," Helen said. "But yeah, he did. Me and Bill, we were both on the cross-country team."

A thought hit me and a feeling like electricity zipped through my veins. I was almost afraid to ask, "And Bill, did he have a letter sweater?"

Helen wrinkled her nose. "I suppose he might have," she

said, and then her expression cleared and she smiled. "Come to think of it, I know he did. I went to his funeral. I remember now. I remember that his letter sweater was hanging right next to a picture of Bill."

"Thank you!" Poor Helen probably couldn't imagine why I had an ear-to-ear grin on my face, but then again, I don't think Luella could, either. That would explain why, when I caught sight of Chandra on the other side of the park and took off running, Luella was right behind me.

Since I didn't want Chandra to see me and head the other way, I circled around and came up behind her. "Great party, huh?"

Chandra flinched and turned to me just as Luella puffed her way over to the gazebo near where we stood. Chandra was wearing white shorts and a blue T-shirt that said *Panther Alumni* on it in white lettering. Her blue earrings matched her shirt. So did her blue flip-flops.

"It's always nice to see the old gang." Chandra waved to someone across the park, but when she made a move to head that way, I looped my arm through hers.

"I was just thinking," I said. "About your school colors. Blue and white."

Both Chandra and Luella glanced at the bunting curled around the octagonal gazebo.

"Yeah." Chandra looked down at her own outfit. "Blue and white. So what? A lot of schools' colors are blue and white. Besides, we used to say the blue was for the lake and the white—"

"Was for the snow that buried us up to our tushies in the winter!" Luella laughed.

I was glad—her comment helped put Chandra at ease.

Which didn't mean I was about to let her go. Still hanging on, I did my best to sound just as casual. "I was thinking about other stuff, too," I said. "But then, I suppose I can't help it at an event like this. It's so great to see so many of the old students return. And it got me thinking, you know, about letter sweaters."

When Chandra tensed, I knew I was right on the money, and I pounced fast before I lost my advantage. "That night Kate and I went to Tara to talk to the Twins about the high-boy, we got back and you had a fire going in your fire pit. A really smoky fire that never really quite caught. I can't say I know a whole lot about burning things, but I imagine that's exactly what would happen if someone was trying to burn something made of wool. Smoke—lots of smoke. And a smell like burning hair. I think that's exactly what would happen if someone tried to burn a wool sweater."

Chandra made a move to run, but hey, I may be small, but I am determined. I clung to her and refused to budge a step. Not even when she burst into tears.

Luella might not have understood what was going on, but she didn't question what I was up to. Like the true friend she is, she took Chandra's other arm.

"Is this something we should talk about in private?" I asked Chandra.

She didn't answer. She was too busy sobbing.

By the time we got Chandra home, her eyes were swollen and her nose was red. As soon as we got inside, she went right to the kitchen and put on the teakettle, and though I feared this meant we were in for some stinky herbal concoction, I didn't argue. Chandra needed to calm down otherwise I'd never get any straight answers out of her. If that meant sharing a pot of Indian gooseberry, so be it.

Luella and I settled ourselves at the dining room table, but not before both of us took a long look at the Bill Barone shrine on the buffet. A few minutes later, Chandra put mugs of tea down in front of us and slumped into a chair.

"How did you know?" she asked me.

I hated to admit it was a shot in the dark, so I skirted the question. "What's more important is why. Why burn the sweater, Chandra? You obviously . . ." My back was to the buffet and I turned slightly in my chair so I could motion toward the framed photos of the man who had been Chandra's first husband. "You obviously cherish Bill's memory. Why burn something that belonged to him?"

"Because . . ." The tears started again and Chandra gulped in a breath and her chest heaved. "Because . . ." Her voice broke. She twisted her fingers together and wailed. "Because after Vivien was killed, I knew I couldn't be found with the sweater. Because . . . because I stole it from Vivien's house!"

Not exactly what I was expecting, though after I sat there for a moment, pikestaffed, I realized it made perfect sense.

"Then you were at Vivien's the night she was killed! That fabric I found caught on the doorway—"

"I snagged my shirt." Chandra hung her head and her blond bob hid her face. "I didn't even realize it until you said something about it. Then I checked and saw that my shirt had the tiniest little tear in it. I threw that away, too." She looked up and glanced from me to Luella. "I had to make sure the police didn't know."

There was a lot here to work through and I took my time. "You didn't want them to know because you—"

"Went over there, of course." Chandra wrapped both hands around her mug but she didn't drink any tea. "It was true what I told Hank. I did go out for a walk. I was thinking— thinking about Bill."

"Because of the anniversary."

She nodded at my comment. "I was walking and thinking about Bill, and honest, I didn't even realize where I was headed until I got there. And then . . ." As if she were reliving the moment, Chandra looked all around. "I saw that I was at Vivien's. Like I told you, Bea, I'd been there before. And I don't know what I was thinking—I mean, I sure didn't want to talk to Vivien or anything. But I went up to the door and knocked."

"And what would you have done if she answered?" Luella asked.

Chandra shrugged. "I don't know. I guess I would have . . ." Her shoulders drooped. "You know, when Bill left me, he took everything of his with him. His high school yearbook and, yeah, his letter sweater, too. And a lot of pictures." Her gaze drifted to the display on the buffet. "I was so hurt at the time, I didn't question it. In fact, I was glad he took it all. I wanted it all out of my house. I wanted to get rid of my memories. Then he got sick and Vivien wouldn't let me anywhere near him. And when he died . . ." A tear slipped down her cheek.

"When Bill died, I realized that I had nothing to remember him by. We had some good times," she added quickly as if she thought we might dispute her motives. "Deep down inside, he was a good man, and before Vivien ruined our lives, I really, really loved him. He just went crazy, that's all. On account of Vivien. He lost his mind."

She'd gotten off track and I nudged her back in the right direction. "And when Bill died . . .?"

Chandra tried to talk, choked on the words, and cleared her throat. "I waited a while. Months, I think. I waited until I thought Vivien might feel like talking and I went over there. I explained that I wasn't there because I was mad at her. I told her that all I wanted was one little thing, one little something to remember Bill by."

"And Vivien . . ?"

Chandra's expression darkened. "She told me to get off her property and leave her alone. She told me that Bill was her husband and I was nobody to him. She said she'd call the police if I ever bothered her again."

"And then that Friday night, you found yourself back at her house. And no one was home."

"Oh, Bea, don't you see! It's not like I planned it or anything. Like I said, I was just out walking and pretty soon, there I was. I knocked, and if Vivien came to the door, I was going to say that we should let bygones be bygones. I was going to ask again. For anything. A few pictures. Anything."

"But she didn't answer the door."

"She didn't, and I don't know . . . some kind of craziness came over me when I realized she wasn't home. The house is old. It wasn't that hard to pry open the door. I went inside, and really, I've never been so scared in my life! I knew I was only taking what rightfully belonged to me. I knew I wasn't going to touch anything really valuable or anything that belonged to Vivien. But still, I was so scared and so nervous. I went into the house and I looked around as fast as I could. I found what I was looking for upstairs, shoved in an old dresser drawer. It's like she didn't even care about any of it. It was all just piled up and put away. Bill's year-book and Bill's sweater and all those pictures." Again, her gaze flickered to the buffet.

"Which explains why some of them are in frames that are marked as new merchandise down at the gift shop at the marina," I pointed out. "You haven't had them packed away for years like you told me."

Chandra sniffled. "You would notice that, Bea. Nobody else would. I never thought of it. I never looked through any of the stuff I took from Vivien's, either. I mean, not there at her place. I was too freakin' scared to do anything but scoop up what I could and run."

I reached over and put a hand on hers. "That's why you couldn't tell anyone where you really were at the time Vivien was murdered."

"I didn't want to get in trouble," Chandra admitted. "And if Hank found out I broke into Vivien's house . . . well, you know Hank. He's pretty much by the book. He'd know I didn't kill Vivien but I'd end up in jail anyway. When I saw his patrol car in your driveway that evening, I thought he knew I broke into the house. I thought he was there to arrest me!"

"And that's why you burned Bill's sweater?" I asked.

She nodded and wept quietly. "When I heard that Vivien had been murdered, I was sure Hank was going to question me, because you see, I did stop by Estelle's that night. Or at least I walked through the yard. I didn't see Vivien, I just cut through on my way home, but after I heard what hap-pened to Vivien, I was afraid someone might have seen me. That why I couldn't take the chance of him finding the sweater here. The pictures . . ." Tears streamed down her cheeks. "I told myself I should get rid of the pictures and the rest of the stuff, too, but I couldn't. I couldn't make myself burn up all that's left of Bill's life. Besides, I figured no one would ever question the pictures. I mean, it makes sense, right, that I'd have some photos of Bill?"

She glanced up at me through the fringe of her shaggy bangs. "That night Hank called from the station, I thought for sure he finally knew. I can't tell you how relieved I was when he said all he wanted was lunch." Chandra shivered. "Are you going to turn me in?"

Luella and I exchanged looks, and in that moment, a silent agreement, as well. But still, I felt I had to ask. "What else did you take, Chandra?"

She pulled herself out of her chair and opened the top drawer of the buffet and I saw a yearbook with a blue and white cover, along with more pictures. Chandra gathered them all up and set them down on the table in front of me.

"I framed my favorite pictures," she said. "But there are more pictures of Bill and some other pictures, too."

Before I could sift through the pile of photographs, Chandra leaned over and did it for me. "I was surprised to find this stuff," she said, and she set five pictures down in a row in front of me.

"That's my house!" I stared at the pictures that showed Bea & Bees in the days before I bought it. "These are the pictures that were missing from Estelle's file on the sale of my house. Why would Vivien have them?"

"Like I said . . ." Chandra sat back down. "I didn't look through things. Not while I was at Vivien's. I just grabbed what I could and got out of there. But I didn't see anything else that looked like real estate stuff. Not in the drawer with Bill's things."

Quickly, I shuffled through the rest of the pictures. There were no others that showed my property and, in fact, no others that showed any other houses that either Estelle or Vivien had ever sold.

I turned my attention back to the pictures Chandra had pulled out to show me. "None of these pictures were ever on Estelle's website," I said. "There were others—others that showed exactly how much of a mess the place was—but these . . ." Again I looked them over. The first and second pictures showed the parlor. At the time, the window that looked out over the front porch was broken and Estelle had managed—but just barely—to keep the evidence of a raccoon nest in the fireplace out of the shot.

The others were all copies of the same picture—one that showed some brave souls actually checking out the property: a dark-haired couple, man and woman. From the angle the pictures were taken, I couldn't see the man's face at all, but the woman . . .

I squinted and bent closer for a better look.

She had a slim nose and trim frame, and from what she was wearing, I could tell the picture had been taken in cold weather.

"This must have been right before I saw the place on Estelle's website and made an appointment to come out and look at it," I said. "Estelle mentioned at the time that some other people had already looked at it. Smart people—these two walked away."

I set the pictures aside. Why they'd been taken out of Estelle's file was still a mystery, but not one I was concerned about at the moment.

"So . . ." With one finger, Chandra traced an invisible pattern over the surface of the table. "What happens now?"

"What happens?" I gathered up the pictures of my home and tapped them into a neat pile. "What happens is we all go home and rest up for the gala tonight. I don't know about you two"—I stood, taking the pictures with me—"but I'm going to go take a nap. It's going to be a long night."

It wasn't the only thing I did when I got home. Off the record (and don't ever breathe a word to Hank), I also tossed that envelope with that piece of gauzy white fabric in it right in the trash.

« 19 »

I wasn't sure who was more thunderstruck, me or Levi.

For my part, I'd just thrown open the front door and I stood inside it and stared in openmouthed wonder at the Civil War soldier who rang the bell. He wore a dark blue frock coat with fringed gold epaulets on the shoulders and gold embroidery on the stand-up collar, along with dark pants and knee-high leather boots, and there was a sword—I take that back, on second look, I saw that it was an empty scabbard—hanging from the red sash around his waist. He wore a hat with a Grand Army of the Republic insignia on it and a jaunty golden feather plume at the side, and after a moment of staring at me with his eyes wide and his jaw slack, he whipped the hat off his head and bowed from the waist.

"Ma'am," Levi said. "You are the prettiest thing I've ever laid eyes on!"

Compliment aside (and believe me, I'm all for compliments!), he sounded gallant and old-fashioned and not at all like the bar owner/PI I knew, and I had to laugh.

"I have a feeling we're a mixed metaphor," I told him. "You're a Union soldier—"

"Union officer," he corrected me.

I nodded to acknowledge my error. "You're a Union officer, and I'm wearing—"

"Oh, what you're wearing!" Grinning ear to ear, Levi grabbed both my hands and held them out to my sides so he could get a better look at the replica of the red gown made famous in the scene in the movie version of *Gone with the Wind* when Scarlett attends Ashley's birthday party. It was made of fabric that sparkled in the evening light—just like the gown in the movie—and had the same formfitting style, the same poofy, short sleeves that were accented with fluffy crimson feathers, and the same low-cut sweetheart neckline.

Which was exactly what Levi was checking out.

I slipped out of his grip and spun around. "What do you think?"

He whistled low under his breath. "I think I'm in love!"

I had to ask. "With the dress?"

He stepped over the threshold and scooped me into his arms. "With the dress and with the woman who's wearing it. You're gorgeous!"

"Even though it's Scarlett O'Hara's dress and there's no way she'd ever be seen with a Union officer?"

"We'll call a temporary truce. At least for tonight," he said, and kissed me.

Truth be told, I could have stood there all night and been perfectly happy, but the blast of a horn sounded from across the street and we looked over just in time to see Kate zip by in a golf cart and wave.

"Kate must be picking up Jayce," Levi said, craning his neck to watch her, her straw picture hat flapping in the breeze. "Are you ready to go?"

I was as soon as I grabbed the gauzy red shawl that completed my outfit. One more look in the mirror to check my hair—pulled back from my face just like Chandra had taught me—and I was all set.

I lifted the floor-length skirt and maneuvered my way down the front steps, which was no easy thing considering the dress was so tight and Jerry Garcia was sitting in the middle of the stairs and refused to move. I had another moment of dumbstruck silence when we got out to the driveway.

That is, right before I burst out laughing.

I laid a hand on the top of the golf cart that Levi had outfitted to look like the buckboard wagon Rhett and Scarlett used to escape the burning of Atlanta. Don't ask me how he did it, but he'd somehow attached boards to the sides of the cart to make it look rustic, and he'd added a plush toy rocking horse to the front so that the cart looked as if it was being pulled by the animal.

"It's wonderful!" I told him, and slid onto the bench he'd covered with homespun red-and-white-checked fabric (yeah, I knew it was really a tablecloth from the bar, but I didn't mind). "It's perfect."

"Not exactly." In an effort to settle himself behind the wheel, Levi pushed down the empty scabbard and tried to climb into the cart, but the scabbard immediately popped back up, poking him in the leg and getting in his way. He tried again, holding it down this time and keeping it down while he sat down. "Honestly, I don't know how soldiers did it in the old days."

"They probably didn't ride around in golf carts," I reminded him.

All right, it was a terrible joke and he gave me the look I deserved. "The boots aren't bad," Levi said, "but the jacket and pants are wool, and they're hot and itchy. And this hat and the sword—"

"You look very dashing," I told him, and he actually blushed.

"I have a cousin who's a Civil War reenactor," he confessed. "And lucky for me, we're just about the same size." His bottom lip protruded just a little. "He wouldn't let me bring the sword, though. He said somebody might get hurt."

It was such a guy thing, I couldn't help but smile.

Before he backed out of the driveway, Levi glanced next door. "Does Chandra need a ride to Tara?" he asked.

"She told me not to worry about it, she had everything taken care of. And by the way, she didn't kill Vivien." While we drove, I filled Levi in on the details of Chandra's alibi.

"You going to tell Hank?" he asked when I was finished.

I fluffed my diaphanous red shawl around my shoulders and tried for a Southern accent that was nowhere near worthy of Scarlett. "What Hank doesn't know won't hurt him, and besides, the only things Chandra kept were some pictures and a yearbook." The accent was silly, not to mention terrible, so I sloughed it off. "I can't imagine Vivien's cousins would want any of those pictures of Bill, anyway, which means they probably would all just be thrown away. At least if Chandra has them, someone will remember Bill."

He slid me a sidelong look. "For a detective, you're a pretty soft touch."

"Is that a bad thing?"

Levi settled a hand on my knee. "You've got heart. But you can look at a situation objectively, too. To me, that's a winning combination."

By this time, we were closer to downtown, and from there, we'd drive to the southern part of the island and to Tara. Getting there . . .

Well, that was another story.

The members of the Chamber of Commerce had been absolutely right—the gala and the ban on vehicle traffic for the evening had attracted a lot of attention. Downtown was packed cheek to jowl with tourists, and watching them standing in line for tables at the bars and gathering in the park was a bit of a surreal experience. Most of them wore shorts and T-shirts, sundresses and flip-flops, but there were a good number of them in gowns and uniforms (though none with as much panache as Levi's), and watching them mingle made me feel as if we'd stepped into a time machine that had spit us out in some crazy dimension where past and present were all mixed up.

"The island's really hopping tonight!" Levi inched the golf cart through the crowd and we waved when people pointed at the cart, and when someone called out, "Miss Scarlett, you look beautiful tonight!" I bowed as much as I was able.

Outside of town, the crowds weren't quite as thick. At least not until we got closer to Tara. Then, there were actually people lined up along the road, three and four deep, as if they were waiting to watch a parade go by. There were cameras, too, from the TV stations on the mainland, and when we passed them, I made sure I turned just enough to make sure my face stayed out of the picture.

Besides, no matter how we were dressed, I was pretty sure two people in a tricked-out golf cart weren't nearly as interesting as so much of the rest of the crowd going to Tara for the gala. Ahead of us, I saw a couple of horses prancing along the road, their riders tipping their hats to the crowd. There was a carriage, too, complete with a team of white horses and a driver wearing a top hat.

"All right, I have to give the Twins credit." I hated to admit it, but hey, I can be a grown-up when the occasion calls for it. "They said this party was going to attract a lot of attention, and they were absolutely right."

"They've sure got the clout when it comes to publicity." Levi tipped his hat to a group of ladies standing along the side of the road. I'm pretty sure a couple of them swooned.

We turned onto Langram Road and were met with the sounds of "The Battle Hymn of the Republic" being played up ahead.

"Looks like the school band beat us," Levi said, only now, with the crowds bigger than ever and cheers all around us, he had to raise his voice so I could hear him.

The crush of onlookers was greatest right at the wide drive that led to Tara. In honor of the gala, the trees there had been hung with shimmering bunting. There were bonfires here and there beneath the trees, and the shiny fabric caught the light and winked like a million stars. There were lit torches along the drive, too, and the Tara staff, most of them college students like the kids I'd seen behind the front desk, were dressed in period costumes. They lined the drive and bowed as we drove past.

Levi slowed and we waited our turn for golf cart valet parking, and once we'd given our key to a young guy in a Confederate uniform, Levi hurried around to my side of the cart and offered me his arm just as the band—arrayed along the front portico—broke into the first jaunty notes of "Dixie."

Kate and Jayce were waiting near the front entrance. Kate, in a white gown sprigged with tiny blue flowers and a straw hat with a matching blue bow on it, was the picture of springtime. Jayce was dressed in jeans and a flannel shirt.

"Hey, I'm a Civil War-era farmer," he said before I could ask. "There was no way I was going to wear a costume!"

We were greeted at the door by a young man in a formal black butler's outfit who took our tickets and invited us inside for cider and lemonade. In the lobby, a young lady in a wide-skirted gown proffered a tray. Levi handed me lemonade and took a glass of cider for himself.

"It's like stepping back in time!" Her eyes wide and her cheeks pink, Kate looked around the lobby at the soldiers and surgeons and so many ladies in ball gowns and the black dresses that made them look like war widows. There were a couple of women dressed as battlefield nurses, a nun (I'm not exactly sure how that relates to the Civil War, but hey, a costume is a costume), and a man who was definitely out of the time period in knee breeches and a powdered wig. In my book, he got points for style.

There was no sign of the Twins.

"Your dress is exquisite," Kate told me. "But then"—she gave me a conspiratorial wink—"I suppose you can afford it."

Before I had a chance to thank her, Luella walked in with Frank Tolliver. He wore a dark suit and a white shirt. Modern all the way—but he'd made a nod to the spirit of the evening with a red, white, and blue tie. As promised, Luella was all in black—long skirt, short-sleeved top dotted with sparkling beads. She looked elegant, and call me a hopeless romantic (which I'm definitely not), but I bet Frank noticed, too. That would explain why he smiled every time he looked her way.

"We should have thought of a party like this years ago!" Luella hugged us one by one while Frank went over and got lemonade. "This is really something, isn't it?"

If any of us answered, the words were lost in the strains of piano music and a woman singing "Beautiful Dreamer" in the parlor. Nice choice of a song. Too bad it was sung by the same lady who sang the national anthems in the park that afternoon.

She hit a note that made me cringe, and Kate laughed. "Oh, come on, Scarlett, get with the program!"

"I am, honest." I pulled in a breath that was dripping with the scent of magnolias. "I will be the first to admit, this is the party to end all parties."

"And a great way to raise money for the historical society." Luella lifted her lemonade glass. "The Twins have to be commended for that."

"Agreed." I'd finished my lemonade and Levi took my empty glass and his over to where a young man stood with a tray, and while he was at it, I peered through the crowd. "Anybody seen Chandra?"

As if on cue, the front doors flew open and the chatter that had filled the lobby dissolved in awestruck silence. "Beautiful Dreamer" still oozed from the parlor but I hardly paid it any attention, even when the singer hit a particularly sour note.

Like everyone else, I was too busy staring at Chandra.

Gold satin gown, decorated with filmy fabric leaves on the sleeves and along the low-cut neckline in a color that reminded me of burnt cinnamon. A tiara of fake jewels on her head. And her cheeks rouged to a color that gave *fire-engine red* a whole new meaning.

I clapped a hand over my mouth in surprise and thought about the book we'd just read. "It's Belle Watling!" I announced. "The madam from the Atlanta brothel."

Chandra spotted us and sashayed over, unfurling her lace fan as she did. "Why, good evening, y'all," she purred.

"Only you could pull off a costume like that!" Kate squealed her delight.

"Well, y'all didn't expect me to come as Scarlett, did you?" Chandra whisked the fan in front of her face. "I knew every sweet young thing on the island would do that." She crinkled up her nose when she looked at a woman in a (bad) replica of Scarlett's dress made from the curtains at Tara. "Although you"—she rapped the fan closed so she could tap me on the arm with it—"you, my dear, are an absolute vision. You pulled it off. You are certainly the belle of the ball."

"Don't speak too quickly; we haven't seen Riva yet."

Chandra pursed her lips. "Upstart! Her and that no-good brother of hers. It doesn't matter if they show their faces or not. It looks like we can have a fine gala without them."

She was right, and the point was brought home when the singer (thank goodness!) took a break and a five-piece orchestra took over. The fainting couches and stiff-backed chairs had been removed from the parlor, and there was just enough room in there for dancing.

Levi took my hand and led me to the dance floor.

"You waltz?" I asked him.

"What, you think strippers can't waltz?"

I was afraid the heat in my cheeks gave away what I just

naturally thought about, but Levi was a good sport and didn't give me time to consider it; he swung me into the dance.

Considering his résumé, I wasn't surprised that he was a good dancer. I gave myself over to the rhythm and enjoyed myself.

When I wasn't getting tangled in my own two feet.

"Sorry." I cringed. It wasn't the first time I had to apologize for tripping up. "The dress doesn't exactly help when I'm trying to move around."

He smiled down at me. "The dress is perfect. So is the woman who's wearing it. Although now that you mention it, moving around might be a whole lot easier once you get that dress off and after we leave here tonight and—"

I had no doubts about what he was going to say. Too bad he didn't have a chance to say anything at all. At that very moment, the orchestra switched from the lazy tempo of the waltz to a tune with more of a regal tone to it, something more appropriate for a royal coronation.

Even before we stopped dancing and turned to look toward the door, I knew the Twins had made their entrance.

Quentin walked into the parlor first, looking dapper, indeed, in a Confederate uniform worthy of Robert E. Lee himself. A second later, Riva swaggered in.

"It's the same dress you're wearing!" It's not like Levi had to poke me in the ribs to get his point across; I could see what he could see. He leaned in close and whispered in my ear, "You look way better in it."

It was every woman's party nightmare. There we were, glittering red dress to glittering red dress, gauzy shawl to gauzy shawl. In a tip of a hat to Scarlett, Riva was even wearing a dark wig.

She caught sight of me and her top lip curled, but hey, I was in too good of a mood to let that spoil things for me.

"We have good taste!" I called out, and the crowd laughed, the orchestra started up again, and that was that.

"She'll get over it," I told Levi when he led me to the side of the dance floor.

"I'm not so sure about that." Over his shoulder, he watched Riva make the rounds of the room, greeting each person in turn in between sending death ray looks in my direction.

"She makes a lousy brunette," he said.

"Oh, I don't know." From where I stood, I had a glimpse of Riva's profile. "It's obviously not a cheap wig. She looks—"

"Bea! Excuse me, Bea!"

The voice came from behind me and I turned and found myself face to face with—

Rhett Butler?

I shook away the moment of surprise and smiled a hello to Zane Donahue. That evening, he might just have stepped out of the pages of *Gone with the Wind*. His dark hair was slicked down and he had a convincing fake mustache pasted above his top lip. He wore a black suit, a tan vest, and a black-and-white-checked cravat tied with the sort of flair one would expect from a hero of his ilk. He had a cigar—unlit, thank goodness—clamped between his teeth.

"Sorry to interrupt." Zane tucked the cigar in his jacket pocket. "Bea, can I see you for a moment?"

I told Levi I'd be right back and followed Zane into what was usually the breakfast room. My gaze strayed briefly to the highboy, but not before I saw that everything that had been in parlor—the fainting couches, the chairs, the bric-a-brac—had been brought in there for the evening.

"I hate to do this to you in the middle of the party," Zane said. "But I stepped in here and I saw something and I thought I should tell you about it."

As far as I knew, he couldn't have been talking about the highboy, so I looked around and asked, "What is it?"

"There." Zane pointed to the buffet, where someone who probably wasn't Riva or Quentin had set the silver candlesticks and the oil lamp I had once hoped to purchase from Estelle.

"I was here the other day and saw those things. They used to be in the parlor," I told Zane.

"But they were at Estelle's house," he said.

I nodded. "With my highboy." I gave it a longing glance. "I wanted to buy those, too, but when I got there that evening Vivien was killed, they were already gone."

As if trying to get his thoughts straight, Zane shook his head. From out in the parlor, the music ended, and out of the corner of my eye, I saw a flash of red. Riva had moved to the center of the floor to welcome her guests. Her gaze must have been caught by my red dress, too, because briefly she looked over to where Zane and I stood talking before she launched into her speech.

"Friday. That's what I'm trying to tell you, Bea." Zane glanced Riva's way, too. "I'm not sure what it means, but something tells me it's important. I told you Vivien and I were together that Friday afternoon in the house next door to Estelle's."

I remembered the orange Tic Tac on the bed and nodded.

"But I didn't tell you . . . I didn't think it mattered . . . I didn't tell you that when I got over there at the time Vivien and I arranged, she wasn't at the house next door. Vivien was busy sorting her aunt's things. I went over to Estelle's to let her know I was waiting for her. And . . ."

Zane scraped the palms of his hands against his pants. I wasn't sure what he was getting at but I couldn't fail to catch the tremor of excitement in his voice.

I put a hand on his sleeve. "And . . ?"

When he ran his tongue over his lips, one corner of his mustache came loose. "And those things were still there. The candlesticks and the oil lamp. They were at Estelle's before Vivien was killed."

"But not when we found her dead. And now, they're—"

In a flash, I thought about all the times I'd written scenes of surprise into my novels. I sometimes described the feelings that zipped through my characters as bolts from the blue or frissons of realization or the slap of an icy wave.

I knew now that none of those descriptions was adequate.

In that one moment, the truth dawned, my mouth fell open, and I spun around so I could see what Riva and Quentin were up to.

Bad timing.

Riva had just finished her sweet little welcome to all, then she took one look at me and she must have seen the spark in my eyes. She called out her brother's name and took off running.

❖ 20 ❖

Yeah, it all happened fast.

But it felt like we were moving in slow motion.

I saw Quentin flinch when Riva called out to him, and though he looked plenty confused as to what was going on, he didn't hesitate. He bolted for the door right behind his sister.

I watched as Riva lifted her skirts and took off through the lobby.

I yelled for Levi, but by this time, the crowd was onto the fact that something interesting and perhaps even tabloid-worthy was going on, and everyone surged forward, blocking my way.

"What is it?" Levi fought his way over to my side. "What's happening?"

I grabbed his hand. "We've got to get to them. Quentin and Riva. We've got to catch them!"

He didn't question me. Hanging on tight, he elbowed a path for us between corporals and generals, Southern belles and Northern widows. By the time we got to the lobby, I knew we were too late. Half the partygoers were out on the veranda watching something.

I was only too afraid I knew what.

"They're getting away!" I called to Levi.

We got outside just in time to see Riva and Quentin hop into one of the waiting golf carts, and Levi shouted to one of the valets to bring him a cart—and for all I know, that actually might have happened quickly if we all didn't freeze in our tracks and gasp in horror.

As they motored down the driveway, Riva and Quentin grabbed the torches that lit the path and tossed them. One of them got tangled in the branches of a nearby tree, and in an instant, the bunting decorating that tree caught. The fabric was light and airy and the fire consumed it immediately, then moved along the rope from which the bunting hung, eating up inches of it, catching the leaves and small branches of the tree on fire. Sparks rained down on a nearby planter and the peacock feathers in it went up in flames. By the time we were ready to jump into Levi's golf cart, the front yard of Tara was as bright as daylight, with fires burning on the lawn and above our heads in the trees.

I heard Luella call out to Frank to start herding everyone out the back door and into the gardens for safety just as Levi untied his red sash and handed it and the scabbard to Kate so he could hop into the golf cart unencumbered. I was already there, and though I knew I didn't have to tell Kate, I yelled for her to call the police and the fire department and we took off after the Twins, weaving our way down the drive, doing our best to avoid the flaming bits of fabric that fell from the trees and started a smoldering fire on the head of the toy horse at the front of the cart.

"Watch it!" Levi yelled when a fiery wad of fabric landed on my filmy red shawl and caught instantly. One hand on the wheel, he grabbed the shawl and yanked it away, then tossed it out of the cart, but not before my arm got singed.

A tree limb crashed in flames in front of us, and he screamed, "Hang on!" then veered to the left, rolling over the front lawn and between a couple of the torches that the Twins hadn't knocked over. A peacock screamed its displeasure with the whole thing and darted out in front of us, and Levi put out one arm to keep me from sliding forward and slamming into the dashboard and jammed on the brakes, and when the bird ran to the other side of the drive and disappeared into a thicket, I joined Levi in a hearty chorus of curses.

The crowds that had been having a party of their own out in the street saw the fire ignite, and we heard screams and a couple cheers from people who obviously thought it was part of the planned entertainment. In the distance, I heard the pulsing sound of a siren.

"Where do you think they're going?" Levi yelled above the noise.

I didn't know, but I knew who would. "Twins?" I asked the people who surged forward to try and see what was happening inside the grounds of Tara, and one woman pointed over her shoulder.

"Downtown!" I yelled to Levi.

It was slow going, what with the crowds already there plus the people who came running at the first signs of the commotion, but with every inch, the crowd thinned a bit. Soon there was nothing ahead of us but empty road.

And the dim, red glow of taillights.

"There!" Levi didn't need me to, but I pointed ahead of us. "That's got to be the Twins."

He stepped on the pedal and we shot forward, but let's face it, golf carts aren't the swiftest of vehicles. Our only consolation was that the Twins were in a golf cart, too, and if they were slowed down for any reason, we might be able to close the gap.

We watched them turn on Toledo and head toward downtown. "I think I know where they're going," I told Levi. "Try the marina."

By the time we arrived, we saw their golf cart, empty, parked up against a telephone pole.

By now, our toy horse had a fiery halo. Levi grabbed his hat, filled it with water from a nearby spigot and doused the horse, then took the time to look around. "What do you think?"

There was a loud party going on in the park, with hundreds of people over there dancing and carrying on. On the dock, boat owners sat on their decks and played music and passed plates of food and bottles of wine. Twinkling lights swung over many of the boats to the slow sway of the waves and created soft, undulating shadows, and carousel music from across the park mixed with Beach Boys songs from someone's iPod.

"They could be anywhere," I told Levi, but even though I knew it was true, I listened to my gut. If I wanted to get off an island . . .

I grabbed Levi's hand and jumped onto the dock.

We raced from party to party and boat to boat, sometimes to the sounds of people asking us to join in and a couple times to complaints that if we didn't have a boat berthed there, we really shouldn't be on the dock. Like Scarlett O'Hara and a Union officer are going to pay attention?

We finally found what we were looking for—who we were looking for—on an unattended sailboat at the end of the dock. While Levi pulled out his phone and called Hank, I jumped on board.

And no, it wasn't easy in that skinny dress, but I managed, if not gracefully.

I was just in time to see Riva toss a carpetbag under one of the benches and then run over to the mast and fight to get the sails raised.

"You're not going anywhere," I told her.

"Where I'm going is none of your business." I am not a sailor, but she apparently knew what she was doing; she untied some ropes and came around to where I stood to untie some more, bumping my shoulder—hard—when she went by.

Levi stepped up behind me. "No, you're really not going anywhere," he said, one hand on my shoulder. "The police are on their way."

"Police? Gee!" The lake was calm, but in the light that oozed over from a nearby boat, Quentin looked as gray as the color of his uniform. There was a sheen of sweat on his forehead. "Hurry up, Riva. Can't you do that any faster?"

She shot her brother a look. "Maybe if you helped—"

"I don't know how!" Quentin wailed.

"But you know plenty about what happened to Vivien." Yeah, I was taking a chance but I knew desperation when I saw it. I also knew I was lucky to have reinforcements; a patrol car screeched to a stop at the end of a dock, light bar flaring, and the sounds of running footsteps pounded the dock. Hank hopped aboard just as I closed in on Quentin.

"This all has to do with you two getting kidnapped, right?" I asked him.

Before he could even open his mouth, Riva spit out, "Shut up, Quentin! Don't you dare say a word."

She could intimidate her brother. Me, not so much.

"Come on, Quentin," I said. "You might as well just confirm it all for me. I've got it all figured out."

"You do not!" Riva yelled. She swung a narrow-eyed look at Hank. "She does not."

"It's your turn to shut up," the chief told her. "Go ahead, Bea," he said, and I was grateful that he could bluff for all he was worth with a straight face, since I knew he had no idea what was going on. "Explain."

I looked over Riva, my mirror image in the same red dress and with the same dark hair.

"It was the wig," I told her. "That's what made all the pieces click. You were wearing dark wigs . . . both of you . . ." I looked at Quentin, whose eyes were wide and whose nervous fingers picked at the buttons along the front of his jacket. "You were both wearing dark wigs that day Estelle showed you my house when it was for sale. Before I bought it."

Hank's dark brows slid down over his eyes. "But when your house was for sale . . ."

"Was when the Twins here were being held prisoner by their kidnapper. Yeah." With one slow step, I closed in on Riva. "Only those pictures Vivien found, they proved you weren't being held captive, didn't they? Is that why you killed her?"

"She wanted money," Quentin howled at the same time his sister warned him again, "Shut up!"

I concentrated on the weak link and turned my attention

back to Quentin. "Vivien found the pictures when she was cleaning out Estelle's house."

He nodded. "Picture. Just one picture. And when Vivien saw it, she knew what it meant. Orrin Henderson was stupid. He didn't kidnap us. It was our idea. The whole thing was our idea. Henderson, he was just . . ." Quentin hauled in a breath, and since he couldn't find the word, I supplied it for him.

"He was the patsy."

Quentin nodded. "When Vivien saw the picture of us with Estelle, she knew we'd never been kidnapped. She knew we had—"

"Quentin!" Riva's voice dripped loathing. "You stupid idiot. Keep your mouth shut!"

But Quentin was beyond listening. "Vivien said if we gave her money . . ." Quentin's eyes were moist. He looked toward Hank. "If I tell you this, you're going to help me out, right? If I tell you what she did?"

I wasn't sure which woman Quentin was talking about. "She? Do you mean what Vivien did? Or what Riva did?"

"Quentin . . ." Riva should have known her brother was too far gone to listen. Tears streamed down his cheeks.

"We went there," Quentin said. "We went to Estelle's and we gave Vivien ten thousand dollars just like she wanted, and she gave us the picture that showed us over at Bea's house back when everybody thought we were being held captive. And we thought . . . we thought that was the end of it."

I thought back to everything I knew about Vivien when she was alive, and all I'd learned about her since she died. "She double-crossed you. How?"

"She showed us a receipt from a drugstore. You know,

for copies of the photograph. She had more pictures made," Quentin said. "She said she had them hidden and—"

"And that's why you tore apart her house and her office. That's when you whacked me on the back of the head." There's a reason they call it righteous indignation and Levi must have known it, because he tightened his hand against my shoulder before I could go after Riva.

"She did it!" Quentin blurted out. "Riva, she did everything. Vivien told us that she had those other pictures, and she said she was going to show them to the police if we didn't give her more money. That's when Riva—"

His sister didn't let him finish. Before any of us could move to stop her, Riva raced across the deck, flattened her hands against her brother's chest, and shoved him overboard into the lake.

While the fire department took care of fishing Quentin out of the drink, Hank slapped handcuffs on Riva and had another officer take her out to the waiting patrol car. That's when I pointed out the carpetbag under the bench.

Hank unzipped it and whistled low under his breath. "Coins," he said. "Plenty of them."

I knew better than to touch evidence, but I peeked inside. "Desiree Champion's million-dollar collection of Civil War coins, no doubt."

"Stolen by the Twins," Levi said.

"Who never were kidnapped and were laying low for a while before they came up with the story of how Orrin Henderson engineered the whole thing. They must have hidden the coins in my house that day they were there with Estelle."

"Which explains why they wanted to put you out of business," Levi said.

"And why they offered to buy my place."

"And why they were up in Suite 6 the night of the Chamber meeting," Levi added. "Trying to find a way into the attic."

I shook my head in wonder. "Every inch of every room in that house was restored and redone and redecorated. But not the attic. I bet the coins were tucked under a floorboard."

Hank scratched a finger under his nose. "But then how did they get them?"

I started to tell him I didn't know, but as it turned out, I did. "The ladder was moved!" I said. "When I got back from Tara the night Quentin tried to convince me that I might get the highboy back." I groaned. "No wonder he wanted to talk to me at Tara. He needed to get me out of the way so that Riva could break into the attic and find the coins. Just like she must have slipped out of Estelle's house and tried to break into my place the evening Vivien was killed. I thought Chuck from the hardware store came and fixed the loose roof shingle, but that wasn't it at all."

"We'll need to get over to your place and have the crime scene techs check it out," Hank said, and he knew I wouldn't object.

I never had a chance to, anyway.

By this time, the people who'd been partying on their boats were gathered all over the dock, watching the excitement, and out on the street, I saw a line of golf carts arrive. Luella, Kate, and Chandra made quite a picture pounding down the dock in their gowns.

"It was those Twins, wasn't it?" Chandra fluffed the skirt of her dress. "I just knew I didn't like them."

"We should have known." Kate crossed her arms over her chest. "As soon as they started spreading lies about you—"

"They needed to get into my attic," I explained. I knew I'd tell them all the details later, but for now, that at least got the point across. "That's why they wanted to put me out of business."

The *harrumph* of indignation that came out of Chandra was worthy of Belle Watling herself. "Losers! They tried to put you out of business! They thought they were better than you! Wait until they find out you're really FX O'Grady!"

By the time the words escaped her lips, it was already too late.

"FX O'Grady!"

The name went through the crowd like the fire over at Tara, and before I could move, cell phone cameras were pointed my way and people were calling out questions.

"Are you really?"

"Can I have your autograph?"

"Why didn't you tell us?"

Levi leaned in close and spoke out of one side of his mouth. "Looks like the cat's out of the bag."

Honestly, at that particular moment, I didn't care, because I knew I was surrounded by friends in a place I was proud to call home, and I'd found the man of my dreams.

I wrapped my arms around Levi's neck. "Frankly, my dear," I told him, "I don't give a damn!"

« 21 »

Three weeks later, and my phone was still ringing off the hook. Thanks to Chandra's announcement, word had gone around the island—and farther—that FX O'Grady was in town and her B and B was open for business.

It wasn't what I wanted. I mean, not the notoriety or the goggling fans.

But it sure didn't hurt to have my suites full and satisfied customers singing my praises.

Even if a whole lot of them did want pictures and autographs.

I'd just gotten off another call for another reservation and walked to the front porch, where Luella, Chandra, and Kate were waiting to share a late-afternoon bottle of wine and the yummy-looking hummus and pita chips Chandra had brought over.

"It will quiet down," Luella promised me.

"Yeah, one of these days." Kate crunched into a chip. "Until then . . ."

"Until then, I'm lucky for what I have." I settled on the wicker couch and poured the sauvignon blanc. "I'm lucky to have all of you." I lifted my glass in a toast to my friends. "I'm lucky to have my home and my business—"

"And Levi!" Chandra giggled.

"Yes," I admitted. "Things are going well between us. I'm very lucky about that. Now if we can just keep our lives nice and quiet and murder-free, life here on the island will be perfect."

They agreed, and we sighed and smiled and chatted.

At least until Hank's patrol car pulled into my driveway.

"Uh-oh." Chandra wiped a dribble of hummus from her chin. "This can't be good."

"Just because Hank is here doesn't mean something bad has happened." Brave words, but I didn't sound all that convincing, even to myself.

He bounded up the steps. "What? The four of you look like you're waiting to hear a death sentence."

"It's not"—I swallowed hard—"another murder?"

"Not one anywhere around here." Hank leaned against the front porch railing, and since he was on duty, I didn't offer him a glass of wine but he did take a plate of chips and glop hummus on them. "Here's the thing . . ." He gulped down a chip. "Once we knew the Twins had engineered the kidnapping and made up the story about what had happened to them and what they went through, it got us thinking. And once we got thinking, we contacted the authorities out in New Mexico where the Twins surfaced after their 'ordeal.'"

He gave the last word a twist.

"And . . ?" I asked him.

"Found Orrin Henderson's body. Or at least what was left of it."

Even the wine wasn't enough to wash down the bad taste that suddenly filled my mouth. "The Twins?"

"Riva. At least that's what Quentin says. Henderson never stood a chance. They got tired of depending on their mother for their money and decided they wanted some of their own, so they talked Henderson into helping pull off the heist and promised him a share when they sold those coins. Then they got rid of him the first chance they got." Hank heaved himself away from the railing and set his dish on the table in front of the couch. "Thought you ladies would like to know."

After he left, we sat in silence for a few long minutes.

"That's awful." Luella shivered.

"Terrible." Kate shook her head.

"I never trusted them." Chandra grabbed more hummus. "What's going to happen to Tara now?"

"Gone with the wind?" I suggested, and cringed. It was a pretty awful pun.

"And the maple highboy?" Kate asked.

Ah, the maple highboy . . .

I held my glass up to the light of the evening sun and smiled, and sure, my Miss Scarlett accent was as bad as ever, but hey, it seemed appropriate. "Well, fiddle-dee-dee. Don't you know, that maple highboy is being delivered here tomorrow. The Twins needed money to pay their defense attorney." My laugh was as light as my mood. "Bless their hearts."

ALSO FROM

Kylie Logan

THE LEAGUE OF LITERARY LADIES MYSTERIES

Mayhem at the Orient Express

A Tale of Two Biddies

The Legend of Sleepy Harlow

And Then There Were Nuns

Praise for the
League of Literary Ladies Mysteries

"Logan has fun with this unusual story, intimate setting, and feisty characters, and readers will, too."
—*Richmond Times-Dispatch*

"What could be more fun than a mystery series that is about a reluctant book club? I love how the mysteries run parallel to the book the League of Literary Ladies is reading."
—*MyShelf.com*

"One of my favorite cozy mystery writers… What great characters Kylie Logan has created."
—*Fresh Fiction*

kylielogan.com
penguin.com

1767